Captain Merrick

Cover Photography by TJ Drysdale

Cover Design by Matthew Weatherston

Griffith Cameron Publishing

ISBN - 978-1-955212-00-7

Captain Merrick

Eilidh Miller

Chapter 1

London, 1675

They'd docked, he knew that much.

Henry Merrick let go of a heavy sigh and gently tapped the back of his head against the wall, staring at the cabin's ceiling. Annoyed though he was at even being here in the first place, he could really do nothing about it because the king had ordered his arrest and return to England. The charge was that he'd broken a treaty … a treaty he hadn't even known about. It was ridiculous, but it was the way things were.

Able to hear the crowds and activity outside, he was ready to be out of this room and off this damned ship. Not that they'd treated him badly — he'd suffered far worse — he just wanted to cease being confined to one room. Furthermore, he was very ready to have a bath and a shave, along with some fresh clothes. The sound of approaching footsteps got his attention, and he sat up as the door opened.

"Right, up you get, Captain," said the first mate. "They have a carriage for you."

"Really? They are not parading me through the streets on a hay cart so people can stare at me? How surprising."

Henry's sarcasm drew a small laugh from the man. "Yes,

well, I do not think it is meant to be fun for you."

"You would consider that fun?" Henry asked before he paused. "Well, I suppose it depends on who was doing the looking."

"Come on," the man said, stepping inside as Henry stood and taking him by the arm to lead him out.

The shackles on his wrists clanked as he walked, almost louder than the sound their boots made as they walked through the hold. He'd been left this way for most of the journey, though there had been moments of respite. He understood why: There was always fear that a pirate captain would steal your ship, but what was he going to do on his own? He could try to get the crew on his side, sure, but that was quite a gamble anyway.

Led to the stairs, he climbed out of the hold and onto the deck, wincing at the brightness of the outdoors as they kept him moving across the deck and down the gangplank. It gave him no time to pause or adjust and no time for anyone who may have followed them to set a rescue in motion. On the dock, some of the king's guard waited to take custody of him and marched him to a waiting carriage after the handover by the ship's crew. There were heavy draperies over the windows to prevent him from being able to either see or be seen, and this was a bit of a blessing, allowing his eyes to adjust. He didn't need to see anyway: The smell told him well enough that he was back in London.

He had no idea how long they'd traveled or how far they'd gone before the carriage came to a stop and the door opened once more. Henry stepped out of the carriage and onto solid cobblestones, moving dutifully forward as the guard herded him through the palace halls. What he'd not expected was to be taken straight to the throne room. Couldn't he at least clean up a bit before meeting his king? Apparently not. When the party arrived at a large set of doors, the march stopped. A man standing there surveyed Henry with disdain before he turned and opened the doors.

"Your Majesty, Captain Henry Merrick."

Across the room, a man sat upon a throne, and when he rose, Henry, along with the guard, all took a knee and bowed their heads. Henry couldn't help but consider how much all the finery dripping from this man might fetch him.

"Well, the great Captain Merrick at last."

"Your Majesty," Henry said, lifting his eyes to the king once he'd been spoken to.

"You do know why we brought you here?"

"I came upon a sinking Spanish ship and thought the best way to assist them was to liberate them of the cargo that was holding them down, sire." He saw no need to mention that he was also the reason it had been sinking.

King Charles looked amused for a moment. "You did so in defiance of a peace treaty, Captain."

"I was not yet aware there *was* a peace treaty, Your Majesty. Word had not reached us at that time."

"I know that, Captain."

Henry couldn't help the look of confusion on his face.

"The Spanish were angry and demanded I do … something," the king said, waving his hand. "The explanation that word hadn't reached the Caribbean simply was not going to suffice, so I had you arrested and brought here. Now they can think I have done something, and you, Captain, can take a bit of a break."

"A break, Your Majesty? In all fairness, sire, I could do so much more for you if —"

"Captain," Charles said, cutting him off. "I feel I am being exceedingly generous here. Are you questioning it?"

"No, Your Majesty," Henry said, his tone resigned as he dropped his gaze to the floor.

"Good. I would hate to have to make you spend the entirety of your time in England lodging at the Tower."

Henry's eyes snapped up. The Tower wasn't a place *anyone* wanted to be.

"I see you agree. Send in Lady Catherine."

A set of doors at the other end of the room opened, and a young woman glided through them, hands clasped at her waist. When she reached the king, she curtsied deeply and then rose. "Your Majesty. You sent for me?"

"Ah, Catherine, there you are. There is someone I would like you to meet," Charles said, directing her attention to the still kneeling Henry.

She looked at him with a mix of curiosity and confusion, and he could understand why based on the way he surely looked: filthy clothing, unwashed, unshaven, his hair likely a mess. What in God's name had he to do with her? Henry took stock of her as she studied him, just as curious about why she was here as he was. She was a beauty, that was certain, her hair so dark as to be almost black, her eyes a sparkling shade of deep green. A dainty thing, she looked almost swallowed in the voluminous skirts she wore, as was the fashion, though the bodice showed off her upper half to its best advantage. More than anything, she seemed tiny next to the men surrounding her.

"Captain Merrick, I would like to introduce you to your cousin, Lady Catherine, distant as she may be."

Her eyes widened, the former trained impassivity slipping for a moment to show her surprise.

"Hello, my lady," Henry said.

Catherine looked to be at a loss for words before she caught herself. "Good afternoon, Captain," she said, her tone clipped yet polite.

"Is he everything you thought he would be?" Charles asked.

"Whatever do you mean, Your Majesty?"

"Do not play the simpering idiot with me, girl; you are better than that. Did you really think I had not noticed how you always managed to be around when news of Captain Merrick's exploits reached us? I know you covertly try to read the dispatches about him. So, tell me: Is he what you expected?"

Catherine looked at Henry for a long moment and then shook her head. "No, Your Majesty," she said.

"Is it not a sad thing when those we are fascinated with do not live up to our expectations?"

Henry did his best to keep his expression neutral even though the circumstances grated on him. He wasn't comfortable being used as a prop to torment a young woman, no matter the reason. He did, however, wonder what she'd expected.

"Your Majesty, I —"

"Did you think he would be a giant?" Charles continued, preventing her from speaking. "Perhaps fiercer looking? A savage?"

"I do not know, Your Majesty," Catherine answered, and it was easy for Henry to see that it was an honest one.

"Your family has a home in London, do they not?"

"Yes, Your Majesty."

"And your parents are away, currently? In the country?"

"Yes, Your Majesty. I stayed behind to serve the queen."

"Very good. You are being reassigned."

"Reassigned, sire?"

"Yes. Captain Merrick will be here in England with us for quite some time to come, and I am placing him under your care, as he is your family, after all."

"Your Majesty —" Catherine began to protest.

"Did it sound like a request, Catherine? It was not. He is to lodge at Merrick House until such time as we see fit to release him, and you will keep him company there. Mindful of your virtue, I will also place a lady within your household to make sure the good Captain does not get any ideas. Your things have already been sent on. Guard, remove his restraints. You are both dismissed."

Charles turned his back, and the guard lifted Henry up, finally relieving him of the shackles he'd worn for weeks. Catherine's face was unreadable, but her eyes showed her distress. This was very clearly *not* what she wanted to be doing. She did, however, meekly follow behind the guard to the waiting carriage. A command from the king was a command, and it was one that couldn't be ignored. Henry was put into the carriage, and Catherine got in after him, taking her seat across from him.

"I am sorry for any inconvenience this may cause you," Henry said, breaking the silence as the carriage started forward.

"I am sure you are," she replied, her displeasure obvious in her tone.

"I did not ask for this."

"I know. From what I have read, you are generally far more subtle."

"I see I disappoint you yet again."

"What does that mean?"

"You tell me. What was it you were expecting me to be?"

Catherine said nothing for a time, letting the question hang in the space between them. "I do not know. You just do not look like someone who would do all of the things they write about."

"Who writes about?"

"The dispatches, the Spanish, the pamphlets. The one described in those seems like he would be a terror of a man."

"And I am not?"

"No."

Henry couldn't help but smile. "You have not seen me at work, so how would you know? Even wolves can be charming."

Henry heard Catherine give a small huff of irritation, and it amused him. To the English Merricks, their Welsh kin was something to be ignored, to pretend didn't exist. They were considerably more well-off than the Welsh Merricks — there was a reason Henry had gone to sea and resorted to piracy, after all — but they still shared the same blood. The ties between the two families might be distant now, as the king had pointed out, but they were still there. Catherine could deny it all she wished, but it changed nothing.

"I will be sure to try and be of as little trouble to you as possible, my lady. So much so that you may even forget I am there."

"Unlikely."

"It is funny; the king was worried about your virtue at home, but not enough to place a watch in here with us for the ride."

There was a sharp intake of breath from Catherine, and Henry said nothing else, content in having reminded her that the person across from her *was* dangerous even if he didn't currently seem that way. However, Henry had heard plenty of tales from this court and wondered how much virtue the woman across from him truly possessed, if any.

When the carriage came to a stop again, the door was opened, and Catherine got out first. Henry followed her, stepping out onto a London street in front of a large house three floors high. He was ushered through the front door without delay, the door shutting behind him to keep prying eyes out. In the foyer stood several household members, all of them looking at Henry.

"Hart," Catherine said.

"Yes, my lady," said an older man as he stepped forward.

"Please see to having a bath set up for the Captain; I am sure he needs it after his long journey."

"Yes, my lady," he said.

"Pogue."

"Yes, my lady." A younger man stepped forward this time.

"Please see to the Captain while he is our guest. This is at the king's command, and thus, he is to be treated as such. Find him some fresh clothes and have the tailor sent for."

"Yes, my lady."

"Show him to his room," Catherine said, and Pogue turned to head up the stairs, the guard following and taking Henry with them.

Once the door shut, one of the women downstairs looked at her. "Lady Catherine!"

Burke, as the head of house for Merrick House, had

known Catherine the longest of any of the staff and was someone the family quite relied upon to keep things running smoothly here at all times.

"I know, Burke, but the king commanded it and thus we have no choice," Catherine replied, weary. "There will be someone else along to ostensibly protect my virtue from the Captain, so when they arrive, please see to it that they are accommodated."

"Yes, Lady Catherine."

Catherine turned and made her way upstairs to her own room, shutting the door behind her and leaning against it. What kind of game was this? Why did he have to stay here? Her own standing at court would be harmed by being gone for God knew how long, not to mention the gossip that would spread about her being here with this man, whether someone was here to guard her or not. It was preposterous that the king should trap her here with this criminal!

Catherine moved forward and sat down in a chair, burying her face in her hands. She really had expected more, but she could never tell any of them the truth about what she wanted. She'd read about Henry's exploits, it was true, but she'd done so because she longed for the freedom he had. She could, in those moments, close her eyes and pretend to be him, to feel what it was like to have the power to do and go where you wished even if only in her mind. The man she'd seen today looked nothing like what they'd said, and she wondered if he'd even done any of those things. The tears came before she could stop them, but they weren't for being stuck here. No, they were for the shattering of a dream, a means of escape sealed up. Inwardly, she chafed against the rules and expectations of her sex even though she followed them to the letter. Those dreams had been her way to be free of all of it, and now it was gone. They wanted to smother any fight in her, and ever so slowly they were succeeding.

Chapter 2

Catherine crept into the room and toward the bed with silent steps, wary. He'd been sleeping for so long they were starting to wonder if he was ill. Drawing near to the bed, she stood looking down at him, and he seemed different now. A bath and some grooming had done wonders, but to see him in the light let her study him in a way she hadn't been able to do when he'd arrived. He was far more undressed than she'd ever seen any man, and she found it intriguing. His skin was a bit darker from all the time in the sun, but not much, and his hair was dark like her own. Through his open shirt, she could see the scars of old injuries on his torso, and that alone told her there was some truth to what had been said about him. Where had they come from? What adventure had he been on when he'd earned them? The parts of his chest she could see were muscular and solid, not at all like the glimpses she'd caught of male courtiers as they cavorted about the palaces.

Reaching out, Catherine took hold of the blankets and pulled them up over him from where he'd shoved them away who knew how long ago. He was breathing, that was easy to see, so perhaps he really *was* exhausted. As she went to release the blanket, Henry's hand shot out and grabbed her wrist roughly, jerking her toward him and bringing a small sound of shock from Catherine. He looked at her for a moment, and then his eyes fluttered closed again, his hand going slack and releasing her. Catherine pulled her hand away and scrambled back from the bed, her breathing rapid, before she hurried out of the room.

***

Henry had no idea what time it was when he finally woke up. The bath had been wonderful, and Pogue had cut his hair and given him a shave. When he'd looked in a mirror, he'd actually seen *himself* and not some crazed barbarian-looking thing. The tailor came and measured him for new clothing, and he'd fallen into the bed, exhausted. He hadn't slept on such a bed in so long, and the comfort of it was quick to pull him down. It was nice to finally get a proper rest with no shackles and no chains clinking to wake him. At some point he'd dreamt Catherine was here, trying to do him harm, but it had just been a flash of a dream. There was no way such a woman would even come into a man's room, much less come in to harm him.

He rose and dressed, finding his way downstairs to the dining room. Upon opening the door, he found Catherine already there, looking surprised to see him. "Good morning, my lady," he said. "May I sit?"

"Yes, of course. You are our guest here. You may call me Catherine."

"Thank you," he said, taking his seat and surveying the food set out for breakfast. "You look shocked to see me."

"You have been asleep for several days, Captain."

"Have I? It didn't seem that long, but it would explain why I am so hungry," he said as he reached out and took a piece of toast, along with a piece of sausage, only to find Catherine looking at him curiously. "What?"

"For someone so hungry, you have excellent restraint."

"Well, I can't offend you at our very first meal by eating like a heathen, now, can I? No matter what you may have heard of me, I do have manners."

"Is there a finishing school for pirates?"

Henry laughed at her joke. "I wish there were, to be honest. Some I know could certainly use it. You are quick."

Catherine allowed a small smile, the first one he'd seen. Perhaps she wasn't always so serious after all.

"I do apologize for having slept so long. It has been some weeks since I have had a proper rest. A bit hard to do with shackles."

"I would imagine it is."

"What shall we do here, Catherine, you and I?"

"Do? Nothing. At least not together. I am sure the king has some sort of plan for you; until then we simply go about our business."

"If I am a guest, should you not entertain me in some way?"

"In what way could I entertain someone like you?"

"Someone like me? What does that mean?"

"I simply mean I have no entertainment that would be of any interest to someone who grew up with sheep in a bog and then went on to spend his time amongst brigands and whores."

Henry looked at her in surprise. It was sharp coming from her and unexpected. "I can think of plenty of ways you could entertain me that would serve you well when they eventually sell you off to be a broodmare for some stranger. Perhaps you could even learn to enjoy it."

"How dare you!" Catherine shouted, standing up.

"How dare I?" he repeated as he stood. "You thought I wouldn't answer insult with insult, did you? Why? Because you are a *lady*? In my experience ladies like you are the worst of them, thinking yourself above everything because your father visited your mother instead of the bawds he would normally frequent for some relief."

Catherine gasped, raising her hand to slap him for such a horrific slander before she could even think of it, and

Henry caught her wrist, yanking her hard against him.

"You listen to me, you primped up little viper," he seethed. "If this is how you want to play, then we shall play, and I will win. *You* are nothing special to me. I do not like this any more than you do, but I was at least trying to be nice. As you will not even give me that courtesy, I will not bother. If you strike me, then you should be prepared to take one back, for I will not be merciful. This is a warning, and the only one you shall get."

With his last words, he shoved her away from him, causing Catherine to stumble and hit her hip against the table hard enough to rattle the dishes. Henry heard the pained sound she made before she smothered it and instantly felt bad for doing it, not having meant to push her that hard. She placed her hands on the table to steady herself, then turned back toward him, her eyes on the floor.

"I apologize for insulting you," she said in a soft voice, though she was shaking. "It was unkind. Please enjoy your breakfast and excuse me."

Catherine didn't wait for him to say anything, hurrying past him and shutting the door to the dining room behind her. Henry realized, based on her reaction, that this was not the first time someone had used violence to quell the fire she'd shown. There was no way it could be otherwise, based on her actions. She'd retreated into herself within an instant, unable to look at him. He closed his eyes and sighed. This wasn't how he wanted this to be, and he cursed himself for giving in to his temper instead of staying calm. Leaving the dining room, he began checking the downstairs rooms, having not heard her go upstairs. He found her at last in a darkened sitting room at the back of the house. The sound of her crying caught his attention, soft as it was.

"Catherine," he said gently, watching her jump and turn to face him, taking a step back with a tinge of fear in her expression, as he held up his hands to show her he meant her no harm. "I want to apologize for what just happened. It was ungentlemanly of me, and I never meant to shove you that hard."

"But you did mean to shove me."

"No." He sighed in slight irritation. "Catherine, stop. Everything I did and said was wrong but so were the things you said. I fear we have very much gotten off on the wrong footing. Shall we try again?"

When there was no response, Henry nodded before he bowed to her.

"Lady Catherine, it is a pleasure to meet you. I am Captain Henry Merrick, here on the king's business."

To his surprise, Catherine curtsied to him. "Good morning, Captain Merrick, I welcome you to Merrick House. I hope you will find your time with us enjoyable, though I am afraid we are quite short on rum. Or is it grog?"

Henry laughed, holding out his hand for hers, and when she gave it, he kissed it with all politeness. "There, now. That is much nicer."

"Yes, it is," Catherine replied, looking down at the floor once more.

"What is wrong?"

"Nothing," she said, her tone still meek.

Henry frowned. "Who is this that stands before me? Not the young woman I met earlier, surely."

"The very same."

"Please do not do this," Henry said, his voice becoming gentle in a moment of candor. "Do not retreat as you have so clearly been taught to do."

Catherine looked up at him with a raised eyebrow. "What is it you want?"

"To know who you are, the *real* you, not the court you. If we have to spend our time here together, we might as well make the best of it, do you not think? I know this meek girl is not you; I saw that plainly enough."

Catherine considered it and then nodded. "Very well."

"Excellent, because meek women make me —" but he

stopped as his eyes fell on her wrist, the same one he'd grabbed moments ago in the dining room. She'd been hiding it behind her back when he'd come in but had forgotten to continue to do so. "Christ, I did not do that … did I?"

Her eyes widened when he so blithely swore in her presence before she shoved her hand behind her back once more. "No."

"Let me see it."

"No."

"Catherine, let me see it, please."

She fidgeted for a moment before she reluctantly produced her hand. Henry took it and winced when he saw dark bruising there, along with fresh red marks.

"Who did this?"

"I —"

"Who?" he repeated, though it was not a question but a quiet demand.

"You."

"You just said I did not."

"Not today."

"Come again?"

Catherine shifted nervously on her feet before she answered. "I came to check on you because we were worried you were ill, and when I pulled the blanket over you, you grabbed my wrist and pulled me toward you before falling asleep again."

Henry's brow knitted. The dream hadn't been a dream. She'd been there, not to do him harm but to check on his welfare. "I am sorry," he said. "I had no idea."

"You were not awake."

"No, I was not. I actually thought that was a dream," he replied with a heavy sigh. "And then I go and grab the same wrist today. That will not help matters."

"I can cover it with a bracelet."

Henry looked up at her with a questioning gaze. "How often do you need to hide bruises that you are so quick with a solution?"

"Often enough."

"From whom and why?"

"From my father and usually because he doesn't like something I have said."

Rather like you. Her eyes said the words her mouth had not, and Henry felt it like a sharp cut.

"You surely do not speak to him the way you spoke to me."

"No, of course not. If I had, I would not be here but dead in a churchyard."

"So, you save your best barbs for unfortunate guests, do you?"

Catherine's laugh was quiet. "I usually say them in my mind."

"You are lucky they have not come out of your mouth by accident."

"I like living dangerously."

Henry gave her a look, and her composure melted entirely as she began to laugh. He couldn't help but join her in it. "Well, it seems my English kin is not as she appears."

"Is anyone?"

"It depends on your line of work, I guess."

"No one I know is, anyway," Catherine said in a nonplussed manner.

"It behooves them not to be."

"Sometimes."

Henry realized he was still holding her wrist and released her. "Would you rejoin me for breakfast so that we might continue our conversation there? I am finding it rather pleasant."

"If you wish."

Henry gestured to the door, and Catherine walked past him back to the dining room, and once she'd taken her seat, Henry took his. "In what way is it not in the best interest of someone at court to not be as they appear?"

"If you are a man, it is not always in your best interest to hide yourself, for the king might find you favorable. If you suspect he would not, it would be smart to hide such a thing."

"And if you are a woman?"

"If you are a woman, it is never in your best interest to be yourself."

"How so?"

"Men expect certain things. Society and court demand a certain demeanor for a woman. If you wish to please the king, honor your family, and appeal to men, then you must be as they wish."

"Oh, but there is where you are wrong. *Certain* men expect certain things from women they have no interest in other than for the sons she can bear him," Henry said, taking note of the way her eyes widened. "Do not look so scandalized as though you do not know it to be true. A man who wishes for more wants a woman who is herself and appeals to him in that way."

"That is not the type of man I encounter."

"How unfortunate for you."

"I suppose it is," she said, looking down at the silver teaspoon she was toying with.

"What is it you want, Catherine?"

"What?" she asked, returning her eyes to his face.

"No one has ever asked you, have they?"

"No, never."

"Well, I am asking you. What do *you* want?"

Asked in so direct a manner, she didn't have an immediate answer. "Freedom," she replied after a time.

"Freedom?"

"Indeed. Freedom to simply be. To do as I please without needing to consult anyone, to not have to remember all of these ridiculous rules or pretend I like something I abhor."

"A little sparrow trapped in a grand cage from which there is no escape."

"Yes."

"Yet, you do not speak of love."

"Love?"

"Yes, the thing that people below you generally tend to

feel for the people they marry, and something most women I have met speak of."

"Love," she repeated with derision. "I know nothing of love."

"What? Impossible."

"Not impossible. Truth."

"You have never once looked at a young man and wished for him to want you?"

"No. Why would I bother when it wouldn't matter anyway?"

"I am sorry to hear it," he said, though he kept the pity he felt for her out of his voice. What sort of life did she lead where she could say such a thing with no trace of sadness?

"Lady Catherine," a dour-looking woman said as she came through the door. "Come away and let him eat in peace. You have conversed quite enough."

"But he asked me to —" she began, but her words faltered when the woman gave her a stern look and she rose from her seat. "Enjoy your breakfast, Captain," she said in a rush as she was nearly pushed from the room.

The woman turned to Henry. "If you think for even one moment that you will be getting anything out of her, you are mistaken. Stay away from her."

She swept from the room, leaving Henry in a silent and empty dining room. It amused him that the older woman thought he'd be frightened of her somehow or, at the very least, severely chastened. No, it wouldn't be that easy, and he'd faced down far worse than she. Catherine was revealing herself to be a mystery he'd very much like to solve. Her answer to his question about what she wanted intrigued him. Freedom. There was more to it, he was sure of that. Why did they want to keep her away from him so badly? Aside from the obvious reasons, of course. He was determined to find out, and finding out called for more *specialized* methods.

Chapter 3

Henry hadn't seen Catherine for the rest of the day, not even for dinner and supper; such was the determination of her warders to keep them apart. It annoyed him a great deal, as he thought he'd at least be able to see her for meals, but it made him all the more determined to find a way around the blockade set up around her. Guarding something so heavily only made that thing more attractive to someone like him, and by evening, he'd devised a plan. He'd discovered Catherine was at least allowed to sleep alone and that they weren't placing the dragon in with the princess … at least not yet. If they eventually did, he'd figured out a way around that, too.

When he was sure everyone had retired, Henry left his room with only a candle. By careful observation he'd figured out which door belonged to Catherine, and it was at this door he stopped, daring a gentle knock. There was a rustle from inside, and then the door opened, leading Henry to place a hand over her mouth before she could utter a sound, keeping his touch light so as not to frighten or hurt her.

"Shh. I mean you no harm, and I know you are surprised to see me," he whispered. "Come downstairs, little Sparrow, to the room we were in earlier, so we can talk. Will you?"

Catherine contemplated the offer before nodding in silence. Henry removed his hand without another word and moved past her toward the stairs. Behind him, he heard the door shut, but he knew she was smarter than to follow him immediately. His suspicions were confirmed when he reached the room and she wasn't directly behind him, though she arrived not long afterward. She looked different this way, her long hair down while she was wrapped in a warm dressing gown, her appearance going against all propriety, and he found he quite liked it.

"What is this about?" she asked, keeping her voice quiet.

"Nothing. I just want to talk to you, and as it seems the dragon will not permit it during the daylight hours, now is the only time I have."

"I really should not be here," Catherine said with a small shake of her head, turning away and heading for the door.

"You said you liked to live dangerously."

She stopped, looking back at him over her shoulder.

"Now is your chance."

Henry watched her inward struggle as she tried to decide before she turned back around and approached him.

"I thought as much," he said, smiling. "Come and sit with me."

Catherine followed him to the settee, where Henry took up a rather leisurely pose he never would've adopted during the day. Catherine, in turn, sat facing him cross-legged, a pose she similarly never would've taken up otherwise, her robe tented around her.

"What did you want to talk about, Captain?"

"Henry when we're alone, and just talk. You intrigue me."

"Do I? Why?"

"You are not like everyone else, no matter how hard you try to convince them otherwise. I can see right through you."

"Is that so?"

"It is rather my job."

"I can see through you, too."

"What?"

"Beneath this haughty display, there is someone else."

Her words gave him pause. He hadn't been expecting that. "Perhaps, but you do not know what."

"Just as you do not know what is beneath mine."

"But you wish to find out."

"As do you."

A small smile played across his lips. "So, we are at an impasse. Very well, I have a proposal."

"I am shocked," she replied, her voice deadpan.

Henry blinked and then laughed. "That was good. Now, do you want to hear it or not?"

"Go on."

"I propose that we are our true selves here, in this room, in the dark. We come here each night, and we get to be as we are and talk to each other, keep each other company. Whatever we must be by day is what we must be, but here that all goes away."

"If we are ourselves, are there topics of discussion that are off-limits?"

"Not at all."

"Then I accept."

"That was fast."

Catherine shrugged. "I am bored with normality."

Henry chuckled. "We are more alike than you would want to admit, I think."

"Are we?"

Henry nodded and, mindful of what he'd just proposed and agreed to, relaxed. He let go of what he knew was expected of him here and became what he normally was: Henry the sailor. "It was why I left, after all."

Catherine looked at him quizzically as his demeanor and voice changed. "Leaving is something you can do, but I cannot."

"But you want to."

"Sometimes," she replied. Her voice was so quiet he almost hadn't heard what she'd said, and he realized it was likely the first time the thought had ever been voiced out loud.

"Then do it."

"It is not that easy for me. As a man, you had ways to leave, to support yourself. I do not have that luxury."

"I suppose that is true. I will admit I am not entirely used to dealing with women of your station in this sort of a way. The women I know could only dream of having what you do."

"But it *is* a dream, not real. All of it is an illusion, everyone pretending to be something in order to move about an imaginary board so as to get closer to the top. There is a high price to pay for this."

"There is a price for everything, Catherine."

"You know that better than most, I assume."

"Unfortunately, yes. Tell me something: What did you really expect of me? Do not tell me you do not know because you do. Tell me the truth."

Catherine worried a fold of fabric between her fingers before she answered. "I suppose I expected someone bold and well-dressed, who did not kneel before a king. Beholden to no one and nothing, free. You would have a sword for fighting and perhaps a pistol, and you would look at once both merry and frightening, for it would be easy to see the danger in you."

Henry smiled. "I had a sword and a pistol, but they took them off me when they arrested me. I cannot answer for the rest."

"No?"

"Well-dressed is not practical for sailing. It would more likely than not end up with you drowned when you are caught up in the rigging because some ridiculous ornament got tangled somewhere. I must kneel before the king because he is my king, just as he is yours. I cannot say whether I appear both merry and frightening, but I am sure I do at some points. As for freedom, well, I do have that in a way. There are still laws, but I tend to break them because there is no one to really stop me."

Catherine's quiet laugh at his last words filled the space between them, and he found he liked it far better than the silence in the carriage on the way here. "I suppose there are not, and that is what makes piracy rather lucrative. I had not thought about that with the clothing, but it is a good point now that you have mentioned it."

"You would not have any reason to have thought of such things. Have you ever been on a ship?"

"Yes, when we came back from the continent with the king."

"Ah, of course."

"I was only a little girl then, but it was exhilarating. I did not want to stay below, and my mother would get so angry," she said, a hint of a prideful smile at her own defiance making itself known for the briefest of moments.

"Do you see danger in me?"

"No. Well, yes, but only when you grab me," she said, looking at him with a wry smile.

"I am sorry about that," Henry said with a small laugh. "Here is some advice: Never sneak up on a sleeping pirate, or you might find yourself sleeping permanently."

"Really?"

"Well, how would I know you aren't there to rob me or kill me? I am asleep. It is just a reflex now."

"Oh."

"I am no danger to you, Catherine. Really."

"Some would argue otherwise."

"I am sure they would, but that's only because I'm treating you like a human being instead of an object to be seen and not heard. The only opinion that matters to me regarding my danger to you, or lack thereof, is yours."

"Which is why I am still here. What is it like?"

"What is what like?"

"Piracy. Sailing. Fighting. The Caribbean."

"Piracy is, well, it can be both fun and terrifying. It is really a bunch of men sailing around and stealing from each other while sinking those same ships. It is all a bit ridiculous when you think about it."

Catherine laughed, and Henry smiled at her. He found he liked it more and more when she laughed, the way it lit up her face and her eyes, a sight he was sure was a rarity with her.

"It is fun when you win and terrifying when you do not. Battles at sea are not pretty. As a captain it is my job to not only find things to steal but to succeed in stealing them and making sure my crew is paid fairly so that they do not mutiny. It is a fine line to walk sometimes. Fighting is fighting, also terrifying, because it is for your life, just as the battles at sea are. You should be thankful you do not have to do it."

"I will take your word for it. What is Jamaica like?"

"Ah, now, that is an entirely different thing. The water is warm and a color I have never seen anywhere else. Many times it is so clear you can see to the bottom. There are fish and sea life in colors you could not even imagine. The sky is blue; the breezes are warm and filled with the scent of flowers. It is paradise."

"It sounds like it. I wish I could see it."

"So do I."

"At least with such a description I can go there in my mind."

"Why do I feel as though you do that often? Escape in your mind?"

"Because I do."

"Why?"

"I cannot be this Catherine, not outside. This Catherine is not desirable to a match and not desirable to my parents. I have to hide who I am behind a mask, much as you do."

"I do, you are right, but we have different reasons for doing so. I hide because no one would fear the man before you and no one would respect him either. There are three of me: the captain, the gentleman, and the real Henry."

"Which one is this?"

"The real one. The captain you, unfortunately, met when you insulted me. The gentleman is who I was the rest of the time."

"I prefer this one."

"Do you? Even though he's not what you expected?"

"Yes. He is real. The captain is the mask you wear to do the things I have read, and I find I did not care for him after all."

"Yes, well, he is a bit of an arsehole if I am honest, but then he has to be."

Catherine stared at him.

"What?"

"That is twice you have sworn."

"I see. I apologize and will try to be more mindful in the future. On the other hand, it is quite useful. Have you ever done it?"

"Certainly not!"

"Maybe you should."

"No, I should not."

"Come on," Henry said. "I promise I will not tell anyone. It is fun."

"No."

"Go on. You know you want to do it, to defy them even if they do not know you have."

Catherine bit her lip. "Arse," she whispered before covering her mouth, eyes wide with shock over having said it.

Henry chuckled. "You can do better than that."

She lowered her hands, took a deep breath, and released it. "Arsehole," she said firmly before she dissolved into a fit of giggles so honest it made Henry laugh hysterically.

"You see?" he said when he'd recovered himself.

"I cannot believe I said it!"

"And yet here you are, still alive, not struck down by the Lord."

"Not yet."

"If I am still here, then it would take a hell of a lot more than one swear word from your lips to bring the wrath of the Almighty, Sparrow."

"That is a very good point, actually."

"I like this Catherine. The real one."

"Do you?"

"Yes. She is alive."

Catherine smiled. "Sometimes I can go hidden for so long I forget what it feels like."

"It hurts to hear you say that."

"Why?"

"No one should ever have to live that way, to hide themselves to the point where they forget what it is like to be alive."

"I feel that way when I go for a ride."

"How often is that?"

"Clearly not often enough."

"Clearly. I think, however, we should retire before we get ourselves caught. There has been enough dangerous living for one night."

"You are probably right."

"Go on ahead, I shall perhaps see you in the morning."

"I will make sure of it. I think so much separation is a bit much. You are our guest; I should at least be able to have meals with you and socialize with you in some way."

"I would appreciate that."

Catherine stood and walked to the door, then turned to look back at him, her hand on the doorknob. "Goodnight, Henry," she said, using his name for the first time.

"Goodnight, Catherine," he replied as she opened the door and walked out.

Chapter 4

When Henry arrived in the dining room for breakfast the next morning, the dour woman was there but so was Catherine. Her smile when he came in was genuine, and it warmed his heart to see a more friendly greeting on the face of the young woman.

"Good morning, Lady Catherine," he said, mindful of properly addressing her before the other woman. To do otherwise could cause problems, and he wanted none of that. Not after last night. He'd enjoyed her company far too much to allow himself to ruin any chance at enjoying it again.

"Good morning, Captain. Did you sleep well?"

"Quite, thank you."

"I am glad to hear it. I was wondering if you might care to take a turn in the garden with me after breakfast?"

"Lady —" the guardian began.

Catherine shot a look across the table that silenced the other woman, leaving Henry impressed by the speed of its success.

"I would, actually. Some air might do everyone a bit of good."

"Excellent, I am glad you agree. As your hostess here, I should at least offer you some sort of cordial interaction while you are our guest. At least you are until the king sends for you."

"Yes, there is that. I am sure it will come eventually."

"Likely."

There wasn't much more able to be had other than polite

conversation under the watchful eye of the guardian, and he was glad to get up and go outside after breakfast. The garden was more expansive than he'd realized, more like a small park, and it allowed some sense of feeling less crowded even in the middle of a city. He offered Catherine his arm, and she accepted it, though the guardian was not far behind them.

"Is it terrible that I want to tie her up and stuff her in a closet?" Henry whispered.

An amused exhalation from Catherine followed his question. "I might actually help you."

"I am surprised she is still living after that look you gave her."

"Not my best work but it did the job."

"You can do worse than that?"

"Never underestimate me."

It was Henry's turn to make a soft sound of amusement, though he wanted to laugh. "I will keep that in mind," he said before dropping his voice to a whisper. "Will you come tonight, Sparrow? I very much enjoyed our conversation and look forward to continuing it."

"Yes," she whispered in return before returning her voice to a normal volume. "I must say, you look quite well now that you have rested and cleaned up."

"Thank you, I do appreciate the compliment. I am not a barbarian … at least not all the time."

Catherine chuckled. "The dispatches say otherwise."

"I am not bothered that they do. Having that sort of reputation makes people less likely to engage with you in a negative way."

"A fair point if one is avoiding being shot at."

"Indeed. I prefer to not be shot at if I can help it. Pistols, muskets, cannons, all things to avoid."

"I would assume so, yes. Tell me, Captain, are you able to read and write?"

"Would it surprise you if I said yes?"

"No, in fact, I should rather hope you can."

"I can and enjoy reading books when I find them or reading pamphlets otherwise. Why, are you considering writing to me once I have gone back to Jamaica?"

"Would it surprise you if I said yes?" she said, repeating his words in a teasing tone.

"No, in fact, I should rather hope you would do so," he replied with a wink that made her laugh.

"I may do, if you wish it. You can tell me things firsthand."

"A bit of vicarious living?"

"Something like that," Catherine said, her gaze becoming as distant as her voice for a moment.

"How far outside of London have you been?"

"Just to our country home in Kent."

"Not far, then," Henry said. "Where would you like to go here if you could?"

"I think I should like to see the north."

"York?"

"Scotland."

"Truly?" Henry replied, intrigued. "And why would you wish to go there?"

"I have heard there is magic to be found, but the wildness of the terrain I have heard described speaks to me in ways I cannot put into words. Have you been?"

"I cannot say I have had the pleasure, no."

"Is Wales like that, too?"

"If I am honest, I cannot really remember what it looked like, so long have I been away."

"Where have you been?"

"A great many places, really. Some I liked, and some I did not."

"Have you been to the colonies?"

"I have a few times, yes, but never to raid them. I stick to the Caribbean for that."

"A wise choice, I am sure."

"Lady Catherine, you should return inside," the older woman said from behind them, and Catherine sighed.

"My sentiments exactly, but let us play her game by day, for the nights are ours," Henry whispered to her. "I will see you tonight." Henry stopped and turned to Catherine, releasing her arm but keeping hold of her hand, bowing and kissing it. "Good day, Lady Catherine."

"Good day to you, Captain," Catherine said with a curtsy before she followed the other woman back to the house.

Henry watched her go, surprised by how much he wished she wouldn't. It was a curious feeling, one he wasn't used to and didn't know what to make of. It wasn't that he was lonely or was dismayed by being alone here; no, he was plenty used to entertaining and occupying himself for long stretches. This was something else, a kindred spirit perhaps, as hidden away as she might be. What he wished was that he was free to explore this, to get to know her in more than short bursts. What would he uncover if he could?

***

As Catherine stepped back inside the house, the walls felt close and almost suffocating, a reflection of what she felt inside. The presence of this woman hovering over her was grating, and it was as if she could sense just when Catherine had been able to relax in order to yank her back from that relief. With quick steps she put as much distance between herself and her minder as she could manage, hurrying upstairs to her room.

Shutting it behind her, she bolted it, having no desire for anyone to just walk in. The anxiety she felt caused her to pace the room, desperate for some sense of calm just beyond her reach. She looked to the door, hurrying toward it but stopping with a shake of her head as she backed away. She couldn't go to him, not now, no matter how she might wish to. Last night, for the first time in her life, she'd felt this weight lifted off her, the weight of expectation and duty, and it was because of him. He'd shown her how it felt to be free to speak, how it felt to have someone genuinely listen to what you had to say when you did, how it felt to be acknowledged as an equal. He'd wanted to hear her, wanted to know who she really was, and given her leave to admit at least one thing she'd never said to anyone. There was a power in that, a draw, that she hadn't been expecting.

The sound of his laughter last night floated through her mind, and she closed her eyes, letting it carry her away for a moment, back to that feeling of relaxation, back to being able to breathe. Opening her eyes again, she went to one of the chairs by the fire and sank into it, covering her face with her hands. The problem now wasn't that he wasn't what she'd imagined; the problem was that he was something far better, something she hadn't known she'd wanted until it was there, and that made him dangerous.

By the time supper was served, Catherine felt as though she could hardly be still, wanting everyone to go to bed so that she could join him in that room where there was no pretense. He sat across from her at the table, but any talk was cursory and she wondered if he was looking forward to it as much as she was. When he stood and bid them all goodnight after the meal, Catherine felt almost dismayed, for he hadn't addressed her directly, but she realized she was being ridiculous now. Of course he wouldn't do so, lest anyone suspect.

Returning upstairs, Burke came in to undress her and ready her for bed, and Catherine let her mind wander as Burke ran a comb through her long hair.

"Are you well, my lady?"

Blinking herself back to the present, Catherine looked into the glass to see Burke watching her with a curious expression. "Yes, I believe so. Why do you ask?"

"You are quiet tonight, distracted. Usually when you are here, you have much to say to me as we get you ready to retire for the night."

"I suppose I am. I find it onerous to have that woman here, always watching me."

"I quite agree. She is breathing down your neck all the time, never giving you a moment's peace."

"Unless I lock myself in here."

"And how is that fair to you? You are already left here to watch over a man who should be nowhere near you, and then this added burden on top of it. I will admit to you that she does not treat us all that much better."

"I am sorry to hear it," Catherine said, frowning at their reflections. "I shall put that right straight away. She is out of line to treat you in any way but respectfully, as she is a guest here."

"Thank you, my lady," Burke said, smiling. "We knew you would see to it once you knew."

"Of course I would!"

"The captain, on the other hand ..."

"What of him?"

"For all his reputation, he has been the kindest guest to have come through here. He treats all of us well and speaks with us as if we are equals. It has been much appreciated; I can tell you that."

Catherine's smile was involuntary but measured. "I am glad to hear it, and I know that such treatment by him earns him extra favor with all of you and thus extra favors."

Burke chuckled. "You know us too well."

"I have grown up with most of you."

"Too true, my lady. You are ready. Do you need anything else?"

"No, thank you. Good night, Burke."

"Good night, my lady," Burke said, curtsying before she departed.

When the door shut, Catherine closed her eyes and let go of a relieved sigh, thankful she'd managed to not slip up in front of someone who knew her so well. As she stood, she picked up a novel she'd been reading, a bit scandalous, but no one would say anything about it. Try as she might, focusing on the words was impossible, and she put the book aside in irritation, worrying her lower lip between her teeth. Crossing to the wardrobe, she lifted the false bottom to remove a far larger tome. With a small smile, she clutched it against her chest before going to sit before the fire. Setting the book on the floor in front of her, she opened it up to reveal a map of the known world. This atlas was one of her most prized possessions, hidden away from those who might think she shouldn't have it, chief amongst them her father. One of her favorite things to do was trace routes across the sea and imagine all of the places she could go if she were Henry.

The sound of a knock brought her head up, and she looked at the door. Standing, she went to the door and opened it, looking out to find no one, and she realized that must be the signal to join him. Catherine hurried back to the book, closing it and creeping out of the room. Her steps were silent, and when she saw the faint sliver of candlelight, it brought a smile to her lips, a smile that only widened when she stepped inside and saw him sitting and waiting for her. Once again, he lounged on the settee in a rather languorous pose, open and relaxed, and it hid both his height and the physical danger he could put you in should he choose to do so. His light brown hair was loose around his shoulders instead of tied back, adding to the informal feeling of their meetings. The only thing about him that remained intense was the richness and depth of the blue color in his eyes.

"Good evening, Sparrow," he said as she closed the door.

"Why do you call me that?"

"It seems fitting, for to me that is what you are, as I said last night. A sparrow trapped in a grand cage. Do you mind it?"

"Were it anyone else, I would say yes, but … with you I do not."

"Very well," he replied, smiling at her before he took notice of what she held. "What have you got there?"

"My favorite item in all the world," she said as she approached him with slow steps.

"Indeed? And you wish to share it with me?"

"We agreed to be ourselves in this room, did we not?"

"We did."

"Then I feel as though you are the one person I can share it with even if you do think I am silly for it."

"I doubt that I will but try me."

Catherine forced herself to hold it out to him, her hands shaking. She'd never shown it to anyone, and to do so made her nervous. What if he thought badly of it? What if he mocked her? She pushed past those thoughts and offered it to him fully.

Henry took it with gentle hands and opened it, then looked up at her with a raised eyebrow. "An atlas?"

"Yes," she answered, fidgeting with her robe. "I told you that you would find it a silly thing," she continued as she reached out for it.

"Hold a moment," Henry said, placing the book on his lap and catching her hands in his own. "What gives you cause to believe I think you silly from just one question?"

"An atlas is a silly thing to prize."

"According to whom?"

"Most anyone I would imagine. My father, for one."

"I am not your father, and something tells me you have kept this hidden from him for just such a reason, am I right?"

"You are."

Henry released her hands. "An atlas is a very valuable thing to any explorer or sailor, and it does not surprise me in the least that you both have one and prize it for its worth. What do you do with it?"

"Now you really will think me silly, but I shall tell you the truth. I like to look at it and dream of all the places I could go if I were …" she began before trailing off.

"If you were …?"

"You."

"Me."

"Yes. If I were you and I had a ship to sail across the sea, where could I go?"

A soft smile appeared on his lips. "I do not think you silly for it at all. I find it flattering that you would read about the things I have done and imagine such a thing."

"Truly?"

"I promise. I cannot and will not lie to you; you deserve better than that from me."

"Thank you," she said in a soft voice, touched by his words and feeling her nervous energy ease.

"May I ask you about something that has been bothering me these last days?"

"No topic is off-limits; was that not the agreement?" Catherine said as she sat down beside him.

"Last night, you mentioned using my description of Jamaica as a way to escape in your mind, and then this morning, your reaction to my suggestion of vicarious living through any letters I might send troubled me."

"Troubled you?"

"Why do you do it? Why do you do those things and look at this atlas while dreaming of being me?"

Catherine faltered for a moment before sighing. "Because when I do, just for a moment, I am not here. I am not me. I am not Catherine, the dutiful daughter expected to be an ornament and a credit to her father by having no depth of feeling or mind of her own but what she is told she can have. You cannot understand what it is like, Henry, how exhausting it can all be, how stifling. How often I feel as though the walls are closing in on me, hoping to squeeze any true life out of my heart and mind. I want so much to be free of it, and I never shall be except in those moments."

The look on his face wasn't pity but genuine sadness, his hurt for her plain. "Catherine, I … I cannot imagine it, nor do I want to. I want even less to imagine you feeling so desperate to live that the only way you can do it is with dreams. What life is this?"

"It is not one," she admitted quietly, "but it is the one I am stuck with."

"How unfortunate not only for you but also for the world you could conquer if you were allowed to be yourself."

"Do you want to know why I was truly upset the first day?"

"Very much."

"Because they took you away from me."

"What?"

Catherine shook her head and looked down at her lap. "Reading those dispatches, imagining your adventures, imagining you … it was one of my favorite means of escape, the one I used most often. The moment the king exposed those thoughts to the light, he stripped that from me, another window sealed up in a house with fewer and fewer openings with which to see the outside."

"I am so sorry," he whispered. "I am sorry he did that, and I am sorry I am not what you wanted or needed, that I am playing a part in it, no matter how unwillingly."

Catherine looked up at him to find his eyes closed, and she could swear he was near tears by the tone of his voice, the thought troubling her. "Henry," she said, reaching out and placing a hand on his. "It is not your fault, for you are who you are, and asking you to be what I expect instead of who you are would be doing the same to you as they are doing to me."

He opened his eyes, turning his hand over so that their palms were touching. "You are right, but if I could be all of it for you, I would."

"Why?"

"Because I want no part in your death, be it heart, mind, or otherwise. Snuffing out the light in another is, to me, one of the worst acts you could inflict on a person. Killing them outright would be a comparative mercy."

"They have closed one window, but you have opened another; they just do not know it yet."

"Have I?"

"Yes, for the reality of you is better than what I could imagine. You speak to me, but you also want to hear me in return. You do not laugh or belittle me; you understand me. To you I am an equal, and I have never in my life known what that felt like until now. I was thinking all day about how, with you, I feel I can breathe. How, for a moment, you lift the weight that is crushing me and how powerful such a thing is. I found I could hardly be still the whole of the day in anticipation of coming here and having that chance again."

"I am glad I can at least do something for you. You are right; I understand you, far better than you may think. You *are* an equal to me, as every human ought to be to another. As you left this morning, I wondered at the notion of kindred spirits and whether I had found mine in the most unlikely place."

"Maybe you have."

"I hope I have, for if I have not, I am terrified of what doing so might feel like if it is not this."

Catherine chuckled. "Time will tell, will it not?"

"I pray we have enough of it."

"So do I."

"You were not the only one who was anxious for the night to come, and I am not used to that feeling in such a, how shall we say … innocent … situation," he said, his voice teasing.

"That is a wicked thing to say," she replied, even though she laughed.

"And yet no less true for all its wickedness."

"You were looking forward to this, too?"

"Very much so. I meant what I said: I want to get to know you, and so far you have not let me down nor have you shown me anything but what I had hoped for when I caught a glimpse of the true Catherine."

"I shall endeavor to keep it so."

"I believe you shall, but you should go," he said, releasing her hand and passing the book back to her. "As much as I wish you would not."

"I wish I did not have to."

"We could talk the night away, could we not?"

"I agree, we could."

"Perhaps sometime soon, we will."

"How will we accomplish that?"

"You leave that part to me. Now, go."

Catherine stood. "Good night, Henry."

"Good night. Oh, and do bring your atlas tomorrow night, beautiful Sparrow."

Catherine paused at the door, looking back at him with silent questioning.

"I promise I shall make it worth it for you, trust me."

Catherine smiled and offered a small nod before she departed. Tomorrow would seem interminable.

Chapter 5

Henry waited in the parlor the following night, eager for her to join him there. He'd started a fire in the grate, having taken to staying here for a time after she'd left, mulling over the things she'd said. Last night had broken his heart for her, the sheer openness of her demeanor and her honesty with her feelings leaving him raw in a way he didn't like. Not because of her but because of how helpless it made him feel. In his world there were quick and easy ways to settle such things, but those methods weren't appropriate here. All the same, he wished he could do something to set her free from a prison she'd been born into.

Waiting for the day to pass had been vexing in the extreme, hours where he had to act as though he knew nothing of the secrets hidden behind those green eyes and layers of propriety theatre. They'd kept their conversation general over meals or if they found themselves in the same place, though a walk after breakfast seemed to be becoming a habit, and it was one he didn't mind. It had allowed him to be nearer to her as well as to confirm her agreement to coming here in the evening.

The door opened, and he looked up, surprised by the relief he felt the instant he saw the slight figure come into the room. She smiled at him, and he instantly did so in return as she shut the door behind her. In her hands, she carried the prized atlas he'd asked her to return with.

"Good evening, Catherine."

"Hello, Henry," she said, making her way over to him.

"Ah, ah, ah," he said, standing before she could sit. "I promised you something, and I fully intend to deliver upon my promise. I am nothing if not a man of my word. Come."

Taking her free hand, he pulled her along toward the fireplace where he'd set out cushions. Taking the atlas from her, he lay down upon the floor on his stomach, opening it up so they could see it clearly in the firelight. Looking up when she didn't join him, he saw her looking at him with a great deal of curiosity.

"Get down here, will you?" he said.

"On the floor?"

"No, on the throne. Yes, down here on the floor with me," he said, laughing.

Catherine shot him an annoyed look, but it was tempered with a small smile as she joined him, taking up the same position. "I do not know if I have ever done this, even as a child."

"First time for everything."

Catherine made a sound of amusement but said nothing.

"Tonight, Sparrow, tonight I shall tell you of adventures, places you can go in your mind that no one can take from you because I gave them to you personally. They are true and thus cannot be exposed as anything else. Are you ready?"

"Yes," she replied, and he wondered if she was even aware of the excitement in her tone.

"Then let us begin with Porto Bello. This was one of my first big actions, though I was not yet a captain. We departed from Port Royal, right here," he said, pointing to a place on the map. "And from there we sailed south."

Tracing the route with a fingertip, he stopped and tapped on a spot on the coast almost due south of Jamaica.

"The ship I was on was part of a fleet of 10, and while

each had its own captain, the admiral of that fleet was one Henry Morgan."

Catherine gave a very small gasp. "I have heard of him!"

"I would be quite surprised if you had not. Anyway, we anchored a good distance away and then got into canoes, getting to shore a few miles from Porto Bello itself just before dawn. We took them quite by surprise, and though we lost 18 men, it was bloodless compared to other raids. We held the city for a month, taking any valuables we could find. Some tortured people to find hidden wealth, but I had no part in that. In the meantime, Morgan negotiated with the Spanish for the ransom to get us to leave. They tried to send a military force, which ended poorly for them, and they gave us the ransom. Each man went home with £120 and whatever plunder he took from the city."

"£120!" Catherine exclaimed, though quietly. "That is a fortune!"

"Indeed, it is, and now you see why piracy is a rather appealing option," Henry chuckled.

"Then what happened?"

"Well, my captain took us off elsewhere. There was an incident, and it led to my becoming captain of the ship."

"An incident?"

"He died in a rather … unfortunate … manner," Henry said with a small shrug, seeing no reason to mention that he'd been the one responsible for that unfortunate manner. He'd had his reasons, and he wasn't sorry.

"Oh, that sounds unpleasant."

"Yes, and not something I want to put in your head. By the time we returned to Port Royal, Morgan was gearing up for another large raid, and after consulting the crew, we joined that voyage. Once again, we were 10 ships, and this time we were for Cartagena, but there was an accident where one of the ships was blown to pieces and made us too small, so we settled for Maracaibo and Gibraltar."

"Blown to pieces by the Spanish?"

"No, a spark in the ship's magazine," Henry said, grimacing. Catherine's eyes went wide.

"Exactly. Now, there were forts that should have been able to mount a good defense," he explained, tapping the spot on the map, "but they didn't have enough men in them to do any good. Once we arrived, we found they'd tried to light a long fuse as a trap, but it was too long and was still making its way. We kicked some dirt on it to put it out and were off. We spent three weeks in Maracaibo, taking whatever we could find, and then five weeks in Gibraltar. Again, as seemed to be Morgan's hallmark, there was torture used, and again neither I nor my crew had any part in it. When we returned to Maracaibo, we discovered there was a Spanish fleet awaiting us in the strait, the only way out."

"Oh no."

"Oh yes. They had 126 cannons with which to shoot at us, so obviously going straight at them would not be the right move. There was a week of negotiations where they wanted us to leave all of our spoils behind, and that was obviously not going to happen. That is when I made the suggestion that would put me squarely in Morgan's notice."

"Which was?"

"Send a fireship directly at the Spanish flagship. We had a ship we had picked up in Gibraltar, and we could use that. We disguised logs to look like crew so that from a distance it would seem fully manned and they would not suspect. We cut portholes and used more logs to look like guns and then loaded it with barrels of gunpowder while putting grappling irons in the rigging. When the ship exploded, those irons would tangle in the Spanish rigging and make them useless."

"That actually worked?"

"It did, yes. The fireship did its job, taking out the flagship and allowing us to capture one of the other ships as plunder.

We still had to get past the fort, and that was something we could not do as we were. Morgan threatened to burn Maracaibo to the ground unless we were allowed to pass, and while the soldiers refused to negotiate, the citizens of Maracaibo did, wanting to pay us to go away. At the same time, we took notice that the fort's guns were set to repel a land attack. So, we began loading men into a canoe to make it look like a landing crew. They would climb down into the canoe, row ashore, and then lie down in the bottom of the canoe as it made its way back, then repeat the process. In truth, all of us remained aboard. The Spanish stripped the forts of men to prepare for that attack, and we raised anchor, drifting out with the tide and raising sail when we were even with the fort. We returned to Port Royal laden with plunder from the two cities, the ransom, and all of the money we had salvaged from the captured Spanish ships."

Catherine laughed, covering her mouth to stifle it. "Clever. But would it not have been easier to send some men to the guns up top, kill the Spanish gunners, and then turn those guns on the Spanish ships below?"

"Are you sure you are not a pirate?" Henry asked, chuckling. "After that, Morgan asked me to join him on his next mission: sacking Panama," Henry said, pointing it out on the map. "This time it was 30 ships."

"My goodness!"

"An army indeed. We took these two islands first," he said, moving his finger, "and then Chagres, where we garrisoned the fort. Then we moved on toward Panama City. The journey was hellish, through jungles and swamps on foot, then transferring to canoes, then back to foot, but after three days we made it. We attacked the following morning, and it was a disaster for them. Their soldiers were green, and we were able to fool them with false movements. As things got worse, the governor ordered a herd of cattle released to try and charge us, but they charged the Spanish instead."

Catherine clapped both hands over her mouth, laughing into them so hard there were tears in her eyes.

"It is rather comical, to be sure," Henry said, laughing with her. "We destroyed them. They lost 500 men, and we lost only 15. The governor had vowed to burn the city down rather than let us have it, and after that battle he did just that. We took what we could from the ruins and headed home."

"Just like that?"

"Just like that. The share per man was low based on how little we'd taken and the sheer number of men involved, but it was really about the clout of having sacked Panama. I decided then that I had no interest in sailing with Morgan again, especially after he took slaves and bought himself a plantation with the money from Maracaibo. Morgan had come to value me as a fellow captain and a sailor and thus did not take kindly to my decision, though I have stood fast by it and not regretted it. As you well know, I now have my own reputation and no need of him."

"I have heard he is a terrible sailor."

"Oh, he is," Henry said, laughing as he closed the book and rolled over onto his back. "I have never known a man who sank more ships by poor sailing than Morgan has while still somehow maintaining his reputation as a pirate, but there you have it."

"Were any of them caused by weather?"

"No, actually, but that is a very good question to have asked. To be quite honest, I always fear the sea more than the men who sail upon it."

"Oh?"

"It can be unpredictable; storms can materialize seemingly out of nowhere and sink you. The wind can die, and all you do is drift slowly while running out of supplies and getting nowhere. At least with other sailors, I often knew who they were and how to fight them; they were predictable in some ways, and it made them feel far less of a danger to me."

Catherine closed her eyes and took a deep breath, releasing it before opening them to look down at him with a bright smile. "What adventures you have had."

"More than my share, I think," he said, though part of him felt a little guilty for polishing these tales as much as he had, leaving out much of the horror, blood, cruelty, and death.

"Not more than your share, for little did you know you were collecting them to share with a distant relation back in England, who will take them most gratefully."

Henry turned his head to look at her, wondering what she would think if he told her the whole of it but having no desire to take this from her. She needed it, and he was happy to give what he could. Without thinking, he reached out and pushed some of her hair away from her face, tucking it behind her ear, his fingertips brushing her cheek as she went almost completely still.

"One who, I think, will go with me on all of my future exploits, carried there in my mind and able to see it all in her dreams as I send it back to her in mine," he whispered.

"Henry, I …" she began in a return whisper. "I should go," she finished, changing whatever it had been she'd meant to say.

"I know, and again I wish you need not, more than the last."

"Thank you for telling me all of this; it was wonderful to listen to."

"You are welcome, Sparrow. Fly away before they see you are gone and lock you away from me."

Catherine sat up, though she seemed reluctant to do so, and part of him hoped she would throw caution to the wind and stay even though he knew she shouldn't. He was still a danger to her in many ways, ways she didn't seem to realize, and he had no desire to bring harm of any sort to her.

"Good night," she said, picking up the atlas.

"Good night. Pleasant dreams of crushing Spanish fleets in your wake," he replied, grinning at her.

Her gentle laugh surrounded him as she stood up and

walked toward the door. "Thank you, I shall endeavor to make you proud."

"I do believe you would," he murmured as the door shut behind her.

Chapter 6

"Tonight, do not get too undressed for bed," Henry whispered to Catherine during their walk the following morning.

Catherine gave him a sideways glance.

"If you want freedom, Sparrow, I will give it to you if you do as I say."

Catherine nodded but said nothing else.

"Excellent."

"Would you care for some archery, Captain?" she said in a normal tone.

"If you are willing."

"Always," she said, letting go of his arm and making her way to where targets had been set up. Bows and quivers waited for them, and he knew she'd planned this.

Henry took up the bow and examined it. "It has been a long time since I've done this. Not something much called for in my line of work."

"No, I suspect it is more swords and daggers and cannons."

"Indeed."

Catherine nocked an arrow and raised the bow, taking careful aim before loosing it and sending it into the target near the center.

"Very good, my lady."

"Thank you."

Henry nocked an arrow and took aim, but when he loosed the arrow, it ended up near the top of the target. He looked over at Catherine, whose lips were pressed together to stifle a laugh.

"At least you hit it?" she offered.

Henry gave her an annoyed look before he tried again. This time he was a little closer but not enough. "Do not say anything," he said, turning to her and pointing.

The gesture only made her laugh. "I am sure you are much better at shooting."

"Definitely. Have you any cannons we could fire?"

"No, sorry, Father does not keep heavy artillery around the house since the footman who was polishing it set one off and blasted the entire back of the house off. It is why we have a garden now."

Henry started laughing. "Damned servants."

"Cromwell took all the good ones."

"Ohhh, careful," he said, laughing harder at the rather subversive joke.

Catherine laughed and then nocked another arrow. "I am sure the king would love to take you hunting," she said as she let the arrow fly.

Henry sighed as she hit the center. She was far better at this than he was. "Perhaps. Or perhaps he should take you."

"Women are not allowed."

"Because you might outshoot the men."

Catherine offered a half-smile as she took another excellent shot.

"What about knives?"

"Knives?"

"Can you throw them?"

"I have never tried."

"Wait here," Henry said, turning and making his way back to the house. When he returned, he was carrying a box of kitchen knives that were waiting to be sharpened. "These will do."

"I do not know how to do it."

Henry picked one up and sent it flying at the target, hitting it dead center. Catherine gasped. "Like that."

"How do you hold it?"

Henry took a smaller knife from the box and placed it in her hand, taking the liberty of adjusting her hold. "Now throw."

Catherine did so, but the knife bounced off and she made a face while Henry chuckled. Taking another knife from the box, he adjusted her grip once more. "Not as hard."

Catherine nodded, and when Henry stepped back, she threw it again, and this time it stuck but to the outside. All the same, there was a little whoop of joy from Catherine, who clapped her hands.

"I did it! Look!"

"Yes, very good. At least you hit it?" he teased.

Catherine narrowed her eyes, reached into the box, picked up a knife, and threw it, burying it in the target right next to Henry's knife. He stopped laughing, his mouth opening in slight shock before he looked over at her.

"Lucky shot."

"Are you sure?"

"If you can do it again, I will give you a sixpence."

Catherine reached into the box, took another knife, and sunk it into the target on the other side of his before holding out her hand for the sixpence with a raised eyebrow.

"How …"

"I told you not to underestimate me."

"Oh. Oh, I see. Rifles."

"Pogue!"

"Yes, my lady!" Pogue said as he stepped out of the house.

"Bring the flintlocks, would you? And the pistols."

"Yes, Lady Catherine," the young man said as he hurried inside.

"Lady Catherine! Such things are below a lady! I said nothing about the knives, but this is too far!" the guardian chided.

"Hardly," Catherine shot back. "Need I remind you that you are only here to make sure the Captain does not ravage me, and given that he has shown no interest in doing so at this time, your input on the situation is not needed?"

The woman huffed but said nothing else.

"Ouch," Henry said as Catherine rolled her eyes at him.

Pogue quickly reappeared with the guns Catherine had asked for, setting them down and starting to load them. Catherine walked to the targets and pulled out the arrows and the knives, replacing them in their boxes before looking at Henry.

"What is our wager?"

"No wager, just a competition."

"What are we seeking to prove?"

"I am not sure if we are seeking to prove more than besting the other."

"Fine."

"Ladies first."

"Oh no. We will do it together."

"Fine."

Catherine held her hand out, and Pogue placed a rifle in it immediately. "Pogue, count us off."

Henry accepted the other rifle and took aim at the target as Catherine did the same.

"3 … 2 … 1 … fire!"

The sound of the rifles firing reverberated across the garden, and both of them lowered the weapons, each having hit the target in the center. Henry's jaw tightened, and he turned, grabbing the pistol and handing off the rifle.

"Again," Henry said.

"3 … 2 …"

Henry turned and pointed his at Catherine, only to find her pointing hers at him, bringing a small scream from the guardian as Pogue ceased counting. The two of them stood there, staring at each other as if daring the other to fire, not wanting to be the first to lower their weapon. Henry, however, finally did.

"It seems there are traits in the blood that not even the English can be rid of," Henry said, his tone dark as he disengaged the mechanism.

Catherine seemed to come back to herself and looked startled. "I … I should go inside …" she stammered, handing the pistol off to Pogue before hurrying past him and the guardian.

As per usual, other than at meals, Henry didn't see Catherine for the rest of the day, though even there she wouldn't meet his gaze. He hadn't thought she could surprise him in such a way, but she had. He wouldn't expect that level of proficiency from any woman, much less a noble one, Henry mused to himself as he made his way down the hall that night. He wondered if she'd even still want to meet with him.

When he knocked on the door, it opened, and he felt relieved when he saw her face peek out. "Put this on. Do not wear anything fancy; leave your hair in a simple plait."

Catherine took the bundle from him, and he leaned against the wall to wait. When she emerged, she was dressed in clothes befitting one of the servants here, not one of the occupants. Henry nodded his approval and threw a cloak over her shoulders, pulling up the hood to hide her face. The two of them made their way down the stairs in silence and out the door he'd taken the key for. They remained silent as Henry hurried them a good distance away before turning and leading them down to the river.

"Where are we going?" Catherine whispered. "And why am I dressed this way?"

"You will see," he replied as he ushered her onto the ferry that would take them across the river.

Once there, he stepped off first and gingerly lifted her by the waist to set her down above the muck. He then took her hand and led her through the streets until he found what he was looking for. Henry swept her inside and pulled the cloak away, and Catherine would see for the first time why she was dressed the way she was. Her eyes widened, and she turned to him, unsure of what to do or think.

"Welcome to an evening of freedom, little Sparrow," Henry said with a sly grin.

"You have brought me to a tavern!" she exclaimed in a scandalized whisper.

"I have indeed."

"I cannot be here!"

"And yet here you are."

"What if someone sees me!"

"If someone you know has come all the way over to Southwark, the last person they will notice is you, I assure you. Now, come on."

Henry took her by the hand once more and pulled her into the tavern after him before she could resist any further. He located a corner for them to sit in and placed her in the darker part of it to shield her even further.

"Rum, please," he said when the tavern girl approached. "The whole bottle and two cups." The girl glanced at Catherine and then walked off.

"Where are you getting the money to pay for all of this?"

"You did not think I had none on me when they took me, did you?"

"I thought they would have taken it."

"No, and if they had, they would not have taken me because they would be dead."

Catherine looked around her at the varying mix of people present in this place. Henry was certain it was her first time seeing anyone lower than the people who served in her household, and her expression told him she didn't really know what to make of any of them or of the place they were in. The bottle and cups were placed on the table, and Henry poured some for each of them.

"Here you are, your next bit of rebellion."

Catherine reached out, hesitant, and picked it up. Lifting

it to her nose, she shook her head. "It smells terrible!"

"Then do not smell it," Henry said, his mouth twisting in a wry smile.

She glared at him and took a small taste before coughing, and he laughed at her.

"Keep drinking. You will get used to it."

"Why did you bring me here?"

"Because this is what freedom looks like for me and I wanted you to see it. It is not all sailing, and this is one way to spend time in a life like mine. A bit of drink and carousing never hurts anyone, and I am certain most of the men in court do the same with fairly good frequency."

"I am sure they do," she said as she took another drink, making a small face.

"Why can you not look at me tonight?"

"What?"

"You cannot look me directly in the face. Why?"

"I can," she said, looking over at him.

"You are looking at my forehead," Henry said, reaching out and pulling her chin down with his thumb. "Why can you not look at me? What is bothering you?"

"I liked today too much."

"Whatever in the hell does that mean?"

"With you. I liked playing with you the way we did, and I liked it more than I should. I —" she squeezed her eyes closed and shook her head. "It is not right. None of this is."

"Why not?"

"What good will it do me? Any of it? So I can do those things, but where will I use them? Do you think that whatever man they marry me to will care? Will he do with me what you did and have been doing? No, he will not."

"He is a fool if he does not."

"And you are a fool if you think he will even care enough to notice."

"I liked it, too," he said quietly.

"What do you mean?"

"It was fun, and you surprised me. You are as competitive as I am. Yet another notch in favor of my kindred soul theory."

Catherine lifted her cup and took another drink without making a face this time. "Some would consider that a fault."

"I am not some, and you should know that by now."

"They are not all like you."

"Would you want them to be?"

"I am not sure if that would make it easier or harder."

"Make what?"

"To be who and what I must."

"That I cannot say," Henry replied as he took another drink.

"Tell me another story," Catherine said, changing the subject.

"About what?"

"An adventure."

"Hm. Oh! I once had a fight with a French ship. They had more guns and were faster, but we somehow managed to hit them. They were not carrying what we thought."

"What were they carrying?"

"Slaves."

"Oh …"

"We killed the crew, towed the ship to shore, and set them free."

Catherine smiled. "You did?"

"Of course. I cannot tolerate slavery and will not. I would never carry human cargo."

"So, pirates have some honor."

"Some of us, yes, others no."

Catherine finished her cup and pushed it to Henry, who filled it up and pushed it back. "Do you think I could be a pirate?"

"I do not see why not, though there would certainly be some obstacles you would need to overcome."

"Such as?"

"Well, you would need a ship, for starters, and a crew. A ship I could help you get but not a crew, and you would have to find a crew willing to serve a woman as their captain. Do you even know how to sail, Sparrow?"

"Um … no."

Henry grimaced. "Well, let us just say you do. So, you have a ship, you have a crew; now what?"

"I attack another ship?"

"How do you know if you want to? Ammunition is not cheap."

"What flag has it got?"

"Ah, now you are thinking. The flag is Dutch."

"Pass."

"The next one you come across issss … French."

"Shoot it!" Catherine shouted, which made Henry laugh.

"Shoot it where?"

"On the side?"

"Which side?"

"I have no idea! One of them," she said, waving her hand dismissively even as she laughed, the rum doing its work.

Henry was still laughing, the game amusing him. "Right, so you shoot it on one of the sides, and they shoot back."

"How do they shoot back? They have a hole in the boat!"

"They would shoot back, I promise."

"Right, right. Where are they shooting me?"

"On the side."

"Which side?"

"One of them," he said with a grin, which turned to a laugh when Catherine kicked him under the table.

"Take some sort of evasive action."

"Good! You were successful. Now what."

"Shoot them again."

"Where?"

"The captain's arsehole?"

Henry stared at her for a moment before he started laughing hysterically as she did. "Oh Jesus, Catherine …"

"Would it work?"

"If you had that good of an aim, I would commend you."

"What do I win?"

"Gold, silk, wine. What would you do with it?"

"Sell it."

"Keep none for yourself?"

"Maybe a little. We could all get drunk on the wine."

"Like you are right now?"

"Maybe," Catherine said, laughing.

"You are ridiculous, do you know that? But in a very sweet and innocent way."

"Innocent!"

"You know so little of the world, Catherine. So little of how ugly it can be, how hard. You wish for freedom, but you do not realize that no one is ever really free. Everyone is constrained by something, even me."

"Some have less constraint; you have less."

"Not always." Henry sighed. "I wish you could stay this way. I wish there would never come a point where you would find out what it can really be like."

"You speak as though I have never seen any of the ugly side of humanity, but I have. I have watched the duplicitous games played at court to get ahead; I have watched people destroy each other, and over what? A title and a better set of rooms at the palace?"

"That is one thing, but you have never played those games yourself, never had to think your way out of them because your own survival depended upon it."

"Have I not?"

"In what way?"

Catherine looked down at her cup. "My father is … he is not a good man and never has been. He is all ambition and will do whatever he must to get ahead. He cares nothing for me as the only daughter except what connection I may one day earn him when he sells me to the highest bidder. The violence he has inflicted upon me to bend me to his will is heavy. I know ugliness, Henry. More than you might wish I did."

Henry reached out and placed a hand on her arm where it rested on the table. "I cannot put into words how much I hate that you have experienced such things at the hands of the ones who should care for you most."

"I am a commodity and nothing more. Why should he care?"

Henry shook his head. "You deserve so much better than this. Yet, I still feel you have not truly seen how dark it is. You have never had to live without food or shelter, never had to sell yourself to get it. There has never been a time where you lived in a rat-infested slum where the rats are as hungry as you are and see you as a meal. You have not seen what it looks like when your last hope is snatched from your fingers, have not heard the desperate screams of pain while witnessing the horrors we can and do inflict upon each other. I have, and I pray you never do."

"But I cannot stay that way, can I?"

"No, you cannot. You will see it in your own ways, that ugly cruelty and lack of regard for decency, and my heart aches for what it will take from you when you do."

"Then let us not think about that and only think about right now and the fun we are having," Catherine said, offering him a smile, and the adroitness she displayed at putting on a far sunnier demeanor than she felt amazed him.

"Are you having fun?" he asked, more than willing to banish those dark thoughts rather than imagine them.

"Yes, actually, I am."

"I am glad to hear it."

"May we come again tomorrow?"

"That would be pushing our luck, do you not think?"

Catherine's expression turned curious. "What are they doing?"

Henry followed her gaze to where a man sat with a lady he seemed to have hired, kissing her. "What do you mean?"

"What are they doing? Why are they doing that?"

"Why are they kissing?"

"Kissing? Does that not just go for cheeks and hands?"

Henry raised an eyebrow. "You cannot be serious."

"I am," she said, unable to take her eyes off them.

"You have never seen a man kiss a woman?"

"Not like that."

"Catherine, do you —" he paused. She couldn't be that innocent, could she? Not in a court like Charles'. "Have you any idea what men and women do?"

"Well, I …" she began, but then gave a small shake of her head. "No, I do not."

Henry's eyes widened. What were her parents doing to her? Were they planning on serving her up like a lamb with no idea of what was coming? Who would do that? He realized in an instant that his wonder at just how much virtue she possessed had been very, very wrong. She might spend her days in a court known for debauchery and licentiousness, but she'd clearly been kept far from it.

"We should go."

"No, I do not want to."

"Catherine," he began but sighed when he realized he'd have to drag her out.

"He is touching her!" Catherine exclaimed in a scandalized whisper.

"Yes, that tends to be what comes next."

"She seems to like it. Are you supposed to like it?"

"If we did not, we would not keep doing it."

"My mother once said it was just a thing to be endured and it would be over quickly, though she never did tell me what 'it' was."

Henry sighed heavily and rubbed his forehead. "The only people who say that are people who do not like each other and do not know how to enjoy themselves. It is what happens when women like you are kept under lock and key until you get handed to a husband whose only use for you is to make sons. Women who love a man, women in the ranks below yours who marry for love? They enjoy it because they want to be with that person."

"I will not ever know that, will I?" she said. "What she feels."

"Probably not."

Catherine lowered her head, and Henry saw a tear land on the table. It wasn't fair what was happening, that such a girl with such a spirit would be shuttered up, cold and alone, never knowing what it was like to feel anything beyond what she was allowed. It was a sort of cruelty he'd never dreamed of, and he was watching it unfold right before his eyes, a murder happening in slow motion.

"Catherine," he said, reaching out and touching her cheek. He knew it was a liberty, but his desire to ease her pain drowned out that reasoning. When she looked up, he brushed her tears away. "Please do not cry. I am sorry it has to be like this."

"Me, too," she whispered.

A sudden commotion broke the moment as a table was flipped over and two men began shouting. Catherine went silent as the two screamed about being cheated, unwittingly moving closer to Henry and gripping his arm even as he put his free arm around her to keep her close to him and thus safer. The entire tavern seemed to stop moving as the two argued over money. When someone tried to step in to calm the situation, he was summarily shoved away, and before anything else could be done, there was a glint of light on metal. Henry inhaled sharply, knowing what was coming, but before he could move to shield Catherine, one man buried a knife deep into the eye of the other. Catherine, along with many other women, screamed in terror, and the whole of the tavern exploded into chaos. Henry yanked her up and out of the chair, hurrying for the door, but the surge of others also trying to get out pulled them apart.

"HENRY!" he heard Catherine scream, but he couldn't see her.

Henry pushed his way through people even as the surge spilled out onto the street, people running in every direction, but he didn't see Catherine. "CATHERINE!"

***

Catherine was pushed along, running with the others because she had no choice, and to do otherwise felt as though she'd be swept underfoot and trampled. As the wave of people spilled into a broader street, it broke apart, emptying into side streets and leaving her standing alone, trying to catch her breath. Turning in a small circle, she realized she had no idea where she was. There was a moment of panic before she realized she needed to act. Beginning to walk back the way she thought she'd come, none of the scenery looked familiar to her, and she couldn't be sure if she'd chosen the right direction. What would she do if she hadn't and had instead wandered further into a part of the city she was unfamiliar with? The figure of a man coming toward her brought a sense of relief, and she hurried toward it.

"Henry?"

"No Henry here, darlin'," the man said. "Are you lost?"

"Yes, I was … I was with a friend, and we got separated. Please, could you help me? How do I find the river from here?"

"What is a girl looking like you doin' over 'ere?"

"My friend —"

"Are you tellin' me a story?"

"No, I —"

"You are not from over this side of the river, I can tell that much."

"I am not. I really am lost and —"

The man grabbed her arm and yanked her into a small close, bringing a small scream from her before he clamped a hand over her mouth, pulling at her skirts with the other. Catherine twisted her body away from him, screaming against his hand and trying to shove him away from her.

"Shut up, tart!" he hissed, moving his hand to now cover her nose.

Catherine choked on her screams, her lungs burning, desperate for blessed air even as she kept struggling to get away from him before he could touch her. In the next moment, the man's heavy weight fell against her and then away from her, his hand dropping from her face as another hand grabbed her arm and pulled her out.

"No, do not touch me!" she gasped out, chest heaving as she took in huge gulps of air.

"Catherine, it is me."

It took her a moment to process that it was H+enry before she started to cry in fear as well as relief. Henry pulled her close, and she buried her face in his chest. Propriety didn't matter in this moment as she threw her arms around his waist.

"You are safe now," he said in a soft voice, stroking her hair. "I have you. Let us get you home."

Chapter 7

The following morning, Catherine wasn't at breakfast, and her conspicuous absence concerned him. When she hadn't even shown up for their normal walk, he'd gotten it out of Pogue that he'd been told Lady Catherine wasn't feeling well and had decided to skip breakfast, but he'd seen her going out to the garden. Henry wasted no time in leaving to seek her out, wanting to see for himself that she was all right. He had a feeling her distance had everything to do with what had happened the previous night and nothing to do with feeling unwell. They hadn't spoken on the trip back; he hadn't known what to say. So much had happened it had been difficult to know where to begin, and he'd had no idea how to put his contrition into words.

When he found her sitting on a stone bench, he sat down beside her, remaining silent for a long moment. "You were not at breakfast," he finally said.

"I am not feeling well."

"Is that the truth or just what you are telling everyone."

"Both."

"I am sorry for what happened, Catherine."

"It was not your fault."

"Yes, it was. I should not have taken you there in the first place; it was foolish of me."

"Why was it foolish?"

"It was not a place where highborn ladies ought to be. Then, when the worst happened, I lost hold of you, and you disappeared. I am glad I found you when I did."

"So am I."

"It happened."

"What did?"

"The moment I dreaded, the moment when you first learned how ugly the world can be. It happened right there in front of me; it happened in that close."

"Yes," she whispered.

"So, you see? I should not have taken you."

"I am glad you did. I was having fun before that."

"So was I, if I am honest. I seem to have fun with you whenever we are up to some sort of knavery."

"Maybe everyone is right. Maybe you should stay away from me."

"Because I am a terrible influence?"

"Yes, but not in the way you think."

"Oh?"

"You made me realize how dull life is here and how dull it will be again when you are gone."

"I wish I could change that."

"No, you do not. Not really."

"Yes, I —"

"I am your current amusement," she said, cutting off his protest. "Useful to you for as long as you are here and then easily forgotten about. You tell me you wish you could change things, but those words are as hollow as the man you pretend to be with everyone else."

"No, they are not. I would if I could; I swear it. If I had any power here, I would do anything I could to change it. If we were in my world, I would be able to do something, but here? Here, I can do nothing."

"Your world," she repeated, her voice as flat as her expression.

"Catherine —"

"Stop. You do not get it, do you? Every day, every moment, they try to smother and kill in me the very things you try to draw back out. You breathe life back in, but what will happen when you are no longer there? You will sail away for new adventures while I will go on here knowing what is there but forever being barred from it. I will let them cover the colors in grays and blacks, so I can see only what they wish me to see, and I will die in that world. I will die, and all that will be left is a shell that answers to the name of Catherine."

Henry was silent, her words cutting sharper than any blade he'd ever encountered.

"I cannot keep doing this. I cannot keep trying to hold on to what I will never have. It is best I just go back to being what I was."

"Why are you giving up so easily?"

"What other choice do I have!" Catherine said, anger flaring into her voice to replace the dullness that had been there only moments before.

"You could fight."

"For what?"

"For yourself, for your soul."

"For nothing! None of that matters! I have less power here than the lowest monger, and do you know why? Because I had the great misfortune of being born a woman. It is better to just accept my fate than to fight for nothing."

"Please, Catherine," he said, reaching out and touching her hand.

"No!" she shouted, standing up and pulling away from him as though his touch had burned her. "Stop it! Stop teaching me how to feel! Stop reaching things in me and drawing them out! Stop being everything I wanted you to be!"

The last words were sobbed out before she hurried past him and back into the house. Henry closed his eyes, and there were tears of his own. What was he doing? What game was he playing? She was right; he would go, and she would stay. He was showing her a world she'd never known, giving her a taste of what she wanted, and then slamming the door in her face on his way out. She'd be married off and sent to the country, never to be seen again but as an ornament whenever her husband felt kind enough to bring her to court.

At the same time, it was more than that. Where he was reaching her, she was reaching him, too. He'd been far more honest and open with her than he'd ever been with anyone. It had been so easy to talk to her, to relax in her presence, and to let down his guard because he knew she didn't want anything from him but himself. He would miss that when he was gone, that honesty. He knew how exhausting it was to live a life where you had to be what you weren't because he had to live it, too.

Henry remained in the garden for quite some time, and when he went in, Catherine was nowhere to be found. She wasn't at dinner or supper; she wasn't anywhere, and it struck him how lonely it made him because he'd grown so used to her company so quickly. He looked forward to the setting of the sun, holding out hope that she would come again so that he could at least speak to her, so that he could explain and let spill all the words that sat so heavily on his heart and mind. When the night finally came, he went to her door and knocked before going to the parlor to wait for her. His ears were trained on every sound, listening for her footsteps or the rustle of her dressing gown, but there was nothing. He didn't know how long he waited there before he returned to her door, giving it a gentle knock.

"Catherine," he whispered. When there was no response, he knocked again. "Catherine, please come out. I just want to talk to you."

The door remained shut, and he placed his palm against it. "Please," he whispered. When silence was the only answer, he sighed and returned to his room to sit in the dark, watching the sky and, for the first time, wishing he were home.

In the morning, a page arrived to tell them that Lady Catherine and the Captain were summoned back to court. Henry was to leave right away, and Catherine would come later after she'd gotten her things together. He knew that no matter what they said, this was a deliberate attempt to separate them, and he wondered what the dragon woman had reported. Catherine didn't emerge to see him off or to even speak to him, and the pain that brought him was acute and unexpected.

This time, the carriage he rode in had uncovered windows, and he could see the streets as they went through them toward Whitehall, teeming with life and humanity, no hints at what darkness hid beneath it to emerge with the setting of the sun. When he arrived, he was once more ushered before the king, but this time he was not hidden in any way, stares and whispers following him as he walked, only to be silenced by the doors of the throne room shutting behind him.

"Your Majesty," Henry said, bowing.

"Welcome back, Captain Merrick. You look much better than when we last saw you."

"Thank you, Your Majesty. Rest and the kindness of my hostess did much to restore me."

"Is that so? I understand you and our little Catherine were a bit at odds."

"No, Your Majesty, quite the contrary. Lady Catherine and I got along quite well once we understood each other."

"Well, it will not matter now. You will be staying here and will be attending events and such with the other men of court. Lady Catherine will resume her duties here."

"Yes, Your Majesty," he replied, somehow able to keep the resignation from his voice.

As the first days went by, Henry hadn't so much as caught a glimpse of Catherine, no matter how he'd tried. Each night was a different supper or party or entertainment, and Henry allowed himself to get lost in it and in the debauchery that came with it, playing the role of the pirate captain they all expected from him. In those moments he couldn't think of her, and for now that was what he wanted. It was easy to drown his sadness and the memory of her in the bodies of willing women, though it never lasted. When he finally found himself alone, it all washed back in, made heavier with the weight of his guilt and his shame at all of this, and it often left him in tears. It wasn't something he was used to, never having once felt either of those things when he'd spent time in many a brothel after coming back from raids, just as everyone did. Now it made him feel dirty, unworthy of her company should he ever see her again, as if he had ever been worthy of it to begin with.

A few weeks after his return, he'd finally seen her on a hunt, riding with the queen and the ladies, but he hadn't been able to get near her. He suspected that was very much on purpose, and it angered him. All he wanted was to go and pull her from that horse so he could take her away and either demand she speak to him or simply put them both on the next ship to Jamaica. Instead, he watched her from afar, able to see her smiles and know they were false, knowing she was hurting as much as he was.

When it was announced that there was to be a grand party for the king's birthday, a general sense of excitement swept through the court as everyone set their minds to wardrobe and who would be there. There was talk of the infamous Captain Merrick being there, and the information reached him that many of the ladies were excited to see what he really looked like. He wondered if she would be there or if she would be kept from it and from him once more.

The question was answered the night of the party when, as he approached the entrance to the hall, he saw Catherine standing behind the heavy curtain, waiting her turn to be announced. Through a seam, she was watching the other partygoers mingle and talk and laugh. His heart in his throat at the very sight of her so near once again, he stepped up behind her in silence, sliding his hand over hers where it rested on the curtain.

"My little Sparrow watches the world go by but no longer wants to be in it."

The words whispered against her ear made her close her eyes, her hand tightening on the curtain beneath his own, and he thought he heard her sigh in something like relief. She opened her eyes and turned to find him behind her, so close his chest had been touching her back.

"Henry," she whispered.

"Hello, Catherine," he said. "It is good to see you."

"Is it?"

"It is. I have missed you a great deal."

"That is not what I have heard."

"No matter what you have heard, it does not change the fact that I have missed your company."

"You have been far too busy for it, I would think."

"They have kept you away from me. Deliberately," he said, refusing to let her shy away from the topic with barbs meant to wound him.

"Yes."

"By their design or yours?"

"Mostly theirs, but sometimes mine."

"Why would you want to stay away?"

"You know why."

"You are afraid."

"Of what?"

"Of me, of yourself, of everything you feel but do not want to."

"Henry, please do not do this. I cannot —"

"Walk out with me."

"What?"

"Let them announce us together. Walk out on my arm."

"I cannot!"

"Why not?"

"It would be —"

"Scandalous? Oh yes, yes it would. It would be a scandal, it would be rebellion, it would be perfection. This is your chance, my lovely little bird, your one chance to show them some color."

Henry stepped away from her and walked to the curtain, and in the next moment, he felt her arm in his, and he smiled, giving a nod to the footman.

"Captain Henry Merrick and Lady Catherine Merrick," he announced as he pulled the curtain back.

Henry stepped through with Catherine and fought the urge to grin as the room went silent. He could feel Catherine trembling beside him, and he wasn't sure if it was from fear or excitement. They paid courtesy to the king and queen before he escorted her down the stairs.

"Well done," he said. "They will be talking about that for weeks."

Henry didn't miss the small smile that passed across her lips.

"Kitty!"

Catherine turned just as a bubbly young woman came bounding up to them. "Hello, Frankie! Let me introduce you to Captain Henry Merrick. Captain, this is Lady Frances."

"Oh! Oh, my goodness! I have heard of you! How exciting it is to meet you! You do not look like a pirate."

Henry couldn't help but be amused by this bubbly, child-like girl. "Do I not?"

"No. Are you not supposed to have a scarred face or look frightening? You do not; you look very nice and not mean or frightening at all."

"I had no idea there were physical requirements. I shall see to meeting them forthwith."

"I think you should be how you are. There are enough scary old pirates that it only seems logical that there should be young handsome pirates."

"I am happy to oblige then," he replied, chuckling.

"Kitty, will you not come dance with us?"

"Yes, go," Henry said, releasing her arm. "I will be sure to find you later."

"Thank you, Captain!" Frances called out as she grabbed Catherine by the hand and pulled her away.

Henry smiled at her as Catherine looked back at him over her shoulder, while he began to mingle with the rest of the crowd. As he did, he watched Catherine dance with the other young women, laughing and smiling. These were true, like the ones he'd seen from her when they were alone together, and it made him happy to know that, at least for a moment, she felt joy.

It wasn't long before he felt her arm slip into his again, her hand resting on top of his arm. He covered her hand with his own, not really thinking about it, but happy to know she was near him again. He hadn't realized how cavernous a hole she'd left in his soul until she'd been returned to him. It amazed him how the moment she was there, everything felt right again, as though these last weeks without her had all been some horrible nightmare. She remained by his side, walking with him as he spoke to different guests and joining the conversation when warranted.

"Good evening, Catherine," a smooth voice said.

Henry turned with Catherine to find a young woman standing there of obviously high rank. She was a beauty, that was certain, and it was clear she was well aware of it.

"Good evening, Lady Mary. Please let me introduce Captain Henry Merrick. Captain, this is Lady Mary Downey, the daughter of the duke."

"Yes, I know who he is, Catherine, thank you. Captain, a great pleasure to meet you at last."

"The pleasure is mine, Lady Mary."

"I have heard a great deal about you, Captain."

"Have you?"

"Yes, from others who have been fortunate enough to have already made your acquaintance."

There was something in the way she smiled that told Henry precisely what she meant, something he knew Catherine wouldn't catch, and he was thankful for it. "I hope I do not disappoint."

"Somehow I doubt you will. Catherine, my father is requesting you join his set for the next dance."

"It would be my honor," Catherine said in a quiet tone that made it obvious to Henry that she felt quite the opposite, releasing his arm with great reluctance before threading her way through the crowd to where the duke and several others stood.

Henry watched as the duke traced a finger along Catherine's bare shoulder with a wolfish expression that did nothing to mask his thinking. He could tell Catherine fought the urge to pull away from it, and it made him angry that anyone, even a duke, should make her feel that way. It was tempting to go and remove her right then, though he knew he couldn't.

"Captain."

Lady Mary's voice drew his attention back to her. "Yes, please forgive me," he said, offering her a charming smile.

"You seem distracted."

"There is much to see."

"I think you have yet to see the best of it."

"Is that so?"

"I would be more than happy to show you."

"I would be honored to take you up on your offer in a while."

Lady Mary smiled, walking away from him, and Henry sighed before he looked over to the dancers. Catherine's smile looked strained, and he made his way over to them so that when the dance ended, he was right there.

"My lady," he said before the duke could say anything. "Might I have the honor of dancing with you?"

"Yes, of course," Catherine said with a relieved smile, though the duke looked less than pleased at being preempted.

"Shall we?" he asked, offering his arm.

"Thank you," Catherine whispered as Henry led her away.

"You are very welcome, though I did want to dance with you. Irritating him was a bonus."

Catherine laughed and took her place across from him. It wasn't the dance he'd expected, but a dance between single couples, slow and somewhat stately. It required him to be in close proximity to her, as well as to pick her up. It was easy to forget there were others there, easy to forget everything but her, and when it ended, he bowed to her and kissed her hand.

"You dance very well, Henry."

"As do you."

"Kitty, come! It is our favorite next!" Frances called from across the room.

Henry smiled, nodding his head toward Frances, and Catherine chuckled and departed. It was then that he felt another arm in his and looked over to find Lady Mary. "You are ready, I see."

"Quite," she said, following it with the same wolfish smile her father had worn not long ago.

"Then lead the way," he said as they began walking toward one of the doors across the room.

"Kitty, where are you going!"

Henry heard Frances call out just as he and Lady Mary reached the door, and he turned in enough time to see Catherine hurriedly making her way through the crowd and out of the door they'd come in.

"Excuse me," he said to Lady Mary, pulling away from her without bothering to wait for her leave.

"Captain!" she called out after him, though he ignored her.

Henry passed through the same door Catherine had used and saw her running down a hallway. His long strides allowed him to catch up to her easily, and he caught her by the arm to stop her movement. "Catherine —"

"Do not touch me!" she hissed, yanking her arm away from him. "I am sure Lady Mary is waiting, so why not go and make your next conquest?"

"I was not —"

"You do not have to lie to me, Henry. I know what she wanted!"

"Yes, she did, and what of it? Why does that upset you?"

Catherine glared at him and shook her head, turning to walk away from him again, but he grabbed her and pulled her back.

"Answer my question!"

"What does it matter why it upsets me! Go and do it! It is what you want!"

"It is *not* what I want! Damn it, Catherine!"

"Then what *do* you want!"

Still holding her arm, Henry dragged her around the corner, pulling her into a darkened alcove and pinning her against the wall as he kissed her hard. He heard her sharp intake of breath, felt her body stiffen in confusion, and then her hands on his face as she responded to him. The intensity of the connection flooded through him, the relief of finally giving in to what he wanted making him momentarily weak. He pulled back from her and placed a kiss against her neck, hearing the sound it drew from her and loving the way it twisted his insides to hear. If he were going to hell for this, it would be worth it. He moved his lips back to hers, and this time she wasn't surprised but met him in it, pulling a small moan from deep within his chest.

"I want *you*," he whispered when they parted.

"You cannot have me."

"I do not mean like this. I mean all of you. I want your heart, your soul, everything they want to take from you. I have missed you so much it hurt, Catherine, and I have never in my life felt that. You have no idea how hard I have tried to forget you, how hard I have tried to let you go, but I cannot."

"You cannot have me that way either."

"For now, right now, I can. For as long as I am here, you can be mine."

"But you will go and —"

"I will, but I cannot let you die in front of me and know I

could have at least let you know how it felt to have someone love you even if only for a little while."

"Henry, stop, please. I do not want your pity," she said, her whisper strained with emotion and tears.

"It is not pity. If I could take you away from here this moment, I would. You are too good for this place, but there is nothing else I can do that would not end up with us both in the Tower. Do not die yet. Stay with me, Sparrow, *please*."

Catherine sobbed in the darkness, putting her arms around him and resting her head against his shoulder. Henry held her close to him, his cheek against the top of her head. He wasn't sorry for this, and he never would be. This Catherine was *his* and always would be.

Chapter 8

"I win!" Frances said in excitement, clapping her hands together.

"Indeed, you do, Lady Frances. Well done," Henry said, smiling as he gathered up the cards.

"This is a fun game. Thank you for teaching it to us, Captain."

"You are very welcome. It is fun to play with all of you. Shall we play again?"

A chorus of agreement came from the ladies seated around the table, and Henry shuffled the cards before dealing them out once more. Over the last couple of weeks, he'd pulled himself away from the tumult and hedonism of the other men, instead ingratiating himself with the ladies of the queen's household. It had meant spending more time near Catherine, and to his surprise he'd found it a good deal more enjoyable in many ways than the previous scenario, though it, too, had its benefits.

He'd managed to spend time alone with Catherine most days, and it was what he always looked forward to. They'd done nothing entirely untoward, though Henry had certainly pushed the limits with what he *could* do. He was well aware he could never have her that way, no matter how badly he wanted to or how badly she might. Such a thing would ruin her, and he wanted no part of that, both knowing this time was borrowed. He sometimes wondered if it would make everything worse for her in the end, when she had to be sold into a life she didn't want to a man she barely knew, but he loved her and he wouldn't deny either of them the memory of it. There were times he'd considered asking her father or the king for her, but he knew it would be pointless to do so and would only serve to ensure that she was removed from court and away from him. There was no way they'd marry a girl like Catherine to a man of no rank who also happened to be a pirate.

As Henry walked through the deserted palace halls that night, keeping to the shadows as much as possible, he felt relieved that the night was finally coming once again. It meant that, just as before, Catherine was waiting for him, and he could hardly wait to get to her. They'd found a place to meet, a room he'd discovered during one of his escapades with the men, and it was in an area that was all but empty at this time of night. He could bolt the door, and if anyone tried to enter, there was a place to hide Catherine while he got rid of the interloper.

"Sparrow," he whispered after he'd shut and bolted the door behind him. Catherine emerged from the darkened corner, and he grinned. "Hello, my love."

She smiled and hurried across the room to throw herself into his arms, and he wrapped her up in them, taking a moment to revel in the feeling of being able to hold her again. Taking a step back after releasing her, he drew her into a kiss and felt her melt into him.

"Mmm, I have missed you," he whispered against her lips when they parted. "I have wanted to do that all day."

"Good, because I have wanted you to do that all day."

Henry chuckled. "Well, I can do so all you want now."

"You say that as though you do not want to do the same."

"I will never deny that I want to spend an entire night doing exactly that."

Catherine made an amused little sound and kissed him this time, holding him in it even as he backed her against the wall. As he pulled his lips from hers and kissed the rise of her chest just above the neckline of her dress, he heard her sigh as she closed her eyes and let her head fall back. Her skin was so soft it drove him mad with the desire to touch the rest of it, but he couldn't. At one of the kisses, he heard her stifle a small moan by biting her lip hard, and his hands flattened against her back before his fingers curled inward to grip some of the material of her dress.

"Jesus, Catherine," he murmured before he forced himself back from her. "I need a moment."

She nodded and stepped away from the wall, crossing to a chair to sit down and catch her own breath. She was a quick learner, and it had left him tension-filled more than once as he fought his desire to show her what such things could earn her. Though he could take those desires out on another woman, he'd never once considered doing so. He was hers alone, and that was the way it would stay.

Henry joined her, sitting on the floor at her feet. "May I ask you something?"

"Of course. Our rules have not changed, have they? No topic is off-limits," she said.

"If I could … Sparrow, if you were allowed to marry me, would you?"

Catherine blinked in surprise. "But they would never allow that."

"If they did."

"Yes," she said without hesitation.

Henry smiled at her. "I would ask you if they would allow it."

"Truly? The infamous Captain Merrick would give up his life of debauchery to take a wife?" she said, laughing.

"For you? Yes. You are the only one for whom I would ever consider it, though."

"I am flattered."

"You should be."

His answer made her laugh a little harder. "You are ridiculous."

"And yet, you love me still."

"I do love you; you are right."

"Marry me, Catherine."

"What? Henry, come now, we just —"

"I know what we just said, but hear me out. Let this Catherine always be mine, and I shall always belong to her. Let whoever goes to the cold marriage that one day awaits her not be *this* Catherine, for she already has a husband, one who loves her with everything he is. Let him save her in the only way he can."

"Henry," she whispered, her eyes filling with tears.

"I do not say this to hurt you, and I know it could never be official in the eyes of the law or the church, but I love you and I would do it in a heartbeat if I were allowed to. God will know, Catherine, He will see this, He will know you belong to me, and when the day comes that we have both left this earth, it is to me you will go and not to whatever unworthy bastard they have sold you to."

Catherine nodded, causing the tears to roll down her cheeks. "How? When?"

"Right now," he said, rising to his knees. He pulled a delicate ring from the smallest finger of his left hand and held it up to her. "I found this in a chest in one of the first raids I ever did on my own as a captain. I have worn it ever since, a bit of a talisman for protection."

"But if it protects you, then you should keep it!"

"No, for you will wear it and your spirit will protect me now. It will keep you always with me," he said, sliding it onto the ring finger of her right hand, where she'd never have to remove it. "The beloved wife of my soul, my Catherine."

"I am yours always," she said. "I always have been."

Henry smiled and kissed her before kissing the ring on her finger. "And so it is and shall be. Our secret. It will protect you, hide you from whoever he is, just as I would hide you, were I there with you."

Catherine wrapped her arms around him, and he held her against him. Every word he'd spoken was true, just as it had always been between them. They were the words written on his heart, a heart that would now always be hers, shut away from any others once the reality of their world pulled them apart. He had the privilege of never needing to marry, and within himself he swore never to do so, these vows as binding to him as any made in a church. He would go to his grave, wherever that may be, as Catherine's husband.

Not long afterward, just as he was starting to wonder if he might end up staying at the king's command forever, Henry was released; he was to go back to Jamaica in the next few days. He hadn't expected how much it would hurt to hear those words or how much he actually hadn't wanted to hear them. Though he'd known deep down the time would come, so much of him had wished it wouldn't even if that meant being here to see Catherine handed over to another. When he'd broken the news to Catherine, she'd reacted as emotionally as he'd expected her to do, and he couldn't help sharing in that grief with her.

They spent as much time together as they could find, but it would never be enough, and on the day he was to leave, they walked together in the gardens to a quiet spot they'd found and sat there in silence for a long while.

"I want to stay," he said softly.

"But you cannot."

"No. Catherine, I am not sorry. I do not regret this."

"I do not either. I will remember this time, and it will be the thing I cling to when I need it."

"I have never ..." he paused to steady himself. "I have never felt for anyone the way I do for you, and I never will. You may be the only person in all the world who knows the real me. Not even my parents knew him."

"As you are with me. Thank you for letting me escape in the only way you could, a ghost wife taken back to Jamaica with you. She cannot live when you are gone."

"I know she cannot, and I hate that the time has come for

her to perish after I worked so hard to save her all of this time."

"You *have* saved her. She is with you," she whispered, placing her hand over his heart.

"I must go, Sparrow," he said, the words feeling like poison on his tongue.

"I know. I have something for you," she said as they stood up, taking his hand and placing something inside of it, then closing his fingers around it. "Look at it later, when you are gone from London."

Henry kissed her and then stroked her cheek. "Always remember that I love you, Catherine. I always will."

"I love you," she whispered.

Henry kissed her again and then forced himself to turn and walk away from her and from the gardens as fast as he could and not look back.

As he was not a prisoner this time, Henry made his way to the deck and watched London drift away as the Thames carried them out to sea. He had no idea if he would ever be here again or, if he were, if she would be. It seemed unlikely either way, but the Henry who had come here was *not* the Henry who was leaving. This one was empty, all that made him what he was left in a garden with a beautiful woman who was also leaving all of herself there. From his coat pocket he pulled out what she'd placed in his hand, having stuffed it there to keep it close but not look at it, as she'd asked. Opening his hand, he found a small, oval locket, and inside was a miniature painting of Catherine. Henry closed his hand tight around it and turned to go back below.

***

Catherine returned to the palace but, unable to contain her grief, cried herself sick. She forced herself up to her duties each day, but her heart wasn't in them. She smiled, but there was no warmth in it, no life in her eyes, but no one cared enough to notice. She retreated once more and became the meek woman Henry had asked her not to be, the woman she'd been with him dying of a broken heart, set free to go with the one she loved even as her body remained. Whenever his name came up, Catherine found a way to leave the room, praying he would fade as a topic of conversation soon enough.

"Catherine, there you are," her father said one afternoon as she walked into the rooms her family occupied at the palace. He'd returned with her mother just after Henry's departure, and his presence only served to make her grief more acute. His callous treatment of her, while nothing new, was a stark reminder of the love she'd lost, and it caused the hole in her heart to become deeper and darker.

"Father, you called for me?" she replied as she curtsied.

"Indeed, I did, my dear girl. I have news for you."

"Good news I hope."

"Very good news. You are to be married."

"Married …?"

"Yes! We have made an excellent match for you. The contracts were signed this morning, and the king has given his agreement."

Catherine felt as though the room were spinning. "To whom?"

"The duke of Downey. You are to become a duchess!"

"But … but Father he is …"

"Old enough to be me? Yes, he is, but he needs a son, and a young wife can provide him that. It has been unfortunate for him that his last wives have met their ends in childbed, but you shall not."

"No, please, Father I do not want —"

"It does not matter what *you* want, Catherine," he replied, speaking over her as his voice took on a menacing edge. "The contracts are signed, and you are marrying His Grace in three weeks. There is nothing else to say about it."

"Yes, Father," Catherine whispered before she turned and walked away from him.

Catherine knew she was supposed to be happy, but she wasn't. All she felt was dread. The tide was coming in, and she hurried to the palace walls to watch the ships come in with it, just as she'd done every day since he'd left her. Every day she prayed Henry would be in one of them, though she knew he wouldn't be. He was gone and would likely be home by the time she became a duchess. Sagging against the wall, Catherine gave over to the emotions that seemed to be swallowing her whole. Fear, heartbreak, helplessness, loneliness, all of it spilling out with the tears that flooded her cheeks. For the briefest of moments, she wondered how easy it might be to fling herself from the wall and free herself forever, but reason shoved that away in an instant. If she did something so rash, she would never see Henry again in the afterlife; it would part them forever. A plan began to form in her mind, her tears ceasing as she sat up straighter.

She wasn't dead yet.

Chapter 9

The docks were crowded, swarming with sailors and merchants loading and preparing ships for the night tide's departures. The small cart carrying several trunks was unremarkable amongst the rest, as was the liveried household accompanying it. The group stopped at a slip where a ship was loading both cargo and passengers, and one of them slipped from the back of the cart in search of the ship's captain.

"Begging your pardon, Captain," the young woman said, the hood of her cloak up against the evening chill.

"Yes? What may I do for you?"

"Is this ship going to New Netherland?"

"It is."

"I would like to book passage if there is room. I am going ahead of my mistress with some of her things to prepare the house for her and her new husband."

"There is room," he replied, surveying the woman before him. "You are in luck, as this is the first journey where I have had a cabin left open this close to departure in quite some time."

The young woman produced a few coins. "I take it this will cover it?"

"And then some, miss."

"Keep it," she said as she gestured to the young men waiting with the cart. "Her trunks are there."

"Caroll, James!" the captain called out to two men who stopped what they were doing to look at him. "Load those trunks there into the hold."

"Aye, Captain," both men said as they headed for the cart and picked up the trunks with the help of the young men in palace livery.

"What is your name, miss? For the manifest."

"Frances Smythe."

"Very good," he said, writing it down in the logbook. "Welcome aboard, Miss Smythe. Let me show you to your cabin."

Following the captain aboard without looking back, she was shown to a small but comfortable-looking cabin, though she hurried back out onto the deck when she felt the jolt of the ship's sails catching the wind and taking them out onto the Thames. Standing at the back of the ship, she pushed the hood from her head as she watched London drift away. Reaching out, she pulled a ring from her right hand and switched it to her left, a dark smile appearing on her lips before she turned on her heel and walked back to her cabin.

***

The day of Catherine's wedding dawned clear and bright, but Catherine hadn't seemed to rise with it. Her father, having grown tired of waiting for her to emerge, threw open the door to her room and stormed inside but was taken aback for a moment when he found it empty. Her wedding gown lay upon the bed, but the bed hadn't been slept in.

"Where is she!" her father roared.

"What do you mean?" her mother asked as she came into the room.

"She is not here, Margaret!"

Her mother gasped. "What!"

"My lord," one of their household said as she cautiously

entered the room. "We went to make sure that all of the silver plate for Lady Catherine's dowry was polished, as you asked, but it is gone. There is nothing in the chest but some stones. Did you move it, sir?"

"No, of course I did not move it!"

"Oh, dear God, Catherine, what have you done?" her mother cried.

"CATHERINE! FIND HER! NOW!"

***

Sitting in a room at his villa with his first mate, Barnes, looking over a map, Henry tried to decide where they wanted to go this season. There were always prospects, shipping, things like that, but it was getting more and more difficult to pull off the large raids they'd previously been doing now that treaties had been signed and one of their own was the knighted governor of Jamaica. They'd all celebrated it at first — it had come just prior to Henry's own arrest — until the man suddenly turned on his former associates and began hunting them down like dogs.

"Captain Merrick, sir!" one of his lower crew called out as he approached.

"Yes?" Henry replied as he looked up from the map.

"Someone here to see you, Captain."

"Send him in."

The man who entered looked nervous to be in Henry's presence, and Henry couldn't blame him. He was meeting a rather notorious pirate on ground that was anything but neutral. "Captain Merrick?"

"Yes?"

"I have a message for you, but I was paid handsomely with explicit instructions to give it only to you."

Henry frowned at such a strange request and held out his

hand for it. "Thank you," he said when he took the letter, not recognizing the handwriting on it, before handing the man a few coins. "Here is more for your loyalty."

"Thank you, Captain," the man said with a smile before he turned to leave.

Henry took a knife from the table, breaking the wax seal to open the letter.

Dearest Captain Merrick,

I hope this letter finds you well and that the man I gave it to was trustworthy. Kitty has run away, but I don't know where she went or how. She gave me a letter and made me swear not to read it but to write to you and enclose her letter with mine. I went to the docks myself — it was rather scary there — but I wanted to make sure I put the letter in someone's hands so no one else got it. By the time you read this, I will probably be married, but I do want to say that court is lonelier without you to play cards with. You were great fun, and I hope you come back.

Lady Frances

Henry dropped the letter onto the table in shock. Catherine had run away? No, that couldn't be right. He snatched up the other letter that had been enclosed with the one he'd just read and opened it.

Henry,

I can only hope that Frances was able to do what I asked of her. I wanted to write and tell you that if you ever come back to England, I will not be there. Not long after you left, my father signed a contract for me to marry Lady Mary's father, the duke. I refuse to let myself be sold to a man old enough to be my father, who has left a long line of young brides in early graves behind him. I will be on a ship bound for the Colony of New Netherland before they all wake in the morning to marry me off. Thank you for making me brave enough to fly when I had the chance.

Your Sparrow

"Jesus Christ."

"Captain?" Barnes questioned, looking at Henry in concern.

"Barnes, get the men ready to leave. Now."

"Aye, Captain, but where?"

"The New Netherland colony."

"What? Why are we going so far north? It is winter there soon, and what in the hell have they got there that we would want?"

"I am aware of that, and we are not going raiding. This is personal. Go."

"Aye, Captain," he said, hurrying off to alert the crew.

Henry's mind was reeling from the words in the letter he still held in his hands. Catherine had fled England to avoid marriage, and as far as he knew, she was alone since her letter had said nothing of being with someone else. What if she hadn't made it? What if the ship had floundered? Even if she *had* made it, how in the hell would she survive on her own? She'd never had to do a thing for herself, and if she were as clever as he knew her to be, she wouldn't be living anywhere with household. The thought of how much danger she'd put herself in both on the journey and once she was on land made him sick to his stomach.

Henry stood from his desk and picked up Frances' letter, holding it to a candle and letting it go up in flames before he dropped it onto a platter. He'd leave no evidence here for anyone to find, no evidence that he'd received it. Clutching Catherine's letter in his hand, he strode from the room to help prepare his ship to sail, as well as himself.

Once they were underway, Henry lost himself in the work of making sure they arrived. The journey wasn't the easiest, but they'd made it, and he was glad to set foot on the bustling docks of the colony. There was a light snow falling now, and he pulled his greatcoat and cloak around him.

"Barnes, go ahead and finish up, and I will be back as soon as I can."

"Aye, Captain."

Henry made his way from the docks to the place where the locations of everyone in the colony would be known: the postal riders. If Catherine were here or had passed through here, they would likely know about it. He shook himself off as he stepped into the building.

"May we help you, sir?" one of the clerks asked, looking up from his sorting.

"I hope you can. I am looking for a young woman, a Miss Catherine Merrick. You would not happen to know where I might find her or if she has passed through here on her way elsewhere?"

"The young widow Merrick? She has a small cottage on the park road. She is a fine seamstress and a sweet young lady. A terrible pity she lost her young man to the sea in the English king's service, but she is not the first nor the last I am afraid."

"No, she is not," Henry said, though he kept his excitement under the surface. She *was* here. She'd lost her love to the sea, but he'd come back after all. "Could you tell me how to get there? I have an urgent message for her."

"Up the hill to the bluff, then a quarter-mile to your right once you reach the park, which you cannot miss."

"Thank you very much," Henry said, leaving the office and merging into the crowd of people at the docks again.

The walk itself wasn't difficult or long, and as Henry neared a little cottage, the door opened, and a cloaked and hooded figure stepped out. Henry's heart nearly stopped as he watched her shut the door and lock it, then tuck her hands into a warm muff and start off down the road away from him. It *was* her; he knew it was. Catherine. *His* Catherine.

"I did not realize sparrows could fly so far from home," he called out.

The small figure stopped moving and slowly turned around. "Henry?" she said, taking a few steps toward him in disbelief. "Henry!"

Henry caught Catherine up in his arms as she ran to him and held her tight.

"What are you doing here!" she asked, full of excitement.

"I got this very odd letter."

Catherine grinned, and he set her down on her feet. "Come in out of the cold!" she said as she hurried back up the path and unlocked her door.

Following her inside, Henry looked around at the small space. It was a charming little place, neat though sparse. It wasn't even as big as Catherine's old room at the palace. What a change that must have been for her. What a change *all* of it must have been. Catherine pulled her cloak off and hung it up, followed by her gloves, and went to re-stoke the fire.

"This is very nice."

"Thank you," she said, smiling as she grabbed a kettle and hung it over the fire.

"How long have you been here?"

"Not long. A few months."

"A few months? You must have left right after I did."

"I did."

"You brought no one with you?"

"No, of course not."

"How did you survive? You have never done a thing for yourself, have you?"

"I had not, but I had to learn, and I have."

Henry grabbed her hand to stop her bustling and pulled her close to him. "What in God's name were you thinking?"

"I could not marry him, and they were forcing me to."

"Of course you could not, but why did you come here? You could have come to me!"

"It would have been the first place they would have looked for me. Any ships going to Jamaica would have been searched, and if they went there in search of me, I wanted no trouble for you. Jamaica is still an English colony, and they could just as easily force me to marry him there as they could back in London."

"I knew you were clever. Tell me how you did it."

"I had three weeks. At night, I would take a little bit of the plate they had put aside for my dowry and put it into another trunk, then put a stone in to make the weight the same. Once I had it all, I paid some lads from the kitchens to come and take it and had them have a wagon ready for the evening because one of my ladies was going to see it to the docks for me. I took some of our livery and put it on, then I went down to the wagon and left. Once I got to the docks, I paid for passage on a ship coming here. No one noticed a serving girl named Frances."

"You … Catherine, you stole your dowry?"

"Part of it, yes."

Henry started laughing. "I wore off on you, did I?"

"Perhaps a bit or, as you said, perhaps there are traits in the blood that even the English cannot erase."

"You are brilliant, you know that, right?"

"Resourceful under pressure more like."

"How much do you have left?"

"Most of it. I took all my jewelry, too. I've been living comfortably but frugally."

Henry smiled and shook his head. "You really are my little pirate."

"Yours?"

"Yes, mine, just as you were and have remained."

"I am not so sure."

"Is that so?"

"You left."

"Now, now, let us not act as though I had some sort of choice in the matter."

Catherine chuckled. "I forgive you."

Henry reached up and cupped her cheek before kissing her. "Oh, my little Sparrow, how I have missed you," he whispered.

"I have missed you, too. I hoped you would come, but I never let myself hope *too* much."

"You had to know I would come for you once I knew. It is why you wrote me."

"Yes, but it might never have gotten to you, or you might have forgotten me or perhaps found someone else."

"The last two are impossible. I promised myself to you, and I meant it."

"When must you go again?"

"Never."

"What?"

"I think, perhaps, the time is right for a change in vocation. They made Morgan the governor of Jamaica, and he has taken to pirate hunting. Things are getting a bit … difficult. I have plenty of money to stay here and perhaps start a farm or perhaps even a shipping company."

"You want to retire?"

"I want to be Henry."

Catherine smiled and stroked his cheek. "You *are* Henry."

"Only when I am with you."

"Then stay."

"There are things I must do first."

"What things?"

"I need to relinquish command for one. Two, I need to have my things brought here."

"You brought things with you?"

"I was coming here to retire. Of course I did."

Catherine grinned. "Very well."

"Third, you need to not be the widow Merrick."

"Oh, right. It seemed the best option; I have a lot more

freedom to be left alone that way," she said, holding up her left hand to show him the ring he'd given her.

"That is actually true."

"I know. What shall I be instead?"

"I will not even dignify such a ridiculous question with a response."

Catherine laughed and rolled her eyes. "Get out."

Henry grinned. "There she is, my Catherine, my feisty wife."

"Not yet."

"Not long."

"Go!"

"You had best be here when I return. No fleeing to God knows where with the rest of your dowry to avoid marriage a second time."

"I will be, I promise."

Henry kissed her and then departed, making his way back down to the docks where he found Barnes and the rest of his crew waiting. They headed to a nearby tavern, where Henry bought a round of ales for them all.

"Lads, thank you for your service and a successful journey here. Barnes, I am turning command over to you."

"Captain?"

"I am staying here."

"Why?"

"Because my wife is here."

The men all looked at each other in confusion. "What wife?"

Henry chuckled. "I promise you will meet her, and when you do, I will let her tell you how she got here. That said, it is time for me to retire. Things are getting tight out there with Morgan on the hunt."

"Aye, that is true," Barnes conceded.

"While I still have life enough and health, I might as well make a life somewhere solid."

"Why did you not say so on our way here?"

"I was not sure if she would still be here or if she had even made it. She sent her letter from England, not from here."

"She must be quite a someone to make you take that sort of thinking."

"She is."

"We will be sad to see you go, Captain," another of his men, Rogers, said. Rogers was, after Barnes, the highest-ranking sailor on his crew and one of Henry's closest friends.

"It will be a change for me, but I wish you all the best. Stay here if you wish or sail back with Barnes; it is your choice."

"We will be here a short spell, as we need to provision, so there is time to think about it," Barnes said.

"Of course, and I will help with that. I need to get my trunks moved as well."

"I think you need time to situate yourself before you do that. That is a lot to move, Captain."

"Hm, I suppose you are right, but how do I know you will not simply vanish with it?"

Barnes looked at him as if he'd lost his mind. "Because I know if I do, you will come after me, and I prefer being alive to what I know you would do to me, Captain."

"Fair."

"It is yours by right; you earned it, same as we did."

"You are a good man, Barnes. All of you take a room at an inn and let me know where you are by sending a messenger to the young widow's cottage on the park road. In the meantime, I do need to move at least one trunk with my clothing, but I can handle that on my own."

"Aye, Captain."

"I am not your captain anymore."

"You will always be the captain. You could never be otherwise."

Henry smiled and then gave a small nod. "I shall see you tomorrow."

"Aye," the men said in a small chorus.

Henry finished his ale and stood, returning to the dock

where he paid two men to help him load the one trunk onto a wagon and take him and it to Catherine's. She opened the door when she saw them coming, stepping out with a small smile.

"Still here, I see. Good. You are obeying me already." Catherine shot him a look, and he laughed. "I know, there is no need to look at me like that."

Once the trunk was inside and they were alone, Henry pulled her close to him just to hold her in silence. He'd never expected this, but he was thankful for it all the same. Somehow this woman in his arms had escaped the cage and made it halfway across the world on her own, where she'd not only managed to survive, but also seemingly thrive. She hadn't let fear stop her, or the unknown; she'd acted to save herself when she had to.

"Have you anything you were meant to do today?" he asked.

"No, when you arrived, I was going to go and pick up a few things at the general store but nothing important."

"Come sit with me then, as we did? I just want to be near you now."

Catherine nodded her agreement, and they moved to the two small chairs by the fireside. Henry went to his trunk and opened it, retrieving a bottle and two glasses and bringing them back. Into each, he poured a little bit of port, handing one to her before he sat down across from her.

"I can hardly believe you are here," she said.

"Somehow I am not surprised. You never did let yourself hope for too much."

"I never had a reason to."

"No, you did not. In fact, you only ever had reason to doubt. How long was it before they signed you away?"

"Not long. A few weeks, perhaps."

"You said something in your letter that I found curious."

"What was that?"

"You said the duke had a long line of young brides in early graves behind him. What did you mean by that?"

"The duke has married many times over after the death of Lady Mary's mother. Each one died in childbed, supposedly, but then not one of them had died after bearing a male child. All of them had daughters, and all of them died within a week, along with the children."

"Are you suggesting that —"

"I am not suggesting at all. I am stating it. You know full well that he would be capable of such a thing and that so many in a row is more than coincidence. I was not about to be the next one, should I have failed to produce a son."

"I would have killed him."

"It would have made no difference. I would still be dead."

"It would have made me feel better. I swear to you, Catherine, if I had gotten such news, I would have come to England with a fleet of bloodthirsty men to avenge you."

"Somehow I believe you would have. After you left, I would go to the walls when the tide came in each day, hoping against hope that one of those ships was somehow bringing you back to me."

"If only that had been possible. I still have your portrait; it has never left my neck," he said, lifting it from beneath his collar to show her. "It was a beautiful gift."

"I am glad you liked it."

"It is strange, but even as painful as parting from you was, it was better than having had nothing at all. After I left, I spent so many nights watching the sky and wondering if you knew I was thinking of you. So much of me was left behind in England with you."

"You were not the only one," Catherine said. "I would leave when anyone spoke of you; I could not bear to hear your name. Even so, I was well aware that the Henry I knew was not the Henry they spoke of."

"No, it was not. I considered asking for you myself so many times before I left, but I knew there was no point."

"We both know they never would have allowed that. You said as much."

"I know, but now they cannot stop me and I will have you if you want it."

"Of course I do," she said. "Why do you think my story was that I was married to a young man who died at sea?"

Henry smiled at her and reached out to stroke her hand. "He did not die at sea, my Sparrow; he died on a beautiful sunny day in an English garden, on the lips of a woman he loved more than he could say."

"It seems he did not die at all."

"She called him back from the winds with a letter, across the sea to a new world and a new life."

"A new life sounds the perfect thing, a life where neither has to be what they are not."

"At least not all of the time. As Barnes said just a while ago, I will always be the captain."

"Of course you will, for he is the one who is the warrior. Henry is the poet of your soul."

"That is a beautiful way of putting it."

"I really have missed these moments."

"So did I, my love. So did I."

"Will you be able to lead so tame a life?"

Henry chuckled. "Yes. It is not so tame here in the wilds, I think, so I will have plenty to keep me busy. Speaking of which, there is something we must discuss."

"Oh?"

"This cottage, my darling, as sweet as it is, will not be sufficient for us."

"Why not?"

"Many reasons, not the least of which is the 10 trunks full of money that are sitting in the harbor at this moment. They won't all fit here."

"How many!"

"You heard me right. Money is not a concern of ours and never will be. There is more I did not bring."

"Henry!"

"I will have Barnes bring the rest. The point is, we need a bigger home and some land. You can keep the cottage if it pleases you, perhaps to continue being a seamstress if it brings you happiness. We will have our own Merrick House where we may live comfortably but not ostentatiously. You are out of place in such surroundings."

"Only because you know me in other ones."

"And everyone else should, too. My men want to meet you, by the way."

"If you wish," she said, laughing.

"Where is the magistrate?"

"Up the road a bit, why?"

"Come with me," he said, setting his cup aside and taking hers before pulling her up from the chair.

"Where are we going?"

"Cloak and gloves and muff on, come on."

Henry pulled his cloak and greatcoat on and ushered her outside even as she playfully protested, having her lead him to the administrative center of the town. "Is the magistrate available?" he asked as they stepped inside a building.

"Yes, sir, what do you seek?"

"I would like him to perform a marriage."

"Now?"

"Yes, now."

The clerk got up and disappeared, then reappeared to guide them into the magistrate's office, and he looked at Henry with great curiosity. "My clerk said you wished me to perform a marriage for you?"

"Yes, sir. I would like to marry this young lady, and I have waited long enough to do it, nearly a year."

"Do you agree, miss?"

"Whole-heartedly."

"Very well," he said, pulling things from his desk. "This is a bit unorthodox, but I can do it."

"I have only just returned from sea, sir. I do not know if I will be gone again, and I want to waste no more time."

The magistrate opened his book for the two of them to sign, but when he looked at Catherine's lineage, he gave her a puzzled look. "Your father is a Lord Merrick of England?"

"Yes."

"Then what are you doing here, my dear?"

"I am here in service of my king, sir."

"I see. So, that makes you Lady Catherine."

"I was, but I am no longer."

"Have you your father's consent?"

"I do not need it, sir. I was married and then widowed, so I am free to make my own choice now."

"Ah, very well then. Join hands."

Henry took her hands in his and held them as the man performed the brief rite. It was a civil marriage, but it was all that was needed. He would marry her in a church if she wished it, but he had a feeling that it wouldn't matter. Within a moment it was done, and with their signatures witnessed and signed by the magistrate, Catherine was now truly Henry's wife, leaving nothing for anyone to do to change it. He supposed her father could try to force the king to annul it, but he was certain Lord Merrick would have no desire to lay claim to a daughter who had stolen her dowry and fled the country. He likely had entirely disowned her, and she was all the better for it.

Once they'd departed the magistrate's, he found the jeweler's row and commissioned a band of gold to place upon her finger, physical proof of her marriage to him. In a move that was entirely out of the ordinary for men, he had one made for himself to wear. It would remind him every time he saw it that she was his and he was hers. Both of them were made with a gold piece of eight Henry produced from his pocket, something of his old life becoming something of beauty in the new.

Chapter 10

The following morning the sun was out, and though the air was sharp, the fresh snow glittered like diamonds. Snow. Henry had forgotten what it could look like; so long had it been since he'd seen it as a child in Wales. Catherine was still asleep, and he'd decided to sleep on the floor before the fire in order to let his beautiful new wife get a good night's sleep after an overwhelming day. He had no intention of pushing her into bed, wanting to take his time with her because he knew full well she had no idea what to do there or even what would happen. There was time for that without rushing.

When he woke, he put water on to boil and had tea ready for her. There were eggs and bread, and when he heard her stirring, he put the eggs in water to poach. When she came out, she was in a robe and dressing gown, as she had been the first night he'd coaxed her from her room.

"Good morning, Wife," Henry said with a soft smile. "Did you sleep well?"

"Quite, thank you. Did you?"

"It was nice and warm by the fire, and I knew you were here and safe, so yes. I put an egg on for you, and there is tea."

"Thank you," she said.

Henry made his way from the window to slide an arm around her waist, pulling her against him and kissing her. "You are so beautiful like this. Of anything it is my favorite way of seeing you. It reminds me of that first night we talked together."

"Mmm, I remember," she said, resting her cheek against his chest, her fingers stroking his neck in a way that drove him mad after having been so long away from her.

Henry stepped back and removed her hand, kissing it. "I was thinking perhaps we might hire a wagon and drive around looking to see if there is any property we like."

"You could always ask if there is anything available in town. They would know."

"That would give us a good starting point, certainly."

"Henry."

"Yes?"

"Are you displeased with me in some way?"

"Not at all, why do you ask?"

"It is just that … well … were we not supposed to … were you not …" she stammered.

"No, no, my love. No. I am not displeased with you; please do not think that. I am not going to rush you. You were overwhelmed enough, and I refuse to add to it. What you need is time and patience, gentleness. You do not know what to do; you cannot even say it. I want the experience to be pleasant and pleasurable for you, not something to be endured. When the time is right, I promise you it will happen."

"You are not avoiding it because I do not know?"

"No. I am waiting because I love you and it is what you deserve. Believe me, there is a part of me that wants more than anything to pull you back into that bed and make sure you do not leave it today but not yet."

"I trust you."

"I will not lie to you, Catherine. I never have."

"I know, and that is why I trust you."

Henry smiled and stroked her cheek with a finger. "You silly little soul, to think I was displeased with you in some way. If I were, I would tell you; you know better. Now, let us have our breakfast and see what we can find, shall we?"

When they went back into town, Henry learned of a Dutch planter who was returning to Netherland, his wife and children having already gone ahead of him. As such, he'd been searching for a buyer for his land and the house on it but had yet to get any inquiries from any advertisements placed here or on the Continent. A short trip out to the property was enough to sell Henry on it.

The land was rich river soil, good for corn and potatoes. There was a small orchard with apple and cherry trees, the stock in good health. There was land as yet unplanted, which Henry saw as an opportunity to put to use for livestock, switching the land back and forth in use in order to let it rest. The house itself was constructed of a rather stately-looking brick, new in design and construction, with two floors and an attic. The inside was rather plain in decoration, but he would give Catherine a bit of leave to make it beautiful, a home befitting the lady she truly was. The furnishings were all new and offered as part of the sale. The best part for Henry, however, was what was in front.

In front of the house stretched the small valley below, down to the docks themselves and the sea beyond. You could see for miles here and watch the ships coming into the harbor. The river that ran along the back and one side of the property swept gently down to empty into the sea. He could smell the salt on the wind, and he knew it would feed the sailor in his soul. Henry was happy to pay what was being asked, offering extra if the man would be willing to vacate the home as quickly as possible so that he might take possession. Details were agreed upon, and papers were signed, deeds handed over then and there. The planter appreciated the offer to live in the cottage until such time as he was ready to depart. As Catherine packed up the cottage, Henry went into town and hired a Scottish couple, Iain and Fiona, to work for them. Fiona and their young daughter, Màiri, would tend to the house, and Iain would assist Henry with the farm work. With that done, he located his men and rallied them to assist him, and by evening they were installed in the house with the planter in the cottage with their thanks.

"Love," Henry said, entering their bedroom as Catherine, Fiona, and Màiri busied themselves hanging clothing and getting the upstairs rooms ready for the night. "Would you consider it an undue hardship if the lads lodged here until they sail rather than an inn?"

"No, I would not. You forget that I lived in a house with many other people and a palace with many more," she said, chuckling.

"Excellent point. You are an angel. Would you come down and meet them when you are ready?"

"Yes, of course. I will be there shortly."

Henry kissed her head and headed back downstairs to where Barnes and the men stood in the kitchen. "The lady of the house is more than happy to allow you to stay here with us," he said.

"Much appreciated, Captain. It will certainly save us some coin. We had the rest of your trunks brought from the ship, and we put them in a room upstairs for you."

"Thank you, Barnes," Henry said, clapping him on the shoulder. "When you return, I will need you to bring the rest."

"I thought you would say that," Barnes said with a small smile.

"Because you know me. I will also need to have you pack up and sell the house. I trust you to get the best price for it."

"Of course."

"We have all decided to stay on, Captain," Rogers said.

"Is that so, Rogers? I am glad to hear it."

"Those of us with family will return for them, the rest for our belongings, and then back here. There are new lives to be had here, opportunity for things we could never have had back home. As you said, things are getting tight, and I know you feel as I do that the kind of life we lead will soon come to an end," Barnes said.

"You are right," Henry admitted. "You would be smart not to raid any ships on your way back. Run clean so you make it back alive."

"Aye, I agree."

"Come in, let us start a fire in the main parlor."

It wasn't long before Catherine came down, though Henry wasn't expecting the way she looked. To his surprise, she was dressed as he'd remembered seeing her at Merrick House, in a mantua made for wear at home, not ostentatious but made of warm fabric in rich colors. He realized she must have brought her finer clothing with her, stowed away with the silver plate in case she ever had need of them to wear or to sell. With Fiona here, she had someone to help her dress and thus could wear them.

All conversation in the room ceased, and Henry rose, crossing the room to take her hand and bring her further into the room. "Gentlemen, please allow me to introduce to you my wife, Lady Catherine Merrick."

"A great pleasure to meet all of you," she said, her smile warm and genuine.

They all just stared at her for a long moment before Barnes shook his head and stood, bowing to her. "Forgive me, my lady, I wasn't expecting a —"

"A lady?" Catherine said with a small laugh.

"Precisely."

The other men scrambled up and quickly bowed to her, but Catherine shook her head and held up a hand to stay them.

"Please, do not trouble yourselves. I may have been Lady Catherine once, but the title was left behind in England as was the rest of my life."

"It does not matter that you left it there, Sparrow. You are and shall always be Lady Catherine because that is what you are, what you were born to."

"How did a fine lady such as you end up with a rogue like him?" Barnes asked, his expression amused.

"Do let me tell this part," Henry said, laughing as he

brought her to sit beside him, and the other men sat down again. "When I was arrested and returned to England, the king had me put under house arrest with my very distant English family. My darling Catherine was at court serving the queen and was sent to be my jailer. She was vastly displeased by this and, when I asked if she might entertain me, told me she had no entertainment suitable for a man who grew up in a bog with sheep and spent the rest of his life with whores and brigands."

"Henry," Catherine chided, grimacing.

"Ouch," Barnes said, though they were all laughing.

"My pride was wounded, to be sure. However, we resolved our differences and became quite good friends. Except for the point where she tried to shoot me."

"What!" Rogers said, aghast, as Catherine rolled her eyes.

"Lady Catherine challenged me to some archery one morning, which, of course, I was not particularly good at. I suggested knives and brought some out, then showed her how to throw them. This little minx threw her first one terribly so as to fool me, for her next throw was perfect. I bet her a sixpence she could not do it again, and I lost that bet. So, I called for firearms, and she obliged. Rifles ended in a draw, and pistols … well … we had the same idea and ended up pointing them at each other."

Barnes and the others stared at her. "She …"

"Trust me, Barnes, she is a better shot than most men I have seen. Do *not* challenge her. Anyway, things followed as they did, and I realized I loved this enchanting creature, though she was never going to be mine. Her father and the king would never agree to such a match, but we were together in our own way when we could be. When I was ordered back, I thought I would never see her again."

It was so much deeper than that, and part of him hated himself for making it seem so lighthearted, but there was something still so raw and painful in the memory of the night at Merrick House when she'd refused to speak to him again, as well as in the memories of having to bid her farewell. He could still find the shame and the guilt over the things he'd done with the other courtiers, and there was no way to put all of it into words someone else could understand. How could he explain what it felt like when he knew he'd met his match only to know she could never be his? How would he explain the connection? He was also, he realized, putting on the persona of the gentlemen these men knew when they weren't on the water, and he hadn't truly realized how false it was until this moment.

"No wonder you were not yourself when you returned," Rogers said.

"I will let Catherine tell the rest," Henry said with a sly smile.

"After Henry departed, my father arranged my marriage to the duke of Downey, a man old enough to be my father in his own right. The duke supposedly had a tragic history of young wives dying in childbed, but everyone knew he got rid of them when they birthed a daughter instead of a son."

"He murdered his wives?" Rogers exclaimed.

"Oh yes, and the infants so that he might marry another young bride and try again."

The men frowned, and Catherine went on.

"I had no intention of marrying this man and becoming yet another dead duchess, so I devised a plan. Each night, I took a bit of the silver plate set in a chest as part of my dowry and moved it to another chest I had hidden. In its place I'd put a stone so the weight would stay the same. Once I had it all transferred, I had it taken down to a wagon and told them it was for me to send north. When everyone went to supper, I put on some of our livery, went down to the kitchens, had the trunk put on a wagon, and went with it to the docks. I put myself on a ship bound for New Netherland and here I am."

"Hold on, are you telling me you stole your own dowry and ran off?" Barnes asked.

"Yes."

Barnes and the other men started laughing hysterically. "No wonder you married her, Captain!"

"You see?" Henry said, grinning. "I told you that you would understand when you met her."

"Oh, I most certainly do."

"The letter I received in Jamaica was from Catherine, telling me she had fled and where she had gone. I did not know how she had done it until I got here, but it did not matter. I had to come to her now so that she could be mine, and even if she could not be, I had to come help her. I could not leave her here alone."

"Understandably," one of the other men said.

"The lads have decided they are going to make lives here," Henry said, looking to Catherine.

"How wonderful! It will be good for you to have people you know here."

"We will need to return to Jamaica first, but when we return it will be for good," Barnes said.

"What will you do with the ship, Henry?"

"I have not decided yet. I could sell it, or I could use it to run shipping back and forth to England as a secondary business."

"That is a thought."

As Catherine charmed the men through continued conversation — just as Henry had known she would — he couldn't help but marvel at how easily she accomplished such a thing. It was hard not to fall in love with her in some way; there was a sweet innocence about her that drew you in, and it was something he knew would never go away. It was miraculously undamaged by the cruelty and politics of court, waking from where she'd hidden it away to protect it now that she was safe and loved. When she was happy, it made those around her happy, and when she was in pain, it made them want to do anything in their power to stop it. That anyone would want to purposely hurt her baffled him, and the idea that those who should love her the most were the ones doing the most harm was maddening. She deserved everything good, deserved the life he intended to give her, a life where she was unconditionally loved by him.

All of it still felt like a dream he'd soon wake from to find himself alone in his bed or staring up at the night sky from the deck of a ship. He'd never intended to marry, hadn't ever even thought about it. While marriage wasn't something unheard of amongst his set, it had never struck Henry as something he wanted to subject someone else to. The uncertainty, the danger, the potential to lose everything. Then came Catherine and all the things he'd never felt before meeting her, and it had become something appealing, something desired. While he'd believed it would remain spiritual when he'd left England that day, fate had seen to it becoming reality, too.

Fiona and Iain returned with food from the inn, as there were no supplies or food here and wouldn't be until the following day, and a merry first supper was had. Afterwards, Fiona led the men upstairs to the bedrooms they'd occupy while they were here, and Henry walked Catherine upstairs, kissing her hand at the door to their room.

"Goodnight my love."

"Henry, please stay. Even if it is only to sleep," she said, holding on to his hand. "I do not want you to go, and we have been apart long enough."

"I cannot possibly say no when you ask me that way. Are you sure it is what you want?"

"Yes, very much so."

Henry smiled and kissed her hand once more before going inside and shutting the door behind them. "I can remain clothed if you wish."

"Why?"

"Well, you have never even seen a man in any sort of a state of undress."

"Yes, I have."

Henry raised an eyebrow.

"I saw you when I went to check on you when you were asleep so long at Merrick House. You were entirely uncovered."

"Define *entirely* uncovered."

"You were only wearing a nightshirt and it was open a bit, so I saw your chest, and your legs were bare. What else is there to see?"

Henry couldn't help the soft laugh that escaped him. "Much, actually."

"Well, it does not matter," she said, a note of defiance in her voice that let him know she wasn't backing down no matter what he said.

With an amused smile, he stripped down to his breeches and pulled a nightshirt over his head, well aware she was watching him curiously. Once it covered him, he stepped out of the breeches and removed the tie from his hair. "This is much more than I usually wear."

"Is it?"

"It is a great deal warmer in Jamaica, love."

"Oh. Well, I —"

"I do not think you are quite ready for that."

"Should I not be the judge of whether I am or am not?"

"In this case? No. Reason being you have no idea what you are asking, and I know you will push yourself to be braver than you are because you feel you must be."

"I am not a child, Henry."

"No, you are not, but —"

"You told me in the tavern it was not what I had been told, and I want to know what you meant. When we were together, I enjoyed all of it, and I know that means you were telling me the truth. I want to know for myself. I know you are trying to protect me, but I am your wife, Henry. I cannot remain this way forever, and I will never know until you show me."

Henry looked at her for a long moment. She didn't know what she was asking, but she was right. She wasn't a child; she was a married woman who had an idea there was something more, something withheld from her, something she was never supposed to have or even know existed. He'd shown her glimpses of it in their time together, but now he could truly show her. He walked toward her with slow steps, stroking her cheek with the backs of his fingers when he reached her. When she closed her eyes at his touch, he brought his lips to hers in a gentle kiss, letting it build a little as his fingers pulled the pins holding her hair. When that was done, he moved to the barest kisses of her jawline, following it to her neck. He heard her gasp, and his fingers involuntarily tightened in her hair as it brought him right back to that room in the palace where he'd tormented them both with this sort of play. It was going to take every ounce of his willpower and discipline to do this properly, but he wouldn't fail her.

Removing his fingers from her hair, he began to unlace the bodice of her dress even as he continued to kiss her neck, and he could feel her breathing quicken. His lips moved back to hers as he proceeded to take his time getting her out of the dress and down to a chemise and stays. Once he had, he lavished attention on the skin at her collarbone and the rise of her chest just above the line of her chemise as he unlaced and removed the stays. She made a small sound of enjoyment, her hands tightening on his shirt. With ease, he lifted her straight up and walked to the bed, placing her on it as he knelt beside her.

"We can stop here," he whispered as she looked up at him.

"Or we can not," she whispered in return.

"You are sure?"

"Yes."

"As my lady commands me," he whispered, the sly smile that appeared on his lips widening her eyes for a moment as she surely wondered what she'd just agreed to.

Henry removed the shoes and stockings she still wore, tossing them away before he kissed one ankle, sliding his hands up her leg while pushing the chemise with it to expose it to him, and he couldn't help the small sound that escaped him. She'd been forbidden to him, and he'd tried to drown his desire for her in other women at court but failed every time because it only made him want her more. Now he finally had her, and it was *he* who would teach her, show her that there could be pleasure in this instead of pain and endurance, and he who could make her want him as much as he would her.

Catherine didn't shy away from his touch but instead seemed to crave it with each passing moment. In a way, it was good that she was entirely innocent of this because no one had told her any of it was shameful or that she shouldn't feel desire from the touch of a lover. Henry lavished attention on each new bit of skin he uncovered, and it wasn't long before each bit pulled a fresh sound of enjoyment from her. When he finally removed the chemise, she didn't fight him, but he fought himself. She was beautiful, and he hated to think for even a moment that such beauty might've gone to waste on a man who wouldn't have appreciated it or likely even cared. What he *did* want was to be near her, pulling his own shirt off and lying beside her, just so he could feel her against him.

To his surprise, she turned toward him and kissed him, pressing herself to him and smoothing a hand down his back. Henry shivered, knowing she'd been paying attention to what he'd done and was copying it, but her hands were soft in a way he'd never experienced. He took the opportunity to smooth a hand down her side, and when he moved it to finally touch her, she pulled her lips from his in a loud gasp before making a sound he had yet to hear, driving him absolutely mad. He didn't stop, kissing her neck as he used his hand to bring her to her first experience of what a lover could give her that an uncaring husband could not.

Catherine clung to him and cried out, and it was only then that he changed position to move her beneath him. The sound she made now was of pain and he didn't move, following it with a kiss to take her mind from it. When he felt her relax beneath him, he began again, and this time it wasn't pain she felt. Now it was he who had those same sounds drawn from him that she'd earlier made, but what surprised him was to hear them also coming from her, and when he felt her body shudder and her hands grip his arms, he was lost entirely. He couldn't think of anything but her and this, and what his end drew from his lips sounded foreign even to him.

Henry tried to catch his breath, to regain some sort of sense even as she lay beneath him trying to do the same. Where some men turned to others for comfort, he knew that would never be a problem he faced, not after this.

"Now you know," he whispered in her ear when he could think again, moving to turn them on their sides.

"Henry, I …"

"Hm?"

"What was …"

Henry chuckled. "The pleasure I would be a very poor lover indeed if you didn't find each time I am with you."

"Would it have been like that if I had married as I was meant to?"

"No, my love, probably not, but you need not worry about that now. Now you are mine, and I would never leave you so cold."

"It is why this is considered sinful."

"It is absolutely why," he said, laughing now. "And it is absolutely why the majority of the world does it anyway."

Catherine joined him in laughter and looked over at him. "Is it always that way?"

"If it is not, then I am doing something very wrong."

She reached out and gently smoothed a fingertip across one of his scars. "So many."

"And each one a story, each a narrow escape."

"Will you tell them to me?"

"Of course, but not now. Now we need to sleep, for I fully intend on waking you again soon."

"If I do not wake you first."

"Well now, look at what I have unlocked."

"Are you not fortunate?"

"You have no idea."

Chapter 11

Winter descended fully before Barnes and the others could sail for Jamaica, trapping them there until the spring. No one seemed to mind, especially not Catherine, as she enjoyed the company and the stories they told. In turn, the men themselves adored their captain's wife and her merry nature, quick wit, and stories of her own. No one, however, loved Catherine more than Henry, nor more than he did with each passing day.

They didn't let the time go by idly, working on preparing for the spring planting while they could. Horses were purchased, a wagon, seed, and other tools. When lambing arrived, there would also be sheep, something Catherine was looking forward to. She spent her free time sewing new dresses for Màiri, who was only seven, as well as a few for Fiona, along with shirts for Henry. She also took time to teach Màiri to both read and write, and some of Henry's men had also joined in those lessons on long winter days when the weather was too rough to be outdoors.

When spring finally arrived, no time was wasted in preparing the fields and getting the seed into the ground, something Barnes and the other men stayed on to assist with. They'd left early this morning to head out to plant the far side, leaving Màiri and Catherine alone in the house while Fiona went into town to buy the week's food stores.

"Hmmm, where could Màiri be hiding?" Catherine asked, grinning as she made a show of trying to find the girl. "Is she right … here!"

Màiri screamed in delight as Catherine pulled the door of the wardrobe open, racing out of it with her laughter trailing behind her. She helped with the housework, but Catherine didn't push her too hard. She was just a child with plenty of time for working ahead.

Laughing, Catherine chased after her into the foyer and around a table before she blocked the only escape back into the interior of the house. "Hah! I have you now!"

"Never! Captain Merrick will save me!" Màiri declared.

"He is not even here!" Catherine said, still laughing.

"That is right, Catherine. He is not."

The voice silenced Catherine's laughter in an instant, her face going pale. "Father," she whispered.

Màiri gasped and turned around to find Lord Merrick, looking tall, imposing, and severe behind her before she ran past Catherine back into the house.

"Do not *dare* call me that, you thieving little whore!"

Catherine's heart raced as her eyes filled with tears. "My Lord, please let me —"

"Explain?" he spat as he cut her off. "There is no way you could possibly explain what you have done, the shame you have brought to your family. Did you think I would not find you?"

"I never meant to shame anyone, but you would not listen to me!"

"And why should I! You were a daughter, not an equal! You were to do what I told you, and that was all!"

"No! I was not going to die for you!"

"Die for me?"

"He would have murdered me if I had produced a daughter, and you know that to be true!"

"Do you think I really cared? What happened to you after your marriage was none of my concern, Catherine! You had done your duty and given your family the prestige and ties that came with it."

"You did not care if I died?" Catherine asked in disbelief.

"No. Why do you think I would? You are a woman; your only use to me was what connections you could bring by your eventual marriage. You were irrelevant otherwise, and had you died before then, I would not have mourned you. You were enough trouble as it was, never content with your place."

A small sob choked Catherine. "Get out of my house!"

Lord Merrick reached out and grabbed Catherine's hair close to her neck and yanked it hard, pulling her close to him as she cried out in shock and pain. "You can order me to do nothing," he hissed in her face. "Remember who you are speaking to. I am above you in *every* way. Where is the plate, Catherine, or did you sell it all already to fund this place you now live in?"

"You can have it! Let go of me!"

"Oh, I *will* have it. Show me where it is," he said, releasing her and shoving her forward.

Catherine stumbled and caught herself on the door frame, shaking as she moved into the house, and he followed her. The trunk where the plate resided was in the main parlor, and Catherine pointed a trembling finger.

"Take it and go!"

Lord Merrick nodded to two men she hadn't noticed before, who went past him and picked up the chest. "Take it to the wagon," he said before he turned his attention back to her. "Now, there is the matter of what to do with *you*."

Catherine looked at him, terrified.

"You thought you would not have to pay for this somehow? You are a thief, Catherine, and back in England you would have found yourself in irons and in the Tower. I could take you back there."

"No!"

"I tend to agree with you. It would mean I would need to

put up with your tears and pleading for the entire journey, and I would find it tiresome."

Without another word, the back of his hand collided with Catherine's face and sent her to the floor. The world felt unsteady, and she could taste blood in her mouth.

"I think, instead, I shall dole out my own justice," he said before he brought the walking stick he carried down across Catherine's back, bringing a scream of pain from her.

Reaching down, he grabbed her by her hair and pulled her up. "I can be rid of my thieving whore of a daughter, and no one will ever know back home."

"I am not a whore! I am —"

"Married?" he said with a dark laugh before he grabbed her hand and ripped the new gold band from it, which brought a pained cry from Catherine. He threw it, and Catherine heard it skitter across the floor. "Hardly. I would never recognize such a marriage, a stain on our bloodline, and if I cared enough to let you live, I would have it annulled."

"Stop!"

"Did you let him have you when he was in England, Catherine? Did you flee so we would not find out on your wedding night what a *whore* you were?"

"No!" Catherine sobbed out. "Please! I never —"

"Shut your mouth," he said, throwing her to the floor. "You are dead to us, and I aim to now make that physically true."

He brought the stick down hard across her back twice more, and Catherine screamed before she returned to a strangled sort of sobbing. The pain washed over her in waves, and it hurt to breathe, though she couldn't tell if it was from the pain or from something else. He reached down and dragged her up from the floor once more by her hair, pulling her face close to his.

"Enjoy your stay in *hell*, Catherine," he said, her name spat like a dirty word.

Catherine felt a sharp pain that took away any breath she

had left, looking up at her father in wide-eyed shock before he dropped her to the floor and left the room.

***

"Captain! Captain!" Màiri shrieked as she finally reached the men.

"Màiri? What is wrong?" Henry asked, a feeling of dread moving through him at the tone of her screams as work immediately ceased and all the men looked at the terrified child. "What are you doing all the way out here?"

"A bad man! He came to the house and yelled at Lady Catherine! He called her a thief and a whore! She was afraid, and I ran to get ye!"

"Catherine," he whispered before he broke into a run, followed by the others. "Catherine!" he called out as he barreled into the house. "Catherine!"

"Captain!" Barnes called out.

Henry turned and saw Catherine unmoving on the floor of the parlor across the room. "No," he choked out, sprinting and sliding to his knees onto the floor beside her. "Catherine! Catherine, my love," he said, frantic as he turned her toward him.

"Jesus!" Rogers called out when he saw her bloodied, swollen, and bruised face.

"Catherine," Henry said, patting the undamaged side of her face to try and rouse her. "Sweetheart, please," he continued as he placed his other hand on her side to shake her, but he froze when it felt wet and warm.

Henry recoiled in horror as his hand came away wet with blood, a scream stuck in his throat.

"Oh, dear God," Barnes said, his voice holding the same horror Henry's expression did before he went to her other side. "Rogers, go with Màiri and find her mother; tell her what has happened. Do it now!"

Rogers ran off as Barnes picked Catherine up from the floor, her body limp and heavy, carrying her upstairs to their bed and placing her in it, Henry right behind him. "Captain, help me undress her."

There was no time for modesty, and Henry didn't hesitate, using a knife to cut through laces and help strip Catherine down. He grabbed a bedsheet, wiping the blood from her skin to find a wound left by a knife, and his heart sank.

"Why …"

"Look, look at the blood. It is bright, not dark, which means whoever did this missed their target. See how the boning in her stays moved it? There's a chip. She may yet recover from this," Barnes reassured him.

Henry put pressure on it, but he noticed the already darkening bruises on her back, and his rage built. "I am going to kill him."

"You do not even know who did this, Henry," Barnes countered, dropping the pretense of rank.

"There is only one person who would call her that," he said as Rogers, Màiri, and Fiona came into the room.

"Sweet Jesus!" Fiona cried out. "Lady Catherine!"

Henry stepped away from Catherine to let Fiona get to her, his breathing heavy, eyes dark with rage and hands crimson with her blood. Without a word, he turned and stormed from the bedroom into the one where his trunks were kept. From one of them he pulled a pistol and a dagger before he hurried down the stairs and out to the barn, saddling one of the riding horses before taking off at a full gallop. He knew full well who had done this, and when he caught him, Henry would make him pay. It was the captain he now needed to deal with.

"Lord Merrick!" Henry screamed when he saw them nearing the docks.

The man stopped and turned around, the two men with him setting down the trunk they'd taken. "You. What do *you* want?"

"Satisfaction," Henry snarled as he dismounted.

"I owe nothing to the man who made a whore of my daughter."

Henry pulled the pistol and pointed it at him. "Wrong. You owe the husband of the wife you have murdered the satisfaction of vengeance."

Everyone around stopped moving to watch what was happening, but Henry took no notice of them.

"Her death is her just reward for stealing from her family, disgracing us in the eyes of the duke and the king, just so she could become another whore for a criminal!"

Henry's hand tightened on the grip of the pistol. "The only one who sought to make a whore of her was *you*, selling her into marriage to a man who only wanted her for his bed, a man who would see her only use as producing a son and dispose of her if she did not deliver. You would send her body to him for money and titles!"

"That is her duty as a daughter! Instead, she ruined herself with you."

"I *never* touched her," Henry growled. "Not once. I fed her heart and her soul, but her body was never mine. I loved her too much to disgrace her, unlike you. It was not until I married her that I took her to my bed, as I am meant to do."

"It does not matter, does it? She is a *disgrace*, as is her marriage to you, a blight we will never acknowledge. She will be erased from our history and never spoken of again, and now that she has been erased from yours as well, I have gotten *my* satisfaction for her crime as well as recovered my property."

Henry lunged for him, only to be grabbed and held back. He tried to lower his arm to fire, but it was shoved up and the shot went into the sky. He screamed in rage and struggled against the hands that held him.

"The plate you carry is covered in her blood and always will be! May it be a curse on you and those who come after you!" Henry screamed as the two men picked up the trunk and continued to the waiting ship, while Lord Merrick smirked and followed them.

"Henry, no," Barnes said.

"He murdered my wife! I demand his head!"

"Henry …"

"NO!" he screamed as Barnes, Rogers, and Màiri's father, Iain, pushed him away, the three men fighting to keep hold of him.

"Do not be stupid! You cannot settle things that way here unless you want to end up in irons. This is not Jamaica! HENRY!" Barnes shouted as Henry continued to try and pull away, slapping him hard.

The blow startled him into stillness, but he glared at Barnes.

"Listen to me: She is badly injured, but she is not dead yet, and if she lives, the last thing she needs is you in prison. Think about it. I know you want revenge, we all do, but this is not the way! She needs you, Henry!"

She needed him. Yes, yes, of course she did. Henry nodded once, and when they released him, they returned to the house in silence. His rage radiated from him in waves, the captain still. As he reached the landing at the top of the stairs, he saw Fiona standing outside, crying into her hands, and Henry hurried into the room. There was still so much blood everywhere; how could it come from her? How could she still be alive? This blood was dark, and that terrified him.

He knelt beside the bed and took her hand, kissing it, but there was no response. Henry stood, running his hands through his hair before covering his face with them. Her blood still stained them, and he didn't know what to do now. What would he do if she died? He couldn't think of it, to think of it might make it happen. No, she *would* live. He had to believe she would, or he'd drive himself mad with grief.

"Captain," Fiona said, sniffling.

Henry looked over at her. "How is there so much blood, Fiona?" he whispered. "What injury did we miss?"

The question made her burst into tears again. "Lady Catherine, she was —"

Henry's heart sank like a stone. "No … do not say it … please, Fiona, do not say it …"

"I am sorry, Captain …"

Henry felt like he could no longer stand, sinking to the floor. The scream that welled up was different from those at the docks, full of pain as well as fury. A child. A child who was now dead, and its mother might follow it soon enough. He crawled to the bedside, forcing himself to look only at her face. He cupped her cheek in his hand and pressed her other cheek to his own, crying in a way he'd never done, and he didn't notice as Fiona removed herself from the room.

"Please, Catherine, please …" he whispered. "You cannot leave me. Do not die now that you are free. I am still here to love you; you do not need to go. Do not die yet," he sobbed, echoing the words he'd said to her once when they'd both believed those moments were all they had.

"God save her," he heard Barnes say behind him. "Henry, come away. You have to let Fiona clean her up."

Henry didn't fight their pulling him away from her. He didn't care if they saw him grieving, it didn't matter, but he wasn't sure he could stand. Somehow, they'd gotten him downstairs, and Barnes went back up to help Fiona so she could move Catherine to a room with a clean mattress. Before they placed her in the new bed, there were rags placed to stop the bleeding from her side and from inside. Her side was tightly bandaged, and she was put in a fresh nightdress. When they allowed Henry back in, she looked as though she were sleeping, though she was far paler than he'd ever seen her. None of them knew if Catherine could or would survive this, and whether she made it through the night was the important part. Someone had thought to summon a vicar to make her ready in case she did not, and Fiona sat in a chair in the corner, praying while Henry sat beside the bed, holding Catherine's hand and stroking it.

A small moan woke him with a start sometime during the

night, and he sat up, lighting a candle. "Catherine?" She made another small sound, and it made his heart pound. "My love, I am here. Come home to me, little Sparrow, come on."

Her eyes fluttered, and she opened them just a bit. "Henry," she mumbled.

"Yes, I am here! Come on, Catherine, you can do this. Fight for me. Come back."

She opened them a little more, and he watched the haze of pain cloud them before she cried out in a way that felt like a knife in his heart.

"I know," he said through tears. "I know it hurts, but you have to wake up. Please."

"Stop," she whispered, tears sliding from her eyes. "Do not hit me anymore …"

He closed his eyes to tamp down the hurt those words caused him. "You are safe; no one is going to hurt you, Catherine. Fiona!"

Catherine suddenly writhed with pain and cried out. "It hurts!"

Henry looked around, frantic, but was quick to roll Catherine onto her uninjured side to take the pressure off her back. He could only imagine how painful it must be, and he did his best to soothe her as her eyes closed again. He wept as she lost consciousness, knowing it was for the best because of the pain, but shattered at hearing her cries and from the fear of her never waking again. She hadn't known he was here despite saying his name, there was no true recognition, and she was trapped in some mental hellscape where someone was still doing her physical harm. Why couldn't her father just let her go? It didn't take more than a second for the thought to follow that none of this had anything to do with some silver plates. No, this was everything to do with pride. She had damaged his, and he sought to make her suffer for it, sailing halfway across the world to do so. It was revenge, bloody and brutal, meant to make her pay for daring to stand up and go against him. Violence was the only way he'd ever known to control Catherine, and he'd spared no effort to use it. This was revenge against Henry, too, for daring to marry an English Merrick and sullying their bloodline with his Welsh heritage and criminal past. For having the audacity to love her and teach her there was another way, another world, if she were only brave enough to chase it, and she had. Part of the reason she was in this bed now was his doing, and the weight of it was nearly unbearable.

The true terror he felt at the thought of losing her was crushing, far beyond anything he'd ever felt, even in his times of worst danger. It combined with the guilt he felt over not having been here to protect her, both things threatening to smother him. This uncontrollable emotion was unfamiliar, and he couldn't remember having felt so paralyzed, helpless, and broken before now. He'd certainly never shed this many tears over anything or anyone, but it wasn't just anyone. It was Catherine. Bright, beautiful, sweet Catherine who had never harmed anyone in her life. How was it possible that she should be in such a position whereas he — who had killed, stolen, destroyed, and thus deserved it — remained unharmed? Henry couldn't help but wonder if this was some sort of penance, a way to pay for his crimes in the most painful way God could manage, and for the first time in his life, he prayed. Prayed for God to forgive him, to spare her and take him instead, to punish the one truly at fault.

Catherine moved in and out of consciousness over the next two days, never lucid and at times delirious with fever. She would scream for him to help her, call out to him to stop whatever it was she was dreaming of, but never seemed to realize he was there, and it broke his heart each time. He held her hand in those moments, whispering encouraging words in the hopes she'd hear them in those nightmares and bring him to her there so he might help her. He refused to leave her side, wanting to be there in case she woke or, on the opposite, in case the worst happened. If she had to leave him, he wanted her hand to be in his when she did, wanted to will her as much comfort and love as he could, wanted her to know somehow that he was with her. Perhaps such a connection would take him with her.

"Henry."

The whisper of his name cut through the fitful sleep he'd found, and he opened his eyes, expecting to have to bathe her with cool water once more. But when he sat up, she was looking at him, eyes open and clear, though she looked exhausted.

"You look terrible," she whispered before she smiled.

Henry stared at her before he broke into something that was a mix of laughter and heaving sobs as he knelt beside her, taking her hand to kiss it over and over. His little Sparrow had lived through the storm.

Chapter 12

As word spread about what had happened to Catherine, those in the town they inhabited showed up to do what they could to help. Men showed up to help Henry finish the planting; women came to help Fiona take care of Catherine and the house. It reminded Henry of the way the outlaw communities of Jamaica would take care of each other when it was needed after hurricanes or other disasters, and he appreciated it immensely. Barnes, Rogers, and the others departed not long after Catherine came back to them, needing all the good weather they could get, though she'd been sad to see them go.

Each day she improved a little more, enjoying being able to leave the bed and return to their own room once a new mattress had been put in. It allowed her to sit by the open window to enjoy the fresh air and spring breeze even if she wasn't well enough to go out in it just yet. Màiri would sit with her when she wasn't helping Fiona and tell Catherine fairy stories her mother had told her or what her father had told her of Scotland. Other times, Catherine would continue teaching her to read.

One late spring morning, Henry bounded through the house with something cradled in his arms, Fiona catching a glimpse of it and shouting after him. "Captain! Dinnae ye take that up to M'lady! Captain!"

Henry paid her no heed, rushing through the bedroom door moments later, laughing and eyes full of mischief with his back to Catherine. "Good morning, love."

Catherine looked up from her needlework as he hurried in, eyeing him with suspicion. "What have you done that has Fiona so upset with you?"

"Set your needlework aside, and I will show you." Once Catherine had done so, he placed a small wooly creature in her lap, and Catherine gasped. "I didn't want you to miss it, and as you cannot come down to it, I brought it to you."

"Oh, what a darling little thing it is!" Catherine exclaimed in delight as she reached out to stroke the nose of the lamb. "Where did you get it?"

"Bought it, of course, along with some ewes and a ram. We need stock for the fallow fields. There are another three where this came from, though this was the most docile."

Catherine laughed as it bleated at her. "Poor little dear, you must be so confused. I think your name should be Columbus because he was confused as to where he was, too."

The joke made Henry laugh. "Excellent suggestion, Sparrow. That's what we shall call him. Ah, but it is so good to see you smile again."

She reached out and placed a hand over his. "There is plenty to smile about."

"There is," he said, giving hers a gentle squeeze. "But I should get this babe back down before Fiona skins me alive. I will, however, return."

Catherine chuckled as he collected the lamb, gave her a quick kiss, and hurried out, and he could hear her laughing as Fiona's strident chastising on his way back reached her upstairs. When he returned, he shut the door and went about cleaning himself up and changing his clothing.

"How is the planting going?"

"Finished and looking well," he replied as he washed his hands and arms, then dumped the dirty water and added fresh to the bowl to wash his face. "If the weather holds, we should have a fine crop of potatoes come autumn."

"Well done," she said as Henry sat in front of her, leaning his head back into her lap and closing his eyes, spurring her to begin stroking his hair.

"Sparrow," he began, not sure how best to broach the topic. "Would you tell me what you remember about what happened?"

It was something they hadn't yet discussed, though he'd made everyone swear to not mention the child to her. She'd suffered enough and didn't need that on top of it. She hadn't known about it yet, and the lack of mention wouldn't hurt her now.

"I do not remember much," she admitted. "I just remember that I was playing with Màiri, and suddenly he was there. He berated me for the shame I brought on them, and I remember him wanting the trunk, then he hit me on the back with his walking stick."

A walking stick. They hadn't known what caused those injuries to her back, but he did now.

"The last thing I remember was him telling me to enjoy my time in hell and then a very sharp pain. I assume that was from the knife you told me about."

Henry's jaw tightened. "Do you remember anything he said to you?"

"No, not really."

"I am glad," he said. She didn't need those horrible slanders in her ears forever.

"I do remember him telling me what happened after my marriage was none of his concern, and he would not have cared if the duke had killed me because I would have done my part."

"What?" Henry said, lifting his head and looking at her over his shoulder. "How could anyone say anything so callous?"

Catherine looked as much at a loss as he did. "I remember my ring and the sound it made on the floor when he threw it."

Henry's brow knitted together, and he sat up fully, taking her hand and only now realizing it was gone. She still had the

126

one he'd originally given her, it having gone back onto her right hand when the commissioned bands were delivered and took its place on her left, and it was the new one that was now missing. In all the commotion, none of them had noticed, and it angered him that it should've been removed at all, much less in such a way. "We will find it, do not fret."

"What happened?"

"When?"

"When you found out."

"I went after him, fully intending to kill him for having taken you from me. Barnes and the others stopped me just as I was going to do it, after he had said horrible things about you."

"What did he say?"

"I will not repeat them."

"That bad then."

"Yes."

"I am glad they stopped you."

"Because you lived, so am I, but Catherine," he said with a heavy sigh, "in that moment all I knew was that you were dead in our home by his hand. The captain wanted his vengeance, and he would have it."

"I cannot blame him."

"I know he left for England thinking you were dead, and perhaps it is best that way. I cannot help but feel as if I failed you. I am supposed to protect you, and the first time you needed me I was not here."

Catherine stroked his cheek. "You did not fail me. We never would have expected this to happen. You did what you could."

He sighed again and kissed her knee. "I know, but the feeling remains and will."

"You could write to the king."

"Why?" Henry asked with a raised eyebrow.

"Tell him what happened and petition for redress, though I am sure he will not look kindly upon it because I did steal."

"You did, yes, but no more than they do from their subjects and tenants while calling it legal. I think it is best to leave England where it is."

"When I am well, do you think we could perhaps have a party? To thank those who have helped us so much."

"I think that is a wonderful idea."

"I promise I will not spend much."

"As I told you before, it is not something you need to worry about, but I appreciate the thought. You need to also oversee making New Merrick House as beautiful as the other. I will see to having tradesmen come to you to begin consultations when you are ready, as you cannot yet go to them."

"Perhaps we should not spend so lavishly as that."

"I promise you; it will be fine. Money is something we will not run out of."

"If you say so."

"I do. Now, let us get you on your feet for a spell, shall we?"

It wasn't long before Catherine was able to walk on her own again, though slowly. He found her ring and returned it to its rightful place, and once she was able to go downstairs each day, true to his word, Henry sent tradesmen to her to begin work on renovating the house. It wasn't long before the place was a hive of activity with walls being covered, chandeliers put in, fine carpets unrolled. Per his request, furniture was ordered built or shipped to them, with Henry's desire to recreate in some way the place where he'd met her and spent so much happy time with her in the forefront of his plans.

Fiona taught her to garden, and she delighted in caring for the plants that would help to feed them and season their food, along with the flowers. There were blueberries and strawberries, carrots, lettuce, and varying other types of small produce, as well as roses and bluebells, two of Catherine's favorite flowers. It amused Henry to see how eager she was to experience all of it, to learn and take on new skills even if she would likely never need them. She enjoyed learning to bake and assisting with basic things like making bread, if her time allowed.

In turn, she passed on her own finer skills of needlework, sketching, and the playing of the harpsichord he'd purchased.

One morning in May, the sound of tiny taps on the floor caused her to look up from the letter she was writing to see a tiny dog making its way toward her, wiggling in excitement. With a grin, she quickly got up and went to meet it, scooping it up in her arms and getting excited licks in return, making her laugh.

"Oh, look at you, how sweet you are! Where did you come from? We must find out where you escaped from, so we can take you home."

"She is home," Henry said, smiling as he leaned against the doorframe. "She is for you."

"For me! She looks like the little dogs the king had at court!"

"Indeed. I had heard tell of a family who made the journey with two of these little spaniels, and the female was ready to whelp soon. I picked one for you, and here she is. A little shadow to keep you company."

"Henry, thank you," Catherine said, though her eyes were filled with tears. "She is beautiful."

Henry came toward her and kissed her forehead. "You are welcome. I thought you might like her, a little friend to stay with you when I and the others are at varying tasks. What will you name her?"

"Frances," Catherine said without a moment's hesitation. "She is so excited, as Frankie always was."

"You know, you are right," he said, laughing. "Do you miss her?"

"Yes, often. I hope she is well wherever she is."

"You should write to her. You knew whom she was to marry; send it to her that way and I'm sure it will reach her. I will disguise the letter for you so that it does not tip off your father that you still live."

"Perhaps I will," she said, smiling and cuddling Frances a little closer to her.

The house was finished in time for a late summer gathering

that Catherine excitedly planned. As it was to be a thank you to the town for their help, she hired musicians and ordered in food of all sorts. The party would be held outside, but the house would be open for people to walk through, though the door to the room of trunks was locked. The weather was fine for the day, and Catherine and Henry greeted each guest as they arrived, thanking them for their particular act of kindness with not only words but also small gifts. Catherine, mindful of the expectation, delivered with one of her beautiful court gowns, another item stashed away from a former life. Lady Catherine should appear as a lady, and she most certainly did.

While she was happy to let the women get a closer look at her attire, Henry was happy to lead people through the house before he stole her away to dance. There were no court dances here, but lively country dances filled with laughter and clapping hands. Henry took a moment to watch her when he stepped out of the sets, and for a moment she looked the way she had that night at the king's birthday, dancing with Frances and the others. It pleased him to see, and he knew that the worst of her ordeal was behind them.

Summer slipped into autumn and the harvest, and Henry brought in his crop with help from the other men of the town, and then he, in turn, helped bring in theirs. Many hands made quick work, and they all shared in the fruits of their labor, trading with each other. Winter arrived, cold and harsh, keeping them often inside. There were, however, snow fights and snowmen with Màiri and Catherine, and Frances flopping around in the snow, turning her normally black nose white. He marked their first year of marriage by giving Catherine the gift of her own rifle and pistol, a call back to their time together in England that served the dual purpose of protecting her if needed. Then came Christmas, and Henry was unable to remember the last time he'd even thought about it. He'd been a child then, back in Wales, but it had never been observed at sea or otherwise.

In February, there was still snow, but the sun seemed to appear more than the clouds. Catherine sat in the parlor with Henry, who was reading pamphlets with the news from the other colonies around them. Frances, true to Henry's word, was Catherine's ever-present shadow and was even now curled up next to her on the settee, snoring. It was the little dog's jolting awake and jumping down from the settee, running and barking, that got the attention of both Henry and Catherine.

"Stay here," Henry said, noting the distress and fear on her face. Unexpected visitors still didn't sit well with her.

He made his way out to the foyer in the direction Frances had dashed to find her jumping and barking at the door. Sliding back the bolt, he opened it, the dog launching herself outside and barking a circle around a group of men standing there and looking bemused.

"Morning to you, Captain," Barnes said with a grin.

"Welcome home, lads!" Henry said with an equal grin. "Come in, come in! Frances, get inside and back to your mistress; no one believes you are frightening. Catherine!"

The men laughed and came inside, Frances scurrying back in upon having realized it was far colder outside than she desired to deal with. She was met halfway by Catherine herself, who let out a squeal of delight when she saw Barnes and Rogers.

"It is so good to see you! Welcome back!" she said, embracing each and kissing their cheeks. "You are absolutely freezing; come sit by the fire."

"It is good to see you looking so well, Lady Catherine," Barnes said, hugging her a bit longer and smiling at her fondly.

"And you, of course. Are you hungry? Tea?"

"No, no. We just wanted to come and let you know we had returned. Our families are back down at the inn, waiting for us."

"What? How dare you!" Catherine chided in her playful way. "You go this very instant and fetch them here."

Barnes looked to Henry, who shrugged with a small smile. "On land, and especially in this house, she outranks me."

"I will go," Rogers said, laughing and shaking his head.

"Take the wagon; I will help you hitch it up," Henry said, walking out with him.

"Where are the others?" Catherine asked as she walked with Barnes to the fire in the parlor.

"A couple stayed in Jamaica; the rest are in town keeping watch on the families."

"I am happy you have returned."

"Are you?"

"It was *far* too quiet here," Catherine said, gesturing for him to sit. "I think Henry was a little lonely."

"Yes, well, he was used to having us around for years. It would be jarring to have us all gone."

"A bit like a family."

"Very much like, yes."

"He could have used you in England, I think," she said, her tone at once quiet and reflective.

"What makes you say that?"

"He had only me, and then when we went back to court, he had the other men. But he seemed so unhappy when I caught glimpses of him. I think he missed his friends."

"He missed *you*," Barnes replied. "It was *you* he wanted, and *you* they were keeping from him. When he arrived back in Jamaica, he was not the same. Sullen, withdrawn, no interest in anyone or anything. We thought perhaps it was his imprisonment and what might have been done to him, but one day, when he had gotten so drunk that he passed out, we found him holding the tiny portrait of you in his hand. I knew then what had happened."

Catherine frowned. "I hate to think of him in such pain."

"It is not as though you were not the same. The difference is you had no one to confide in and you certainly were not getting drunk."

"No," she said, chuckling. "I could not. No, I still had to serve the queen and go on with my life as though he had never been there."

"But he had."

"He had, and try as I might to forget it, I could not. I knew I would eventually be married off."

"Would you have run if it were someone different?"

"I cannot say," she answered honestly.

"What was he like there?"

"As you see him here. He was just Henry. Well, at least when we were alone. In court he played his part, and I am sure he played the part of the captain, too, when people wanted to see it, but with me he was himself."

"I am not sure I had ever seen that one until he got here, but I quite like him."

"Did he tell you he took me to a tavern?"

Barnes looked intrigued. "He did not."

Catherine laughed. "He did. Someplace in Southwark I could not find again even if I wanted to. He dressed me like a servant and snuck me out in the middle of the night. It was the first time I had been any place like that, and it was fascinating to see all of the different types of people."

"I can imagine it would be if you had never seen them. I can only imagine what you might make of Port Royal."

"He bought rum and gave me some, and it was awful at first but then it was fine, though I felt a bit fuzzy."

"He got you drunk," Barnes said, laughing.

"Yes, he did, and then we played a game about what I would do if I were a pirate. But I must admit I was terrible because I do not know the first thing about sailing or what parts of ships are called."

Barnes was laughing hard, unable to help himself. "I would have liked to have seen that."

"Then, well I know what it was now, but I saw a man kissing a woman he seemed to have hired for the evening, and poor Henry tried to explain to me what they were doing because I could not conceive of it and I pushed him to tell me."

"Oh, Jesus …"

"Then everything went wrong."

"What?"

"Two men got in a fight, and one stabbed the other in the eye."

"A tavern brawl?"

"Yes, we tried to get out but were separated. I was terribly lost, then some horrid man found me and pulled me into a close. He covered my mouth so I could not breathe and tried to … well … but then Henry found me and made the man let go of me."

"Made him let go … how?"

"I do not know. He just did."

"I am fairly certain he killed him, my dear."

"What!"

"In that sort of a situation, the Henry I know would not hesitate. He would eliminate the threat."

"You are right," Henry said from the doorway as he entered the room. "I would."

"Did you?" Catherine asked, shocked.

"I did. He was not going to simply let you go without a fight, darling one. As I had no interest in your being in the middle of that, I took care of the problem. He was not worth keeping around if he would do such a thing anyway."

"But … you … I mean …" she stammered.

Henry looked at her with curiosity. "Catherine, did you believe I had never killed anyone?"

"I … well, not up close?"

"You always want to think the very best of me, Sparrow. I have done a great many things, and that is probably the least of them."

"There are worse things than murder?"

"Well, no, but I did not do that exactly. It would have been me or them, and I preferred it to be me. Murder is more killing for killing's sake or killing someone who was not trying to harm you or someone else."

"That is a very fine distinction."

"But a distinction nonetheless."

Barnes snorted in amusement. "Henry, you have to remember this lass has not lived the life we have or seen what can happen in it. She would have a difficult time understanding that concept."

"She saw a bit in that tavern."

"Take her to Port Royal and let her see that, then she would understand."

"Hmm, good point, but there is not a chance in hell of my taking her there."

"You did it for my protection so … it is … well, that is fine," Catherine declared.

"Thank you, Sparrow, for the forgiveness," he said with an amused smile, kissing her.

"It is a good thing we left when we did," Barnes said.

"Is it? What news?"

"The earl of Carbery and Morgan are at odds, of course. Carbery was angered by the salary that the assembly settled on him, and all the while Morgan has kept up good relations with the captains, even investing in some of their ventures. Captains, their ships, and their goods are welcome in Port Royal as long as they are willing to pay Morgan a share. He and his brother-in-law are directing captains to the French in Tortuga to get letters of marque while they get a sum for each one signed."

"Still a criminal but a knighted one."

"Exactly. That cannot hold, and when we left there were rumblings of a coming confrontation between the two in government."

"For what reason?"

"My best understanding is collaborating with the French against the Spanish."

"Carbery should watch himself, lest he end up missing."

"Indeed. But it seems Morgan takes at least some of his

job seriously as he starts to take full control of the defenses and the port."

"I am sure it helps his determination when he is enriching himself in the process."

"You knew he had one plantation and invested in another after Maracaibo. He has since added a third."

"Jesus," Henry muttered. "With slaves, no doubt."

"Absolutely. We are all well away from it. While you and Morgan were civil, you were never what anyone would call friendly, particularly after Panama, and I am sure his dues request from you would be onerous."

"Undoubtedly."

"Things are going to get ugly there before long, and when it does, the infighting will be bloody and brutal. Right now, Morgan might control the island and the Assembly, packing it with family and supporters, but word will get back to England and there will be a reckoning."

"It is best we are not there when it comes."

"And we will not be."

"No. We will be here, making honest lives and living off of the spoils of previous adventures," Henry said, grinning.

"Living the dream."

Barnes and Henry both laughed, and Catherine shook her head with a smile.

"Barnes, tell my wife that money is not a thing to concern herself with. She does not believe me."

"It definitely is not."

"How so?" Catherine asked.

"Has Henry shown you what is inside those trunks we brought the first time?"

"No, but he said they were full of money."

"Indeed, they are, chock full of Spanish gold, and there are 10 more in the hold of the ship down at the harbor, all stuffed full, all belonging to him. That does not even count the money from the sale of the villa."

"So, you see, Sparrow? We are probably richer than the king himself. We just are not showing it, and our money is actual money and not property."

"Good Lord," Catherine whispered, staring at him in disbelief.

"No one can ever say I was not good at what I did," Henry said, shrugging.

"That is one of the truest statements I have heard," Barnes said, laughing. "You have certainly earned a comfortable retirement."

Chapter 13

When Rogers returned with the wives and children of both himself and Barnes and the other crew members who decided to return, there were reunions and introductions with tea and food provided for them. Catherine had it all in hand, along with Fiona, and Màiri was excited to have other children to play with. Those who had been here before admired the changes to the house in their absence, while the wives and the children marveled at it all. They hadn't lived in shacks, but this was beyond even them.

"She looks well," Barnes said as he and Henry stole away to take a walk and talk alone.

"She is. She has healed entirely, as far as we can tell."

"You must be thankful for that."

"Very."

"I had hoped there might be a child of your own around the place by now," he said, and Henry winced.

"Not yet."

"You still have not told her?"

"No. I cannot do that to her; she has suffered enough. What good would it do?"

"If it made her unable, should she not know?"

"If it made her unable, she would feel guilty and blame herself for causing him to come here and do it to her in the first place. It would be perhaps best to simply let her believe she could not from the start. It would certainly solidify her choice to run from that marriage for he surely would have killed her."

"Do you still want to kill her father?"

"Yes, but then I also want more. I want to make him pay, make him suffer, as he tried to do to her. Death is too easy."

"I am sure you have entertained ideas."

"Plenty of them, but I have not settled on one yet."

Barnes chuckled. "When the time comes, be assured we will help you."

"I would hope so. You and Rogers love her as well as I do."

"We do, indeed. I am hoping to find some land near here."

"You have picked a good time. With the signed treaty, we are soon to be a British colony again. You would be wise to move quickly, as some of the Dutch settlers will be returning home."

"Do you know of any?"

"The neighboring farm, I know that, but it sold recently."

"That is a shame. I think I would have enjoyed living next to you."

"Then I suppose it is good that I am the one who bought it, hm?" Henry said, laughing. "I planned on holding it for you until you arrived, and now here you are."

"That is very good of you," Barnes said, his tone showing him to be touched by the gesture. "I will, of course, pay you back for it; just let me know, and we will do the transfer as soon as all the trunks are here."

"Only half of it," he said, smiling. "We are old friends, you and I, and you have always been there when I needed you. This is the least I can do, so please consider it a gift from Catherine and myself."

"Just as you were there for me. It was not a one-way deal and never has been, but I thank you both for your kindness, and I know my wife will be grateful to you."

"I still will be there, Barnes. I am glad you decided to stay; I am not sure what I would have done had you not. You were free to go, of course, but I would have missed your friendship a great deal."

"We have known each other since we started at this as little more than children, Henry. What, 15 years now? From powder monkeys and deckhands to sailors and more. We have always been more like brothers than friends, rank aside. When you became a captain, there was no question in my mind about following you, and when you decided to stay here, there was once again no question as to what I would do."

"I agree. I have always thought of you that way, too."

"I know you have; you never had to say it. I did not want to mention it in front of her because I had a feeling she did not know the full truth of your exploits, but Morgan was asking after you when we returned."

"Why?" Henry asked, wary in an instant.

"My guess is to suss out the depth of any connections you made in England and use them to his advantage, or at least any scandal he could use to hold over their heads. He was, as I understand it, particularly interested in the fact that you had left Jamaica never to return."

"I would have wished him luck at such blackmail, as I am not sure any of them much cared."

"I am sure there was more. We all know he was a wretched sailor, and you were one of the best. He may be governor, but he is still a pirate. You can never take that out of a man, and you know that better than anyone. I promise he still has targets he longed to hit, and he intended for you to hit them for him."

"I never would have agreed to that. I have been very clear on not working with him again."

"You and I both know that with his new power you would not have had a choice if you did not want to swing."

"Do you think he would send someone after me?"

"It would expose him, and there are others who, though less skilled, might get the job done without going to that sort of trouble. I would not put it past him, though, and you should be on your guard. With this becoming a British colony once more, his reach extends even here now."

"If the target were large enough, he might come knocking."

"He very well might. You cannot escape who you are, Henry, no matter how hard you try or how deeply you bury it beneath the veneer of a husband and honest man."

"Can I not? What if I do not want to be that anymore? I left for a reason."

"You left for Catherine. There is a difference."

"That is a reason."

"That is an excuse. Do not dare try to tell me that if that woman died you would not be back on the water the moment she was in the ground, running from grief and venting your pain with the blood of others, and had her letter not reached you, then you would be there still. Do not lie to yourself."

Henry said nothing, eyes trained forward as they walked.

"You left because she showed you there was still good in you, something worth saving. You left to make yourself worthy of her and everything she believed you were. Henry, *this* Henry, was not dead after all, and the reason you left was to save his soul and redeem him. If that were not the case, we would have come here, picked her up, and taken her back to Jamaica, so you could go back to the life you knew so well."

"I could never take her there," Henry said quietly.

"No, you could not, and that is why you are here. The *real* reason. You stayed for her, to protect her from all of it and everything you have done. She would not last a day in Port Royal, and you knew that. People know you there, and she would find out *exactly* who you were when you were not with her. *What* you were. She would be a target for anyone who wanted to hurt you. What would you become in her eyes when she found out the truth?"

Henry closed his eyes and stopped walking. "I do not know, and I do not want to find out."

"But you do not regret a damned thing."

"No."

"And that is exactly it, is it not? All of the blood and all of the death and you regret nothing. There is not an ounce of remorse in you for any of it. You told me that she had seen those dispatches, that she had an idea of you that was so far from reality because those could not tell the truth. Somehow, she saw something in you no one else did, not even you. She made you remember who you were, who you had been, before all the rest buried it. But the rest is still there in the background, waiting."

"Are you saying I should tell her? What would I say? 'Catherine, my love, did you know I used to stand on the deck and listen to men scream as we blew their ship apart, and I was glad to hear it?' Should I tell her about the women and children we saw slaughtered but did nothing to stop it because that was not why we were there? How we heard them screaming for help and still stood there and watched it happen? The last two I will regret until the day I die, but that does not absolve me of the sin, does it? Or you, or any of us who were there?"

"Henry —"

"Maybe we should talk about the way we whored our way through weeks before we remembered any time had passed? Or drank our way through the same? How we did it all to try and forget the horror we saw and the horror we caused? I can tell her how I became a captain by leading a mutiny and killing mine. I can tell her there is no way she will see her beloved husband in the hereafter because he is bound for hell for all of the blood he has bathed in. All in the name of the king, or at least that is what we told ourselves to make it easier."

"You cannot, of course you cannot, and no one expects you to."

"Then what do I do? What will I do if that past comes knocking on our door demanding my surrender again? How will I look her in the eye when she discovers how much she did not know! All I want is to be worthy of her and the adoration I see in her eyes every time she looks at me. I can never make up for it, but I can try."

"It is all any of us can do, and to worry about it coming for you is borrowing trouble. You are not a monster even if you think you are, but it will always be there. Yes, we did stand by that *one* time and did nothing when we should have, but you fixed that, did you not? You could not stand it and killed the captain; you took over and that is where you have been ever since. Mutiny or not, it was the right thing to do. Accept it, embrace it, and then live your life. I see the way you tread so carefully, waiting for the floor to fall out from under you and for all of this to be taken from you. I suspect that even if she did find out about some of it, she would still love you the same. She would find a way to reconcile it, to excuse you, because she cannot do otherwise, just as she did earlier in the parlor."

"I should not be excused. I do not want to be."

"That is her choice, not yours, and she may never have to make it."

"I love her more than life itself and I would murder a million men to keep those truths from darkening our door. I would do it, and I would not hesitate, would not care. Those parts of me remain, but this part of me has shackled them where they belong and that is where I intend for them to stay. God help me, but I would take my own life before I would let her be pulled into that hell after me. Morgan cannot call me if I am dead. I will never, *ever* go back there, and I damned sure will never again be the Henry Merrick who smiled as blood dripped from his hands."

"Unless that blood is her father's."

"That is an exception I am more than happy to make."

Barnes laughed. "It is good to see that the fire I knew so well is still there."

"Could not be otherwise."

Barnes clapped him on the shoulder. "It is all right, you know. You are the way you are, and all that matters is what you do now. If that is protecting your wife and spending the rest of your life in comfort with her, so be it."

"It is all I want. She is my star, the one guiding me on the right course. Without her I *would* go back, we both know that, and you said as much. I like this Henry, this part of me I had forgotten, who can do more than just sail and kill. I love to see her smile and to feel her in my arms at night."

"All of those things you could never have in Jamaica."

"Yes. There was no other way, no other option. I had to walk away from it, and I have not regretted it."

"That is all that matters now."

"And so have you."

"And I do not regret it either. It is time to do our best to pay recompense for our sins by leading lives devoted to the good of others and not the destruction of them."

"Well said, my friend. Well said."

Chapter 14

Barnes, Rogers, and their families began joining Catherine and Henry for meals while improvements for their own homes took place. Rogers and his family were able to secure land a few miles down the road, and it pleased Henry a great deal to know that his two most loyal and longtime friends and associates would still be nearby. The work on both homes started within days, with many of the same tradesmen who had worked on New Merrick House now working on these. They wouldn't be as opulent as New Merrick, but they didn't need to be. The existing houses were fine, strong homes, needing only a bit of expansion and work to suit the needs of the two families.

A pounding at the door interrupted dinner one afternoon in April, and the group gathered around the table ceased talking and laughing, their expressions confused. Henry looked at Barnes and Rogers over the table, all three of them already aware that whatever was behind the door wasn't good. They heard Iain open it, then loud voices demanding Henry Merrick. Henry wasted no time in rising and heading for the foyer, followed closely by Catherine. His stomach knotted when he saw the bright red coats of English soldiers.

"Henry Merrick?" the officer called out.

"Yes."

"You are under arrest and are to come with us."

"What? For what reason?" Catherine said, panicked. "By whose order?"

"By order of King Charles and the governor of Jamaica."

Henry looked at Barnes and Rogers, who stared in disbelief. This was everything he'd feared coming true, everything he hadn't wanted.

"No, this cannot be right; he has done nothing wrong," Catherine insisted, placing herself in front of Henry as if she could protect him.

"Captain Merrick stands accused of murder, treason, piracy, and several other crimes. I suggest you stand aside, madame."

"Murder of whom? He has been here the whole time with me, and I will *not* stand aside! I do nothing by your order!"

The soldiers looked at her in confusion, as did everyone else. Everyone but Henry. He knew this Catherine, and he knew her well.

"The king —"

"The king," Catherine repeated. "As the daughter of a peer and one who loyally served the queen and king in their court and their household, I am not required to do anything by your order."

"Who is your father?" the officer asked, his expression and the tone of his voice making it plain that he found her claims dubious, at best.

"Lord Merrick. As a member of the privy council, I am sure you have heard of him?" Catherine fired back, her own tone of voice becoming ever so slightly mocking.

"Orders are orders. Stand aside. Captain, come with us," he replied, though he faltered a bit as he reached for Henry.

"He will *not*!" shouted Catherine, shoving his hands away. "Leave my house at once and send this colony's governor!"

"It does not matter! Stand aside!"

"No!"

"Catherine," Henry said. "Let me go."

"Henry, I cannot! You have done nothing!"

"You cannot stop this, my love. You cannot. Please."

"What are you saying?"

"I will come with you, please give me a moment," Henry said to the officer, who nodded. He knew well enough that this situation could and would get ugly — and bloody — very quickly if he allowed it to go on. "Catherine," he said cupping her face in his hands. "Everything will be fine. Barnes and Rogers will take care of you, and you have everything in the room to live on."

"You are speaking as if you will not return!"

"Because I will not," Henry sighed. "Remember always that I love you."

"Henry, stop! Please!"

Henry turned away from her without another word and forced himself to walk out, where the men immediately put him in irons and loaded him into a wagon.

"NO!" Catherine screamed as the wagon pulled away, prevented from running after it by Barnes. "HENRY!"

Henry could hear her panicked screaming following him, and it made him want to be sick. It had all been for nothing because in the end it had come for him anyway. He would hang in Jamaica, or he would be killed in a raid directed by one of Morgan's subordinates, but he knew he was never meant to come home again and never see Catherine. He knew why they'd come for him now; the tide was ready, and his departure would be immediate. This time he was treated far less kindly, shoved roughly below decks and into a cell. Henry slid down the wall and buried his head in his hands. All he could do now was pray to die before he ever reached Jamaica.

***

Catherine was taken upstairs, unable to stop her tears. What was happening? Henry was gone. Her beloved taken for who knows what real reason, never to return. She knew well enough that any crimes Henry had committed could've been paid for in England two years ago but weren't. Why now? No, this was something else entirely. She couldn't let this happen, but what could she do? If she were in this situation, what would he do? Catherine berated herself for even needing to think about it for a moment. Henry would come for her and — but her thoughts paused there. Henry would come for her, of course he would! He would come for her and set things right; he wouldn't rest until she was once again safe with him.

Catherine pushed herself up from the bed and threw open the door to their bedroom, sweeping out and down the hallway to the room where Henry's trunks resided. There was only one without a lock, and she flung it open. Within lay a pistol, a dagger, and a broadsword. Without hesitation, Catherine grabbed the pistol and the dagger, loading the pistol before she left the room, and hurrying down the stairs.

"Lady Catherine, what are ye doing?" Fiona cried out upon seeing her.

The commotion caused Barnes and Rogers to turn around, their eyes widening. "Lady Catherine —" Barnes began.

Catherine stopped and aimed the pistol directly at his face, engaging the mechanism. There was no tremor in her hand, no fear in her eyes. "Take me to Jamaica."

The room was still as if everyone had forgotten how to breathe.

"Lady Catherine, you cannot —"

"It was not a request. I will *not* let him die. You are taking me to Jamaica, and you are doing it on the next tide. Or I swear to God I will kill you all for your lack of loyalty to him, just as he would if you defied an order. Provision the ship. We leave as soon as it is done. Do it now."

There was no question as to whether she was serious. She was, and they all knew it.

"Aye, Captain Merrick," he replied as a dark smile spread

across his lips. "You heard the Captain, Rogers. We sail to-morrow. Round up the crew."

"Aye, we do," Rogers said with a smile of his own. "Time to go hunting."

Chapter 15

Henry's fervent prayers during the voyage went unanswered, and he found himself very much alive when they reached Jamaica. The heat was oppressive as they pulled him out onto the deck and not something he'd missed, though it was cooler above than in his cell. At least here there was air moving to help cut the thickness of the stale atmosphere below. Shoved into a rowboat to be ferried ashore, Henry took in the sight of the port city as they approached, and it seemed as though Port Royal had grown since he'd left it. He wasn't sure if that was a good thing, or at least if it was a good thing for anyone but a select few.

Once they reached shore, he was loaded into a wagon for the drive up to whichever plantation Sir Henry Morgan, former pirate captain and now lieutenant governor of Jamaica, was deciding to occupy at the moment. It was on the larger side, and it made Henry angry to see the slaves toiling in the heat as they passed. Inside the house, Henry was unshackled and given an opportunity to bathe and change his clothing, something he appreciated. When he'd finished, the shackles were placed back on his wrists so that they could march him into a large office, and Henry felt resigned to whatever fate awaited him here. He no longer cared because if he wouldn't be going back to her, what did it matter anyway? Behind a large desk sat the man himself: Henry Morgan. All dark hair and steely eyes, he looked fearsome and was exactly as anyone would expect someone like him to be. Henry Merrick was rather the exception.

"Well, well, well. If it is not the great Henry Merrick, dragged back from self-imposed exile."

"Dragged being the operative word. I was quite happy where I was, not that it matters to you."

"You are right; it does not."

"Why am I really here?"

"You know damned well *why*, Merrick. You are valuable in numerous ways, and then there is the reward being offered by the king, the rewards being offered by France or Spain, and your skill as a privateer."

"Why does the king have a bounty out for me when I have done nothing since I left England?"

"Murder."

"Murder. I have killed a lot of people, so could you be more specific? Whom did I supposedly murder?"

"Your wife, according to the dispatch, though I was rather surprised to hear you had taken a wife."

Henry felt as though he'd been punched in the gut. "My … what? My wife is alive and well; you can ask the men who dragged me away from her while she screamed!"

"According to her father, you murdered her in a fit of rage when he came to take her back to England rather than allow him to have her."

Henry shook his head. "No … no, *he* tried to kill her! He beat her near to death and stabbed her! It was a miracle she lived!"

"Can you prove it?"

"She is alive at home! Those men can tell you so!"

"Come, now, you know they will not vouch for you."

Henry's anger was clear. "I *never* hurt her," he seethed.

"I can make this all go away for you."

"Oh?"

"If you do what I want you to do, I will vouch for you myself, tell them I saw the lady and she is alive. Then you can go home."

"And if I do not?"

"Then you hang, Merrick, and I collect the bounty."

"You will collect it either way."

"Yes, I will."

"What is it you want from me?"

"Panama."

"Pan — that is a death wish! We raided it once before; there is not a chance in hell you would do it again!"

"I would not, but you could. Think of it, what glory, hm? Sacking that city once more. You would be a legend."

"I would be breaking treaties, and then the king would want me dead twice over!"

"We could get several ships together, the best crews. You could do it. You were there last time; you know what such an expedition would be facing."

"No."

"Are you sure you want to be so quick with an answer?"

"I refuse."

"Do you not want to see your wife again? Your home?"

"I would not see it because I would be *dead* at the bottom of the goddamned sea, Morgan, and you know it."

"It would be a glorious death."

"Not to her."

"What does it matter? To history it would. History is what matters. When she is dead and gone, the history will live on, and you would be the man who helped sack Panama a second time."

"No."

"I am going to give you a few days to think about it. You are tired after your journey and not thinking clearly. Take him away," Morgan said, waving his hand.

"I will not do it! It does not matter how long you lock

me up or what you do to me! I WILL NOT DO IT!" Henry shouted as he was dragged away.

Taken back down, he was put in the cells at the garrison, and when the door shut behind him, he closed his eyes. It was stifling here, the walls damp with humidity. He didn't know how long Morgan would let him protest before he realized that Henry wouldn't cooperate and killed him. Henry thought back to the conversation he'd had with Barnes just months ago, where he'd sworn he'd kill himself before he'd become what he once was. He'd said he'd never come back here, but that was beyond his control this time. The rest was not. If he could find a way to do it before Morgan did it for him, he would.

***

"My lady! We are here." Barnes called down below.

Catherine stepped onto the deck, watching the island and the port grow closer. She'd heard of this place, the "Sodom of the New World," and she was going into it willingly. In truth she had no choice, or at least no other acceptable choice. Henry was somewhere in this place, and she wouldn't leave until he was returned to her. She'd put Fiona and the wives of Barnes and Rogers in stewardship of New Merrick House while she was away, and she'd made sure to bring money with her in case it was required to pay for his freedom. They were only two days behind Henry, and she hoped it wasn't two days too late.

"I will find out where he is first," Barnes said. "You should not come ashore until we know."

"Why not?"

"It is beyond dangerous for you here. There is a damned good reason Henry never would have brought you to this place, and it is safer for you to stay aboard."

"Once you find out where he is, you will come and fetch me?"

"Of course. There are acceptable places for you to stay higher up the island, and we will take you there. You have come this far; I will not stop you now."

Catherine looked at him and smiled. "Thank you for being here."

"You were going with or without me, and I could not let him down by letting you go alone. It is fascinating; now I see the woman who stole her dowry and fled England. I had always wondered if the sweet young woman I knew could do such a thing, but you are so much like him it is honestly terrifying."

"What you saw was the real me, the person I am when I am with him. *This* is the Catherine who refuses to let anyone take it from her, the one who survived court."

Barnes chuckled. "Yes, well, I commend you for having done so."

"The heat is awful."

"Yes, I have not missed that, and I feel for you having to wear the rest of your clothing once we are ashore."

"I will manage," Catherine murmured. She'd been wearing only her stays, chemise, and a petticoat for the last few days, as the heat had been so unbearable that she had little care for modesty.

"Rogers and I will go ashore and try to find any news about the Captain," he called out to the crew as they made ready to drop anchor. "The rest of you stay here and guard Lady Catherine. If anything happens to her, you will have to deal with *him,* and I would not want to be you," Barnes continued as he started to prepare the rowboat. "Home again, eh Rogers?"

"Unfortunately," Rogers muttered.

"The sooner we find him, the sooner we are out of here. Come on."

Catherine sat on the deck near the stairway leading below decks so that she could duck inside if necessary, but her stomach was in knots as she waited for the other two to return.

What if they were too late and he was already dead or shipped to England for justice? What if Barnes and Rogers couldn't find out where he was or get any information out of anyone? Hearing the crew call out as the two men arrived back snapped her out of her thoughts. Standing, she hurried to the rail, looking at Barnes expectantly as he came back aboard.

"He is here, and he is alive."

"Thank God," Catherine said, her relief clear.

"I do not know for how much longer, however."

"What did you find out?"

"He is being held at the garrison. There was a bounty on him from the king himself."

"On what charge?"

"Murder."

"Murder! Whose?"

"Yours."

"What?"

"It seems your father told the king that Henry murdered you rather than let your father take you back to England. Morgan is planning to collect that bounty by sending Henry to the gallows … unless he cooperates."

Catherine's expression darkened, her green eyes hardening like glass. "Cooperates with what?"

"Morgan wants Henry to lead a second sacking of Panama. Henry refused and continues to do so."

"Why? Why not just do it so he can come home?"

"Because that is a suicide mission and he knows it. Morgan sacked Panama once before; their defenses are surely better now, and there is no way another run like that would succeed. If he went, he would never come back."

"If Morgan knows that, why would he even try?"

"Because he loses nothing in the attempt but gains everything if it miraculously succeeds. It is why he dragged Henry here. He is the best chance Morgan has to pull it off. Henry did not get his reputation for nothing. He is one of the best sailors out here."

"So, Henry dies either way."

"Exactly. He told me when we came back that he would die before he did this again, and it seems he intends to keep that promise."

"Like hell he will," Catherine said. "I need to meet with Morgan."

"I am not sure it will be that easy."

"Oh, I am sure it will. Let us go."

Unloading began at once, and Catherine was the last to go ashore. First, it was the things they'd brought with them, left on the dock with the rest of the crew, then Barnes and Rogers came back for her. The cloaked and hooded figure who stepped out of the boat seemed unremarkable, even in the afternoon heat, but as Catherine would not have been able to disembark in her normal clothing, she remained in her underthings with the cloak to hide that and her. If it got out that the wife of Henry Merrick was on the island, she would become an instant target for anyone who might have a grudge against him. To that end, she carried a loaded pistol in her lap, hidden beneath the cloak, in case anyone stopped them.

The trip to the inn took them through the docks and up through some of the less illustrious areas of Port Royal. Though Catherine sat in the wagon, it was easy to see in the bright light of day the debauchery around her. The prostitutes, both male and female, the taverns, the drunks, the criminal element that considered Port Royal its paradise. She found it hard to believe the Henry she knew had ever made a home here, but she wasn't so naive as to believe he hadn't frequented these areas, moved in them and amongst them, partaken of some of these women or anything else one might do here.

"There is a price for everything, Catherine."

The memory of those words floated back to her, the night she'd told him there was a high price to pay for the life she led. The truth of those words was on display right before her eyes. Everything here had a price for someone willing to pay it. From the sugar that moved off the island's plantations to the bodies of those on this street, all of it was for sale. She was sure this was just as true in London or anywhere else; you'd just have to try harder to find it. A woman's laughter got her attention, and Catherine met her eyes from where the woman sat on the lap of a man who was groping her. She smiled, but it was hollow, her eyes devoid of feeling. Catherine's heart ached, knowing that feeling far more intimately than she cared to admit. The look on her face seemed to, for a moment, cause the woman's to falter, her laughter and smile fading. A moment of shared understanding and shared pain allowing the life to return to the eyes of the unfortunate soul before she looked away.

"Barnes, stop the cart."

"What? Lady Cath —"

"I said stop."

Barnes pulled up on the reins, his posture uncomfortable and wary. Catherine stood, and he tried to grab hold of her arm, but she shoved his hand away and climbed down. Walking back the short distance, she stopped in front of the two. The woman looked confused, but the man grinned.

"Coming to join in, little one?" he leered.

"No," Catherine replied, refusing to look at him. "You need to move."

"Excuse me?"

"You have been outbid."

"What in the hell does that mean?"

"It means I am paying her now, and I promise it will be more than you are offering."

"Now see here, you little bitch! Just who in the —"

Any words leaving his mouth ceased when he found the pistol pointed at him in a range close enough that there was no way she'd miss. Catherine engaged the mechanism and gave him a sideways glance from beneath the hood.

"Are you sure you want to continue speaking? I think it would be wise to do what I say."

The man was unarmed, and anything he could reach he wouldn't make it to before she pulled the trigger. Thinking better of it, he raised his hands. "As you say, little one," he sneered before he stumbled off.

Catherine disengaged the mechanism and looked back into the stunned face of the woman. From the small purse tied at her waist, she pulled out a coin and pressed it into the woman's palm. "This is enough to at least give you an entire night's peace and freedom."

"Miss, I —"

"Please, take it. I know what it feels like to be trapped. Someone set me free once, and now I have the chance to do the same even if only for a little while."

The young woman nodded and closed her fingers around it, though her eyes were filled with tears. "Who are you?"

"No one important," Catherine said, offering a small smile as she squeezed the young woman's hand and walked back to the cart.

Climbing back in, she nodded to Barnes, who got them underway again. "Are you mad, woman? What are you doing!"

"Repaying a favor," Catherine replied.

"With a pistol?"

"The only way some people will listen to a woman."

"Bloody Merricks," Barnes muttered, and it made Catherine smile.

Once they reached the inn, Catherine wrote a letter to Morgan requesting a meeting with him. To the surprise of everyone but Catherine, the response was quick and was an invitation to supper, with Barnes and Rogers attending as her escort, as was fitting of a lady of her status. Catherine bathed and dressed carefully, knowing the image she wished to portray and the impression she wanted to give. She'd packed a fine dress for exactly this reason, because if Morgan had gone to the trouble of transporting Henry here, then he wanted something Henry had, and whatever it was might be something it would seem to perchance be in her power to provide. If he was knighted now, buying up land and trying to be respectable, he was intending to climb the social ladder, and she would be damned if she'd allow him to do it by using her.

Morgan sent a carriage for her, and the ride to the plantation was silent. It was hard not to notice how different things seemed higher up the island, far from the port and its noise, as well as its other activity. As the carriage rolled its way down the long drive, Catherine took note of the slaves — men, women, and children — toiling alongside it, their backs bent, looking exhausted. Some bore scars on their backs as evidence of past punishment, and it made her feel ill. How could anyone do this to another? She wanted to burn this place to the ground and set them free, but she couldn't. She was thankful Henry vehemently disagreed with such barbarism and had actively fought against it when he could. Morgan clearly had no such qualms.

When they arrived, they were shown in by a slave, and it made her uncomfortable. She was used to household, but all of them were paid and not forced to work for them. Maybe she should knock a lantern down on her way out after all.

The doors to the dining room opened, and they walked inside to find Morgan waiting for them, though he rose when she entered, bowing to her.

"Lady Catherine Merrick, I must admit I was surprised to receive your note."

Catherine curtsied in return, taking stock of the man before her. His dark hair and eyes made him look fierce, but there was something altogether unhealthy about his appearance that she couldn't name. "Were you? Why would that be?"

"You are supposedly dead, my lady. At least according to the dispatch sent from the king."

"As you can see, I am very much alive, so you can release my husband from the false charge."

Morgan chuckled. "How can I be sure you are who you

say you are and you are not some tart they have dressed up in order to get him free?"

"I am fairly certain they would be hard-pressed to find a tart with the manners and bearing of the English nobility, but by all means, test me if you wish. Shall I translate Latin for you? A recitation? My family tree?"

"I think you are quite right," he said. "Barnes, Rogers, how good to see you," he continued, though his voice made it clear he felt the opposite. "Please do have a seat."

Catherine took her seat, the stones of the jewels on her neck and ears glinting in the light of the candles. "As I said, you can release him."

"I think not. You see, that would not be his only crime."

"It would be the only one since he was last in England under the king's custody. If he wanted him punished for those crimes, he could have done so then."

"He could have, that is true, but the French and the Spanish do not feel the same way, and they have their own issues with Captain Merrick."

"Everything he did, he did in the king's service."

Morgan laughed now. "Is that what he told you?"

"Governor —" Barnes began before Morgan held up a hand to silence him.

"Answer my question, my lady."

"He told me nothing, but I know he had a letter of marque. I read the dispatches to the privy council. I am not ignorant."

"Oh, dispatches to the privy council only told part of the story, the parts we *wanted* them to know. Let me tell you about your husband, Lady Catherine."

"Governor, please," Barnes said.

"Quiet, Barnes. She should know what her sainted husband is really like and then decide if he is still worth her efforts. Henry Merrick is a cold-blooded killer. I never saw him show an ounce of remorse when he cut down men who were begging for their lives. I saw him laugh and cheer when he was covered in their blood. He craved it, he loved it, and he was good at it."

"Stop," Catherine said.

"What, did you think those ships just handed over their cargo because he asked nicely? Naive girl. The number of dead men littering the floor of the Caribbean who were sent there by Merrick is considerable. All because he wanted what they had. Then he came back here with the two men beside you and he did what we all did: drank, ate, and spent time with every harlot he could find."

Catherine shook her head, tears in her eyes.

"Why are you doing this, Governor? Stop," Barnes said.

"How many women and children do you think fell under his orders, hm?" When Catherine gasped, his smile turned sinister. "Oh yes. Ask Barnes, ask Rogers. Ask them about how those unfortunate souls were penned up in their churches. Ask them who had a torch."

"He did not!" Rogers shouted. "That is a goddamned lie! He had nothing to do with that!"

"Who will you believe, Lady Catherine? Me or the men who have lied and will continue to lie for him?"

Catherine gripped the arms of the chair and closed her eyes, pushing the standing tears down her cheeks.

"Do you still want him freed? Still want him to come home to you and share the bed he brought you to with lies? Bought with the money earned with the blood of others?"

"Enough, Morgan!" Barnes said.

"If you want him, I know a way you can earn it. Come here to me."

Catherine opened her eyes and stood.

"No, Lady Catherine … do not do this …" Barnes said.

"Yes, do. Come here, little lamb, and sacrifice yourself for his sins."

Catherine approached him with slow steps, and when she was close enough, he took her hand and pulled her close to him, looking up at her from where he sat, drawing a fingertip down the back of her arm.

"How badly do you want him? Badly enough to ransom yourself to me for the night? Your body for his freedom? Do you think he would forgive you?"

Catherine's distress was clear on her face.

"What will you choose?"

In a split second, Catherine's entire demeanor changed from distressed wife to cold deliberation, and she pulled out a knife she'd hidden in a pocket, placing the tip against Morgan's throat. Just as quickly, he grabbed her wrist and forced it away, only to find her other hand holding a knife to his throat. At the same time, Catherine lifted her leg and pinned his other hand to the chair with her knee, leaning forward to put some of her weight on it, bringing a shout of pain from him. Barnes and Rogers stared in shock.

"I am more than willing to kill you," Catherine said, her voice taking on an icy and menacing edge that neither of the men with her had ever heard.

"You would do no such thing."

"Would I not?" Catherine said, pressing down harder on his hand and grinding her knee into it, which made Morgan give a pained shout through his teeth. "I have nothing to lose, while you have everything. I know all of your secrets, Morgan, and if you harm me, they will be on their way to the king with you unable to stop it. What do you think he would do, I wonder, if he found out I had been alive, but you killed me to collect a false bounty?"

"You know *nothing*."

"Are you sure? How do you know what he has told me and what he has not? You were willing to believe I was helpless, a weak woman, a poor scared daughter of the nobility, and you were wrong. Are you willing to risk being wrong again? If you honestly believe for even a moment that I do not have plans in place, you are a fool. You have quite the comfortable scheme here; it would be a terrible shame if it all came crashing down, do you not think?"

Morgan stared at her, and Catherine knew she had him. He had no idea what she knew or if she was bluffing, and he didn't want to find out.

"Since Captain Merrick has refused my demands, he is to hang for his crimes, but I will give you a chance to save him. Be at the gallows tomorrow."

"How do I know you are not lying?"

"I swear on the code. Barnes and Rogers know what that means. I admire your dedication and your fire, Lady Catherine, and I will reward it with one final chance to save him. It seems Merrick chose a more fitting bride than anyone realized, perhaps even him."

"Barnes?" Catherine said, not taking her eyes or her knife off Morgan.

"He has sworn on the code, my lady, the code that rules all pirates. If he breaks his word, his own life is forfeit."

"Excellent. I am glad we understand each other," Catherine said. "I want to see him."

"Of course you do, and as his wife you have the right to do so. I will send a letter with you to the garrison, and that will allow you in."

Catherine stepped back, releasing his hand but keeping both knives in hers in case he came near her. Morgan rose from the chair and went to a desk, writing something and signing it before handing it to Catherine. One look at it told her it was precisely what he said it would be.

"Be at the gallows tomorrow at nine. If you are late, he dies."

Catherine backed up a few steps before turning and sweeping from the room, Barnes and Rogers behind her. The carriage was still there, and she told the driver to take them to the garrison once they were all inside, tucking the knives back inside her pockets.

"Jesus Christ, woman!" Barnes exclaimed. "Where in the hell did you learn that?"

"Henry learned once to never underestimate me. Morgan just learned the same."

"The Captain would have been proud of that performance," Rogers said.

"Still will be when we tell him," Barnes said.

When they arrived at the garrison, Catherine showed them the letter, though the guards looked at her with curiosity. Women did not usually show up here dressed in court gowns and dripping with jewels. As they were led to the cell where Henry was being kept, Catherine wanted to scream for the horrible conditions he was staying in. It was dank within, the air stale and stifling in the narrow hallways. There were prisoners huddled in the corners of cells, some looking dead or nearly so, and the smell of sweat and human waste made Catherine want to retch. The sooner she could get Henry out of here, the better.

***

"Captain Merrick! You have visitors."

"I have already said I will not —" Henry began as he turned around, but he stopped, sure he was dreaming. No, it couldn't be. He wanted her so badly he was hallucinating now. "Catherine?" he whispered.

"Henry," she said through tears as she ran the last steps to his cell, reaching her arm through the bars.

"Sparrow!" he exclaimed as he threw himself at the bars to grip her hand in his, kissing it before burying his nose against her skin. "What …. how … I am dreaming …"

"No," she sobbed. "I am here. I came for you as you would come for me. I could not let you die, and I will not."

Henry grabbed her face and kissed her repeatedly. "My love, you never should have come here, but thank Christ you have!"

Catherine cried, holding his hands on her face. She returned every kiss he gave her, as desperate for any contact with him as he was with her.

"How did you get here!"

"She was very persuasive," Barnes said.

"Barnes?" Henry said in shock, looking up.

"She pointed a pistol in my face and told me we were coming to get you. Rather hard to argue with that. Particularly when it is a Merrick doing the pointing."

"You did what! Catherine!"

"Oh, it gets better than that, Captain," Rogers said.

"Damned right it does," Barnes agreed.

"How?"

"Well, there is the part where she just got out of a meeting with Morgan himself."

"No ... Sparrow, you —"

"Where she held him at knifepoint and threatened to expose his dirty secrets to the king unless he let her see you and set you free. He swore on the code he would give her a chance to save you in the morning."

Henry's eyes went wide. "Catherine, you held Governor Morgan at knifepoint? *The* Governor Morgan? *Captain Morgan*? That one?"

"Yes, I did, and I am not sorry."

"Oh, it was a thing of beauty, Captain," Rogers said, grinning. "First, she pulled one knife, and when he shoved that away, she had a knife in her other hand against his throat, and then she smashed his hand against the arm of the chair with her knee and used her weight to pin him there. Every so often she pressed a little to remind him. He was trapped, for if he let her hand go, he was dead, but if he tried anything else, she would still kill him with the other hand before he could do anything."

Henry stared at her. Catherine, *his* Catherine, had just held not one knife but two on one of the most famous pirates to sail the Caribbean. She'd somehow managed to get the wily old goat to let his guard down and not see her as a threat.

"You are the most amazing woman I have ever known," Henry said. "Most of the men here would not have the stones to even *think* about doing what you just did. The husband in me is furious with you, but Jesus, is the pirate in me overruling him right now and bursting with pride."

"I sure as hell would not have," Barnes agreed.

"Nor me," Rogers said.

Catherine laughed through her tears. "I missed you so much. I am going to get you out of here, Henry. I am."

"I believe you. If anyone could do it, it would be you."

"That is enough visiting for now," the guard said.

"There is no time limit on that letter!" Catherine protested.

"I have decided there is. Out."

"Sparrow, it is all right," Henry said, squeezing her hands. "I am fine. Go. You should not be here," he said before he kissed her again. "I love you."

"I love you," she whispered before the guard pulled her up and away, pushing them out in front of him.

Henry rested his forehead against the bars and sighed, closing his eyes. She was here. The last place he'd ever expected her, the last place he'd ever wanted her to be in, the place he'd been so sure would eat her alive, and she was here. She'd walked willingly into hell for him. The wolves had circled, as he'd known they would, but she'd shown them she was to be feared just as much as her husband. The scent of her still lingered on his hands, and his heart ached with wanting her.

"Another letter came," the guard said, and Henry opened his eyes. "Tomorrow is not going to be that easy for you," he continued with a dark grin before Henry heard the sharp snap of a whip.

Chapter 16

Catherine paced the floor of her room, twisting a kerchief in her hands. She'd sent Barnes and Rogers with the crew to make sure the ship was ready, provisioned, and loaded, so they could leave as soon as they'd gotten Henry. She knew she wouldn't be sleeping, not with the way her mind was racing. There were too many thoughts, too many images, and she couldn't be still.

"Everything is ready," Barnes said as he came into the room.

"Thank you," she said without looking at him, her voice distant.

"You are troubled by what you heard tonight."

Catherine stopped pacing and looked at him.

Barnes shook his head with a small sigh. "What did you expect?"

Henry had asked her that once, in a moment which now seemed a lifetime ago. "I do not know."

"You knew he was not innocent. You *had* to know that."

"I did, but —"

"You had never let yourself consider the details. It was easier that way, was it not?"

Catherine closed her eyes, but it didn't stop the tears from escaping.

"I can assure you he never, *ever*, killed women and children. He did not, and for Morgan to say so was a slanderous lie. He knew damned well Henry had never done that. The incident he spoke of was when both Henry and I were only crew, serving under another captain who had no reticence in committing such crimes. The man ordered that massacre, but several of us refused, willing to accept punishment rather than take part in such atrocities. Others carried it out, but we did not. We also did not stop it. We could not. Henry was appalled, we all were, frozen with horror. I will never forget those screams, and I know he will not either. In the end, he did the only thing he could do: He committed mutiny, killed the captain, and took over himself."

"At least there is that," she said.

"Catherine," Barnes said, dropping the formality now as she'd often seen him do with Henry. "Morgan did everything he could to make Henry sound like the worst man to ever sail these seas. He did it on purpose, to sow doubt in you so he could bend you to his own purpose. You saw that clearly enough when he asked you to lay with him to free Henry. You heard what he said, how he called you a little lamb come to sacrifice yourself for Henry's sins. Had you given in, he would not have freed Henry, and you know it. He would have used it to torment him into either leading the raid or to make sure he suffered before he hanged."

"I cannot reconcile the man I know with the man he told me about."

"You had before. You knew enough from those dispatches, and you were able to accept them and the man he was. You will have to do it again, because if you cannot, then you might as well let him hang tomorrow and spare him the grief of losing you and the love he prizes above anything. Without it and without you, he is *nothing*. You saw him tonight, his reaction to seeing you. He has never reacted that way to anyone in his entire life. You are everything to him."

The sound of the door shutting as Barnes left the room,

leaving her alone with his final words, caused her to bury her face in her hands and sob. He was right, of course he was, but it wasn't as easy as he wanted to make it out to be. This had all gone so much deeper than she'd ever imagined, and he hadn't told her the full truth about any of it. It was this that made her angrier than anything else. Had he told her, had she heard it from his own lips, it would be different. She could have been prepared for something like this. To hear it from someone else was crushing.

A knock on the door caused her to look up, and she crossed the room, pulling the door open. "Barnes, if you want to lecture m —" but Catherine stopped short with a small gasp as she found the woman from the street standing there.

"Apologies for coming so late and unannounced."

"No, no … please come in," Catherine said, stepping back to let her in and shutting the door behind her. "What is your name?"

"Evelyn."

"I am —"

"I know who you are," she said, smiling. "As soon as I saw Barnes and Rogers, I knew who you were. You are her, are you not? Lady Catherine?"

"Yes. How did you know of me?"

"Oh, everyone heard," she said with a chuckle. "Captain Merrick leaving the life behind to marry a noblewoman was big news around here. We were sad to lose him down in —" she stopped, looking sheepish. "Sorry, I should not have said that."

Catherine swallowed hard. Before her was a woman she had helped but also a woman who had very likely bedded her husband more than once. "It is all right," she whispered.

Evelyn reached out and took Catherine's hand. "He is a good man, whatever else they may say about him. He was always kind to people when he could be, and we all knew we could go to him for help if he was in town and we were in trouble."

"Go to him for what?"

"Protection. Money. Revenge. If someone was hurting us

or threatening us, all we had to do was tell him and he would make sure it stopped."

"That is not what I heard tonight."

"No, I am sure it was not. He did terrible things at sea, to be sure, but they all did and still do. He was not any worse, and he was certainly better than many."

"I was told he set fire to churches with women and children inside."

Evelyn frowned. "Who in the hell told you that?"

"Morgan."

Rolling her eyes, Evelyn scoffed. "He is the last one you should believe about anything. Captain Merrick did no such thing. Trust me, we would have heard about it. What I heard was that his old captain did it, and Merrick led the crew in a mutiny. Tied the man up in a rowboat, set it on fire, and let it drift so he could suffer the way he made those poor people do."

"He …" Catherine began in a horrified whisper before trailing off.

"Was not as though he did not deserve it, and I am sure he could have come up with worse things to have done. I have certainly heard about worse. There are rumors that Morgan forced nuns and priests to put the ladders to the walls at Porto Bello so that they would be the ones to die first, but I do not know if that is true."

"Good God," Catherine said, sinking down to sit on the end of the bed.

"I know it is hard to understand, being from where you are, but that is the way things are here."

Catherine shook her head. "How did you come to be here?"

"My father wagered me in a card game and lost."

"He what!"

Evelyn offered a small shrug. "He was a drunk. He was also a trader, so we stopped here often. One night I went to sleep and woke up in the morning being told that I belonged to the house now and my father was gone. And he was. Sailed off in the middle of the night and left me here."

"That is … I am so sorry."

"Life is not always pretty."

"Henry told me that once, that I had no idea how ugly it could truly be. He was right."

Squeezing her hand, Evelyn sat down on the bed. "Be thankful you have gone this long."

"I wish I could burn this entire port to the ground," Catherine said, dissolving into angry tears. "I would free everyone here!"

"I am sure some of us would help you, but then what? Where do we go? What do we do that is any different from here?"

"I wish I knew."

"I want to thank you for what you did today. For a moment, just a moment, there was a bright spot. Another Merrick showed up and helped one of us. He would be proud of you if he knew."

"They are hanging him tomorrow, so he may never know."

"Not if you have anything to say about it, I think."

Catherine smiled and then chuckled. "No, not if I have anything to say about it."

"Whatever is between you is something you will need to sort out, but please know that no matter what he did, he was not the worst of them, not even close. You married a man who was good in spite of those things, and we all respected him here. The other captains respected him for his skills as a pirate, but the rest of us respected him for how he treated the least of us. I know he must love you if he walked away from all of this at the height of his renown to be with you."

Catherine nodded. "Thank you for telling me."

"You are welcome," Evelyn said, standing. "Good luck to tomorrow," she said, walking toward the door. "We will all be rooting for you."

"Evelyn, wait."

"Yes?"

"Come with us."

"What?"

"Come with us. Come to New York, start a new life. I will help you. Leave here while you can."

"You … you want me to come to … you really want to help me that way?"

"Yes. I cannot bear to think of you staying here to suffer this fate. It is not fair, and if I can stop it, then I will. I cannot help everyone, but at least I can help you. Please, come."

"What would I do?"

"If you do not mind helping tend house, I am sure there are families around who would hire you, maybe even Barnes' or Rogers' families. If not that, we can find something else; I am sure of it."

Evelyn hesitated for only a moment before she nodded. "I will."

"Good," Catherine said in relief. "Meet us down at the docks after whatever happens at the garrison."

"I will be there," she said before she grinned. "Show them what kind of hell there is to pay when you cross the Captain's wife."

Chapter 17

At the appointed time, Catherine, Barnes, Rogers, and the rest of the ship's crew arrived at the area in the garrison where the gallows sat. Word seemed to have gotten around that Captain Merrick was facing a hanging today because the plaza of the garrison was packed full. As Catherine moved forward through the crowd with Barnes and Rogers, they were forced to stop by an already dense crowd. Catherine caught sight of Evelyn, who gave her a stoic nod. Morgan and Carbery stood on the platform and, at exactly nine, Henry was brought out, but not without assistance. Two soldiers dragged him out, blood covering him from the lashing he'd gotten. He was able to stand, though not well, and a noose was placed around his neck, choking him because of the difficulty of supporting his own weight.

"Henry!" Catherine exclaimed when she saw him before she turned toward Morgan in fury. "You swore I would have a chance to save him!"

"And you shall," Morgan said, flashing a sly smile. "If you can figure out how to free him from where you stand, he is yours. If not, you watch him hang."

A ripple of shock ran through the crowd as Morgan revealed the catch of his offer.

"That is … that is impossible," Rogers said.

"I think that is the point," Barnes replied, both angry and defeated.

Catherine closed her eyes for a moment to try and think about what she could do, though the idea came to her in almost an instant. Opening them, she looked at Morgan. "I will need a rifle."

"What?" he asked her, incredulous.

"I will need a rifle. I have an idea, and if it fails, he will die anyway."

Morgan seemed to consider it a moment before he gestured to one of the soldiers to hand her his rifle. "Would you even be so kind as to load it for her? Remember, my lady, if you attempt to do any of us harm with this little plan of yours, it will do you no good. You will die and so will he, and your efforts would be all in vain."

Catherine knew from that comment that he assumed she'd never handled a rifle, and she planned to use that to her full advantage. When it was handed to her, she made a show of distress, crying and looking at it, hands shaking as she fiddled with the mechanism and seeming to struggle to figure out how she ought to hold it. No one there believed she had any idea what she was doing, and that was the entire point.

"We do not have all day, Lady Catherine," Morgan snapped in impatience.

Catherine looked at him and let all pretense fall away. Gone were the tears and distress, and in its place was a stone-cold adversary with an iron spine. Lifting the rifle, she took careful aim, just as she had done that day target shooting with Henry. Her body was still, as were her hands. If she missed, she would likely shoot Henry and kill him. She took a deep breath, released it, and pulled the trigger. The crack of the rifle was followed by the snap of the rope as the ball cut it, dropping Henry to the gallows platform, where he coughed as his lungs struggled to regain air. There was a loud, collective gasp from the crowd, and they all stared at her as she lowered the rifle, her eyes meeting Morgan's, who now looked absolutely furious.

"Holy Mother of Christ," Barnes whispered.

"How did she …" Rogers said before stopping and shaking his head.

"You were saying, Governor?" Catherine said pointedly. "I will be taking custody of my husband, and I expect a letter detailing the commutation of his sentence *and* his release."

"Give him to her," Morgan growled.

She knew he had no choice; he'd made the deal, and she'd delivered in front of most of the citizenry of Port Royal. If he went against it, they'd have him on the gallows in a second. If he retaliated later, it would be the same. Henry was picked up from the platform as Morgan stormed over to a table and began writing. He signed it, as did Carbery, then sealed it and handed it to her, hands shaking with fury. Henry was passed to Barnes and Rogers.

"A pleasure doing business with you, Governor," Catherine said, smiling before she curtsied and followed Barnes and Rogers, the crowd parting for her as she left a stunned silence in her wake.

As they made their way to the docks with Henry in the back of a wagon, Catherine was beside him, stroking his hair, though he was no longer conscious.

"Let us get back home," Barnes said.

"Not yet," Catherine replied.

"Where are we going now?"

"England. I have a score to settle."

"Why am I not surprised," Barnes muttered.

When they reached the docks, the ship was moored there, allowing them to pull right up to it. Evelyn was waiting for them with salve and bandaging, and both Rogers and Barnes looked at her in surprise.

"Evie, what are you doing here?" Barnes asked with a raised eyebrow.

"Lady Catherine told me to be here," she replied, lifting her chin.

"Wait …"

"I did," Catherine said, stepping down from the wagon. "She is coming with us. Rogers, we are going to need more water, and see if you can get more salve and bandaging."

"Aye, Captain," Rogers said before he hurried off.

"The rest of you, on board now and prepare to sail as soon as he gets back."

"Aye, Captain Merrick," a chorus of voices responded.

They were underway as soon as everyone was aboard, with Henry taken below to the captain's cabin and placed in the bunk. Catherine opened a window to let air in, and Evelyn brought water, rags, and salve. Catherine set about stripping him out of the clothing he had on, and both women cleaned the dirt, sweat, and blood from him. That done, they treated the lash wounds on his back and covered them with bandaging before Evelyn left Catherine alone with him. Catherine broke down in tears, resting her forehead against a part of one of his shoulders that had been spared the lash, releasing all of the tension, fear, and anxiety of the last days. She'd managed to pull him out, though she knew damned well that it was a lucky shot today. A gust of wind, a jostle by someone in the crowd, and it would have all been over. She would have missed, or worse, shot him. Now all she could do was wait.

***

The thing he noticed first was the scent of the sea air and the whisper of it across his skin. Then came the sound of it as it crashed against the hull, followed by the movement telling him he was in a ship at full sail. The pain came next, the skin of his back burning and tight from the lashing and the wounds it had caused. Had Morgan forced him onto a ship headed to Panama anyway? What had happened to his Catherine? Had she been a dream he'd conjured to make his last moments easier? No, she had been real, she had come to Port Royal, and the remembrance made his eyes snap open. Catherine.

To his great surprise, he saw her sitting in a chair, watching the sea from the windows, not realizing he was awake. She looked tired, pale, and in this moment where she thought she was alone, she looked conflicted and sad.

"Sparrow," he whispered.

She blinked and looked at him, offering a weak smile. "You are awake."

"Clearly thanks to you," he said before he frowned. "What troubles you?"

"Now is not the time for discussing it."

"Why not?"

"Your focus needs to be on getting well before we arrive in London."

"London? Why are we going there?"

"Because we are," she said coolly before she got up and filled a cup of water, bringing it to him.

"Catherine, please talk to me."

"Save your strength and your breath, Henry. I have no desire to talk to you beyond this right now."

He closed his eyes, her words cutting deeply. Something had happened, and the thing he'd feared had come true. There was no love in her eyes or her words for him. He'd lost her somehow.

Though she stayed by his side to tend him over the next two weeks, any conversation was short and to the point. The pain it caused him was unlike anything he'd ever known, and he prayed to be released from it. Though she was here, that was all she was, and he would rather be gone than live with this.

When he was finally well enough to sit up, she'd helped him to shave, and as she rose to take the bowl away, he grabbed her hand to stop her.

"Catherine …"

The look she turned on him was withering.

"Talk to me, please, I am begging you. I cannot do this. I cannot live with you looking at me so coldly. What have I done?"

"You *lied* to me."

"What? I have never lied to you!"

"Yes, you did. You lied to me about who you really were."

"I did no such thing! There were things I did not tell you because you did not need to know, because they served no purpose, but I never lied. Not once."

"Yes, you did!" she shouted, yanking her hand from his and throwing the bowl across the room where it collided with the wall, sending water everywhere. "You made me believe you were something you were not! You told me you had done it all in the king's service, that it was just a bunch of men shooting at each other and stealing. That was a *lie*!"

The sudden burst of fury and emotion surprised him. "I did do it in his service! We harassed the French and the Spanish at his command!"

"Did he tell you to murder them, too? Did he tell you to ignore the pleas for mercy from defeated men?"

"If I had not, I would be the dead one! How do you not understand that? This was not a game, Catherine, with little ships you move around a board! This was reality with real stakes and real men, real blood and real death! Who told you this? Who has turned you against me?"

"What does it matter who?" she hissed. "You brought me to your bed with lies, and you made a life for us with blood money."

"That is not true. Answer me, Catherine! Who did this!"

"What did you really want from me? To give you an air of legitimacy for a new life? To lend you prestige and status? You have made me the whore he said I was, and you have done it for your own benefit! Did you even love me?"

Henry stared at her, aghast. "Catherine!"

"I wish you had never come for me. You should have stayed in Jamaica, as it is where you so clearly belong."

"Then why did you not leave me there! Why did you come for me, hm? You should have just let me hang there, or is this to be my punishment? A life with a wife who hates me."

"I came before I knew the truth, and maybe I should have left you there, but I had come too far to stop. Maybe I should tell Barnes to turn around, and we can drop you off there so that you can drink and whore yourself to an early grave!"

"Stop it."

"No! You are a liar and a murderer, and I wish I had never met you, much less let myself love you! I hate you! You have used me to absolve your sins, and I hope you are happy!"

Henry jumped from the bed and grabbed her, shoving her against the wall, the collision bringing a small sound from her before he pinned her there with his body. "You hate me? Is that so? Do not *dare* act as though you did not have a good idea of what I had done. You knew. You knew, and you were willing to ignore it as long as you were never confronted with it, is that it? Happy to play the pirate's wife until you saw what that truly meant, and *now* you hate me?"

"Let go of me," Catherine growled.

"Oh no, it is too late now. You have said your piece, and now I will say mine. I did nothing but love you, truly and completely. I left my life behind in order to make a proper life with you. I gave you everything you wanted. I gave you the love you had never understood, gave you the nerve to break from the life you hated. I came for you when you called for me, and the bed you went to is one you went to willingly. You knew where that money came from, you knew what I had done to get it, and you have the gall to accuse me of using you for prestige and legitimacy? What legitimacy, Catherine? What prestige? You had *nothing*! You had stolen from your family and fled England, and if you think that does not make you a criminal just like me, you are wrong."

Catherine struggled against him, and he stilled her with a hand against her throat.

"There was nothing you could give me that I did not already have without you. *Nothing*. All you had was the one thing I wanted the most, the one thing no money could buy, and that was your love. There is nothing you could do to absolve me of my sins, and they are many. I will admit them freely. Will you? Tell me who has done this. Tell me who has taken you from me. At least give me that. Better yet, admit to me what you did. What did you do to earn my freedom, hm?"

Henry felt the sharp point of a knife at his throat. "Get away from me," Catherine hissed. "How *dare* you. How dare you accuse me of such a thing."

"Do it. Go ahead. I will even help you. I want you to do it rather than let me suffer this. Kill me. Do it, Catherine!" he shouted at her.

He felt her put a little more pressure on the knife, but that was all, and it told him all he needed to know. He ripped the knife from her hand before turning it on her, placing it at her throat the same way she had done at his.

"Shall I really let your blood absolve me? Is that what you want? It would damn me, but it is not as though I am not damned already. I could do it so easily, and it would only hurt for a moment. I would follow you; you would not lack my companionship in hell."

Catherine was breathing heavily, but there were tears on her cheeks.

"Is this what you expect of me? Is this who you believe I really am? Is this who someone has convinced you that you were married to? Tell me, Catherine. It is not, is it? You know better. But I will be this man for you if that is what you want. I will let him be the last thing you see instead of the man who loves you more than his own life. Just say the word."

A soft sob from her was the only response.

"Everything I have done since I met you, I have done for you. Every secret I kept, I kept to protect you. I wanted nothing more than to keep my past where it belonged, and

I would die before I would let myself be what I once was because of what I knew *you* would think of me. I was willing to hang in Jamaica rather than comply, so you would know I went to my death with honor instead of as a renewed criminal. Your opinion was the *only* thing that mattered to me. Do you not see that? Someone has stolen that from me, and I demand to know who!"

Henry removed the knife from her throat and plunged it into the door next to her, which garnered a tiny scream and a fresh sob from her.

"I would never hurt you, and despite your protests I know you love me still because if you did not, you would have taken your chance to kill me. Admit it. God damn it, Catherine, admit it! Admit that you still love me as I love you!" he said, the last words hoarse with his own emotion.

Releasing her, he stumbled back, burying his face in his hands and sinking to his knees. "Please, Catherine," he sobbed.

In the next moment, he felt her throw her arms around him, and he lost all composure, holding her against him as they both cried. She was angry, but she still loved him. She'd needed someone to be angry with, someone to blame for the hurt and the pain this had all brought on, and he was the only obvious choice. Someone had twisted his beautiful wife, turning her against him with words and doubts, and she'd pulled away from him because of it.

"I am sorry," he sobbed. "I am sorry for everything I have ever done. Tell me what you want from me, and I will do it. Anything you want. Tell me what to do to bring you back to me because I cannot have it otherwise!"

"Shhh," she whispered, kissing him through her own tears. "Henry, please … I am so sorry …"

"I want you back. I need you here with me!"

He hated what he'd just done, what they'd done to each other. He'd been careful, so careful even then, not to press too hard with his hands or blade. He didn't want to hurt her;

he'd never want to hurt her. Catherine silenced him with a kiss that took his breath away in its intensity, and he stopped thinking, pressing her back onto the floor and finding no resistance. He wore nothing, she still wore little due to the heat, and Henry shoved the chemise and petticoat out of his way. There was a need in each to possess the other, and there was no room for gentleness in it. When it was over, he gathered her from the floor and brought her to the bed, where he sat with her straddling him.

"Tell me," he murmured against her ear. "Tell me you love me still."

"I do love you," she whispered.

Henry felt as though he could weep with relief, but he didn't. Instead, he very gently pulled her head back by her hair and heard her gasp when she felt a blade at her throat. Henry turned it and slid the flat down her neck, following it with kisses, hearing her sigh and let go of a small moan as he felt her fingertips dig into his arms. The reaction set him on fire.

"I forgot my little Sparrow likes to live dangerously, and I think I now feel quite inclined to indulge her," he whispered.

Chapter 18

Henry stepped out onto the deck later in breeches and nothing else, closing his eyes as the cool wind swept over his bare skin, cooling him off from the heat below. He'd left Catherine asleep, a rest she probably desperately needed, and he wondered how much she'd slept since leaving New York. That sort of exhaustion would certainly not have helped matters, nor set her at ease or let her think her way through all of it. The memory of her words still tore at him, angered him, though not at her. Though she'd spoken them, those words belonged to someone else, someone who had given her cause to feel them and let them fester in her heart, to eat at her until she could no longer stand it and threw them back at him like so many daggers.

"Good to see you up and moving, Captain."

Henry opened his eyes to look at Barnes and gave him a small smile. "Good to be up and able to move."

"It seemed a bit close for a while, but my lady brought you around."

"Yes, she did," he replied in a soft voice.

"What is it?"

Henry moved over to the rail and looked out. "There will be much to repair."

"In what way?"

"She told me she hated me. Asked if I had ever loved her. Accused me of using her to lend legitimacy to a new life and absolve myself."

Barnes sighed. "She does not mean that."

"Part of her did. Part of her felt compelled to call me a murderer and a liar, to tell me she wished she had never met me or let herself love me. She meant it enough to pull a knife on me."

"Henry —"

"I hate what I did to her, Barnes. Hate myself for pinning her against the wall, for having my hand on her throat, for saying the things I did. For telling her I wanted her to kill me and then turning that same blade on her when she would not. For threatening to be what she thought of me and having it be the last thing she saw."

Barnes frowned. "Why? Why would you do that?"

"Because I was angry, because I wanted to hurt her as she was hurting me. I wanted to show her I was none of those things and she knew it, to show her what that person would really be like. I wanted to break her anger and make her see."

"Did she?"

"Yes, but that does not mean I like how we got there."

"The point is that you got there in the way you had to."

"She would not tell me who did this, who put these things in her head."

"I think you know perfectly well."

Henry's hands tightened on the rail, and he closed his eyes. "What did he say to her?"

"Do you want the truth?"

"Yes. Do not leave anything out. I need to know what he said."

Barnes walked to the rail and leaned back against it, looking at Henry. "Most of what he told her was the truth, Henry. All the truth you tried so hard to hide from her. You killed without remorse, you killed men who pleaded for mercy, you loved the life and were good at it, and many a skeleton at the bottom of the sea was there by your doing. That you came back to Port Royal flush with money and covered in blood to drink and whore it all away. None of that is untrue."

"No, it is not."

"It was after all that was said that he turned to lies and cruelty, striking at you where it would hurt the most. He told her *you* fired those churches, that the order was yours."

Henry looked up, his face pale. "That is a lie! I never —"

"And I told her as much later."

"But she believed it. For a moment he made her believe it."

"You cannot blame her for that. She knew nothing, so what did you expect? He made her doubt you, doubt us, questioning whom she would believe: him or the men who had lied for you in the past."

"Damn him," Henry whispered.

"It got worse."

"How?"

"He asked her if, after all of that, she still wanted you freed. Still wanted you to come home to her to share the bed you brought her to with lies, bought with money earned from the blood of others."

"Those words … she said those words to me …"

"And he put them on her lips for you."

Henry shook his head. It was as he'd thought. The words weren't her own.

"At the end, he told her if she wanted you, he knew a way for her to earn it. He bid her come to him, and when she did, he said something that chilled me to the core. 'Come here, little lamb, and sacrifice yourself for his sins.' He asked her if she wanted you badly enough to ransom herself to him for a night, her body for your freedom, and questioned her as to whether she thought you would forgive her."

"He did what …"

"You cannot be surprised he would try. If she were desperate enough, she would do anything. On top of that, she is beautiful, the perfect prize; that she is yours made her even more so. She let him believe it, that she was indeed that desperate, and that was his mistake. But, Henry, think about what he said: a sacrifice for your sins. He would have killed her after he had taken what he wanted, he would have killed her and shown her to you as proof you had nothing left, that even the woman you loved would betray you, and her death would be on your hands."

"It is worse than that. He would have used it to show me that I had no reason left to protest his plans. I told him I would not do it because of her, and he said it did not matter because when she was dead and gone, only history would remain, and I would be a legend. She would be dead at his hands, and now there would be no worry for what she might think of me."

"It was all of it; I am certain. He wanted to break you, and he felt no remorse in using her to do it. She, however, had other ideas."

"She is clever."

"She is you."

"What?"

"Even he said so, that you had chosen a far more appropriate bride than perhaps even *you* realized. Henry, that woman is so much like you it is honestly frightening. She is the reason we are here. She walked into that hellhole without fear and walked out with you. Do you have any idea what she did for you?"

"I do now."

"But the end, Henry. It was not over after that meeting. He told her he would give her a chance to save you, and when she got there, he told her that if she could free you from where she stood, you were all hers. He thought he had given her an impossible task, and his face when she proved him wrong was glorious."

Henry looked at him with curiosity. He remembered nothing of that day. "How did she do it?"

"Called for a rifle. Made a big show of crying and fiddling with it. She had all of us believing she had no idea which end fired the shot. He told her he did not have all day, and she

186

dropped the act, squared up, took aim, and shot the rope. If she missed, she would either shoot you or not completely sever the rope, losing you in both cases. Instead, it snapped, you hit the floor, and she looked at him as though he were an idiot for challenging her. 'You were saying, Governor?' I would have laughed if I was not both shocked and terrified by what I had just witnessed."

He dropped his head and smiled, shaking it a bit. "I know that look well. She gave it to me once when I made the same mistake."

"All I am saying is that it took balls none of us have to take that shot and she did it without a tremor. She made Henry Morgan eat his own words in front of a garrison packed full of Port Royal's finest criminal element and demanded a written release and commutation of your sentence."

Henry started to laugh, softly at first, then louder. "Ah, God help me, but I love her for all of it."

"You should. I do," Barnes said, laughing. "Fairly certain some of the crew are going to be dreaming of that at night, if you know what I mean."

"Cannot blame them," Henry said. "If I ever see Morgan again, I am going to kill him slowly and painfully, and I am going to enjoy it."

"Pretty sure you will not be hearing from him again."

"What a shame. Any idea why we are on our way to London?"

"Lady Catherine has a score to settle, she says."

The smile that crossed Henry's lips was dark and cold. "God help them then."

"Well, if it is not Henry Merrick. I have not seen you this undressed in quite some time."

Henry raised an eyebrow and turned his head toward the new voice. "Evie?"

"The one and only," Evelyn said, grinning.

"What are you doing here?"

"I had the same question," Barnes said.

"Lady Catherine told me to come."

Henry stood up straight. "She … Evie, how do you know my wife in any sort of way that she would even be able to say such a thing?"

"Why do you say it as though I am somehow sullying her by even saying her name?"

Henry sighed. "That is not what I meant. I apologize. What I mean is how did you have an opportunity to even speak to her with everything going on?"

Evelyn fidgeted for a moment. "It was in the street. She must have been on her way to the inn higher up, but she saw me with a customer. We locked eyes, and it just … it was like she could see right through me and understood what I felt. She had Barnes stop, and she came back to me."

"That was you?" Barnes asked, incredulous.

"Yes. My customer thought she was coming to join us or something, but she set him right in an instant. Told him to move because he had been outbid. When he asked her what that meant, she said she was paying me now and it was more than he was going to pay so he needed to move on. He did not take at all kindly to that, and when he raised his voice, she put a pistol in his face and asked if he was sure he wanted to continue speaking because it would be in his best interest to do what she said. Then he left."

"Jesus, Catherine," Henry said, running his hands through his hair in disbelief.

"I know," Evelyn said, chuckling. "But then she did something that told me in an instant who she was even without having seen Barnes or Rogers."

"Which was?"

"She pulled a piece of eight out, a whole one, and put it in my hand. 'This is enough to at least give you an entire night's peace and freedom,' she said. She clearly had no idea how much money she had given me, but that did not matter. It was just like you used to do. She said someone set her free once, and she was going to do the same for someone else even if only for a little while. I knew it was her, the woman we had all heard about after you left, because *you* were there and only a Merrick would do something like that. So, she must have come for you."

"You see?" Barnes said. "I told you. Just like you."

Henry shot him a wry smile.

"As if just like him is a bad thing?" Evie shot back.

"Fair," Barnes conceded.

"I think it depends on what part of her is like me, but go on," Henry said with a chuckle.

"I saw her get back in the cart, saw Barnes and Rogers, and that confirmed it. I went to the inn to thank her, and we talked for a while. I told her what you used to do for us, that you were a good man no matter what the job required of you."

"Thank you, Evie," Henry said in genuine appreciation.

"That bastard Morgan told her you set those churches on fire! Well, I fixed that."

"What do you mean?" Henry asked, even as Barnes raised an eyebrow beside him.

"Told her the truth," she said with a shrug. "That you killed the old captain for doing it by tying him up in a boat and setting it on fire."

"How in the hell did you know that?"

"*Everyone* knows that, Henry," she said matter-of-factly.

"Right."

"Anyway, I was getting ready to leave when she stopped me and asked me to come with you back to New York, that she would help me start a new life. I agreed because I knew she would keep her word, just like you would."

"I would," Henry said, smiling. "And we will."

"You are lucky to have her."

"You are right; I am."

"I feel honored by her help and honored by her wanting to be my friend in spite of who I am. Most fine ladies would not even notice I was alive, much less acknowledge me."

"That has never been her way. She sees people, not rank."

"Even people who accidentally admit they have bedded her husband."

"Christ! Evie!" Henry said, aghast.

The way he said it made Evelyn laugh. "She took it pretty well, honestly, and I was not lying when I said we missed you down at the docks. Rather hard not to."

Barnes started laughing, and Henry joined him after a moment. "Thank you, I think."

"You were one of my favorites, you know that!"

"I cannot believe we are even having this conversation, much less that you had it with my wife and somehow we are all still living."

Evelyn shrugged. "Not like I am trying for it now."

"Very wise," Henry said, chuckling.

"She did say she wanted to burn the whole of Port Royal to the ground, though."

The laughter of both Henry and Barnes ceased immediately. "She what?"

"Can you blame her?"

"No, but —"

"She wanted to burn it down and set everyone free, whatever that might mean. I have a feeling she even had a plan, but I did not ask. Pity she could not, now that I think about it."

Henry leaned back against the rail and rubbed his face. "Jesus, my wife really *is* a pirate. How in the hell did I manage to find the one woman who would qualify amongst the nobility in England?"

"Luck?" Evie offered.

"Cannot disagree there," Barnes said with a shrug. "She can shoot, she can throw knives, she commanded a ship and a crew, she outsmarted another pirate, and she raided a city to take what she wanted and then felt like burning it down on her way out. Sounds about right when you sail with a Merrick."

Henry started laughing hard. "I suppose that is true. Then you add in the part where she has no problem threatening other people with knives and pistols when they get in her way, and you really do have a version of me in female form."

The other two laughed with him. "God help the world that there are two of you, that you managed to find each other, and that you are now sailing together," Barnes said through laughter. "We could be even richer with the both of you working together. You sure you want to give up now? Maybe you can run a few raids with her first."

"Stop," Henry said, laughing so hard he was crying. "Yes, I do want to retire. The world is not ready for dual Merrick piracy."

"That is for damned sure," Evelyn said.

"Just think of how furious her father would be, Henry," Barnes said, wiping tears from his eyes.

"Oh, well, that makes it tempting."

"I have a feeling you are going to get your chance soon enough."

"I am looking forward to it, believe me."

"So am I."

"I am glad you came, Evie," Henry said, hugging her. "If anyone deserved to get out, it was you."

"Thank you, Henry, for everything you did for me and for the rest of us when you were still there."

"I had to do something to redeem myself, hm?" he asked.

"If that is what you want to call it, yes."

Henry laughed and stepped away from her. "I am going to do a round of the ship."

"Aye, Captain," Barnes said.

Henry walked at a slow pace around the deck, talking with the crew, checking the provisions and the ship to see if anything needed attention. It served a dual purpose of giving him something to do in order to get his mind right and process all that he'd heard from Barnes and from Evelyn, as well as made him feel useful. He wasn't accustomed to not being in charge on his own ship, and he found he couldn't let go of that sense of responsibility.

Once he was satisfied, he returned to his cabin, and upon opening the door, he found Catherine awake, sitting up in the bunk with her back to the wall. She hadn't dressed, and the sheet covered only part of her legs. She was beautiful, reminiscent of the sirens so often seen as figureheads on ships, and it drew him to her, where he took a seat in front of her at her feet.

"I want to apologize," he said. "For what happened in here. I never meant to ..." he said but then stopped. He didn't know what to say.

"I forgive you," she replied, her voice quiet. "I understand, and you did not hurt me."

"I am glad. I was worried I might have."

She gave a gentle shake of her head and looked down at her hands. "I am the one who should be apologizing for the horrible things I said. You were only responding to that."

Henry reached out and ran a fingertip down her leg. "I understand why you said them now. I know what happened."

Catherine closed her eyes, her lower lip trembling. "The things he said —"

"Were not untrue, but you knew that. You wanted to believe otherwise, and I let you because I did not think it would do any harm. I was wrong even though I never could have imagined this. I need you to understand that I was not the only one, that this is the way it was for everyone and the same way it would have been had I ever been captured. There were far worse than me, and Morgan was one of them. Well, L'Olonnais is far worse than either of us, but I digress."

"I think I have heard of him."

"I could tell you stories, but not right now. Sparrow, I never ordered the firing of those churches. You *must* believe me. I would never do that. I have done a lot of things but never that. In fact, I quite happily killed the man who did."

"I know," she replied. "Did you really set him on fire in a boat?"

"I did, yes. Wrapped him in burlap, spread pine pitch around the inside for fuel, lowered it into the ocean, and tossed a torch in so he could feel what it was like to be trapped in flames. He deserved no less."

Catherine grimaced. "It seems a horrible way to die."

"It sounded like it was, certainly." Henry moved closer to her and draped her legs over his. "That I was good at what I did, that I loved it, that is all true. I will not deny it; I will not deny anything to you anymore. You deserve to know the truth and I will give you all of it."

"You returned to port to —"

"Yes," he said before she had to say it. "Yes, I did. We all did. It was the way you could forget what you had done for at least a little while. If you were lucky, you were able to forget even that part." He looked down for a long moment. "I cannot say I am ashamed of that either."

"Did you love any of them?"

"No. Aside from the few of them I had dealings with outside of that, most of the time I did not even know their names."

"I am not sure that makes you any worse than the men of court."

"It does not. Trust me, I know; I was there."

Catherine frowned, and he sighed.

"What I did there I did to try and forget about you, to try and drown how much I wanted you, but all it did was make me want you more because none of it could do what I wanted it to. For the first time, I felt guilty and ashamed of it because I felt it made me unworthy of you. I had never felt that before."

"I can forgive that."

"But not the rest."

"The rest, too. My not knowing did not make it less true, and you are right, I did know deep down."

"Believe me when I tell you that I have never lied and

193

never would. I love you, and I have loved you. I never would have given up my life there if I did not. I did not use you, and you know that, too. You were angry, you wanted to hurt me, but you know that is not true."

"Yes," she whispered.

"Sparrow, there is no money in the world that is clean. All of it is covered in the blood of others, from the blood of the slaves who dug the ore to the blood of the men who died to transport it, to the coins that change hands every single day to pay for the toil of others. Even the dowries paid to trade women like slaves to the highest bidder. It is all dirty, every piece. Ours is no worse, and we are using it to do some good."

"You're right. I hadn't thought of it that way."

"You hadn't needed to," he said as he reached out and stroked her cheek. "I heard what you did for Evie."

Catherine looked up at him. "I forgot to tell you she was here."

"You did, but she found me, and I am fine with it. What made you stop?"

"She looked at me and I just … I saw myself. The hollow smile, the eyes devoid of any feeling. I knew how it felt to be stuck, and I wanted to help her the way you helped me."

"By putting a pistol in someone's face?"

"Well, no, but he did not leave me much choice. I have had quite enough of men yelling in my face, so getting to do that was a bonus."

"A bonus! Good lord, Catherine, I really have rubbed off on you."

Catherine chuckled. "I rather liked the power it gave me."

"Trust me, I understand."

"You would."

"I heard you also wanted to burn down the whole of Port Royal."

"I still do. It is a horrific place."

"You do realize that, as Barnes said, that makes you sound just like me?"

"I take that as a compliment," Catherine said, raising her chin in slight defiance.

"My little pirate," he said, chuckling.

"And I once wondered if I could do it."

"Clearly you can and quite well at that. Barnes asked if I was sure I wanted to retire before you and I were able to run some raids together."

"If I said yes, would you want to?"

Henry looked at her, taken a bit aback by the question. "I … maybe? It is so dangerous, and I would never forgive myself if something happened to you. There is no amount of glory or money worth it for me to risk your life in such a way. On the other hand, I am curious as to just how well we could do."

"I am not sure I could really go that far. I am too soft-hearted for that; I would be trying to stop you from hurting anyone."

"Yes, you would, and that is what makes you a far better person than I am. However, I am perfectly content to have a pirate captain for my wife and consider myself fortunate to have located one amongst the nobility."

"Or at least one who is honest about it?"

"More like one who is my type of pirate and not the court games and intrigue kind of pirate."

"I happen to be both."

"Indeed, you are. I want you to know that if you had done what he asked of you, if you had felt it was the only way, I would have forgiven you," he said. "God knows I would have felt unworthy of such a price."

Catherine looked up at him with tears in her eyes. "If it was the only way, then I would have."

"I know, but you showed him you are a Merrick, and not only a Merrick, but also my wife. You were not going to accept that, and you made that clear. It is a good thing, too."

"Why?"

"Barnes and I both agreed that if you had, he would have killed you afterward and used it to punish me."

Catherine went pale and looked sick.

"Shh, now, it did not happen because you were too clever for that. I am impressed. You will have to show me how you held him because I am rather curious what that looked like."

"I will," she said with a small smile.

"And I heard about the gallows. Well done. Though when Barnes told me the look you gave Morgan afterward," Henry said with a laugh, "I remember it well."

"You should; I gave it to you the last time you underestimated me."

"The *only* time. I will not make that mistake twice. And now we are to England with a score to settle."

"We are."

Henry nodded and then looked out the window for a long moment. "Tell me true: Are you mine once more, or has he put a rift between us that will never heal?"

"I always was. I would have gotten over it eventually."

His chest relaxed at her words. "Eventually."

"Though I must admit I enjoyed what came afterward."

He looked back at her and grinned a little. "I could tell. I will have to do that again."

"Please."

He kissed his way up her leg before moving to sit beside her, and she snuggled into his side. "There is one more thing I need to tell you," he said, "in keeping my word to withhold nothing."

She sat up and looked at him. "What is it?"

They were words Henry had never wanted to say, but he had to now. She deserved that from him. "There is something I have kept from you about what happened with your father, something I had sworn everyone who knew to secrecy about."

"Henry … what is it …"

Henry closed his eyes. He could still see it, all of the blood, still smell the metallic tang of it. "You," he began but stopped, swallowing hard. "There was a baby, Catherine."

"A wh —" she began before she realized what he was say-

196

ing. He watched it sink in, wash over her like some horrible wave. "I was …"

"Yes, my love. I am sorry."

"No. No, no, no, no!" she cried out, getting up and making it halfway across the cabin before she stopped, covering her eyes, a soft wail leaving her lips and shattering his heart.

He got up and went to her, wrapping her in his arms as she screamed with the anguish she felt and had every right to. "I know," he whispered. "I know."

"Why!"

"My best guess is the shock of the beating and the stabbing caused you to lose it. It … it was not very far along, probably why you did not know but —"

"Henry, no! This is not true; you are trying to hurt me!"

"Sparrow, no. I am not, I swear it to you. Ask Barnes or Rogers. They know. I would *never* use something like this to wound you."

"No!" she sobbed turning away from him and resting her hands on the table.

"I did not want to tell you because you had suffered so much already. Why add to it with something you could not change?"

"Stop!" she cried out. "Please!"

Henry retreated, sitting down on the bunk and resting his head in his hands. He didn't know how to fix this, how to take it away from her. Perhaps he shouldn't have told her. It had never settled with him, the loss of a child he hadn't known about. It would have been a child he wanted, a child he would have loved, and it had been taken from both of them. God only knew if the chance would come again.

"He is going to pay for this," he heard her sob out, and he looked up.

"Who?"

"My father. He is going to pay for this and for everything he has done to us. It is just one more thing he has taken from me, just as he tried to take you."

Revenge. She wanted it, and he knew she would have it. It

was in her voice, that determination, a thing he knew well because it was the same as his own. Barnes was right. She *was* like him. Henry rose and went to her, placing a hand on her back.

"You have my support in it, you know you do, but until then, tell me what I can do. Tell me what I can do for you, to ease your heart."

Catherine turned to him and put her arms around him, crying into his shoulder. "There is nothing," she whispered. "Just be here."

"As long as you need me. Come lie down. I will stay with you."

Henry guided her back to the bunk and sat with his back against the wall, allowing her to rest her head in his lap. He stroked her hair with slow, deliberate movements and listened to the sea before he sang her a lullaby in Welsh, the first time he'd spoken it in he couldn't remember how long. He should remember. Someday he could teach their child, if they had one, a reminder of where he'd come from. He wondered if his parents were still alive or any of his siblings. He'd never gone back, never written. They probably thought he was dead. It had been cruel of him to do that to them, he realized that, but he wasn't sure there was a way to change it. Catherine cried herself to sleep, but he remained, and when she woke, he was there to greet her. She smiled, though she kept her head where it was.

"So, what did you think of Port Royal?" he asked. Anything to change the subject.

"It was wretched, and I do not know why anyone would willingly live there."

Henry laughed. "You are not wrong. Summer is brutal, and you seem to have escaped without meeting the mosquitoes."

"It sounds like something I am glad of."

"Oh, believe me, it is."

"It was not like what you said. There were no flowers on the wind, I saw no brightly colored fish, but the water was clear."

"You would have to go to another part of the island,

less populated, to experience that. Had I been able to do so, I would have taken you. You could have bathed in the sea like a mermaid."

"Without fins."

"Details."

She laughed. "What I saw was dirty and sad. Everything had a price; remember how you told me that once?"

"I do."

"Everyone tried to act happy, but it was not in their eyes. They were all unhappy, hollow. I thought it would be a place where people were free to be who they were, but it was just like everywhere else. People pretending, playing games."

"It was why you were so well-prepared for them. You saw it clearly because you had lived it already. The machinations, the intrigue, the infighting. The lust for power, the greed. You had trained in that world since your first steps; there was no way Morgan would be any match for you there."

"I saw his slaves. I wanted to set them free so badly."

Henry sighed. "I understand that all too well. I also understand being in the position where you are helpless to do anything at all, no matter what you want, but at least you saved one person."

"So, you have told me all now?"

"All, and if I forgot anything I will answer you honestly, if you think to ask it of me."

"Would you like me to show you what I did to him? To Morgan, I mean."

"Very much so."

Catherine sat up and left the bunk, picking up two knives from the table. "Sit in the chair."

Henry did so dutifully.

"Pretend I'm in a dress; that will help."

"All right," he said with a soft chuckle.

"I came near to him, here," she said, stopping. "He ran a fingertip down the back of my arm and asked me if I would be willing to trade myself for you." Catherine then moved her left hand, bringing a knife to his throat. "Then he grabbed my wrist and pulled it away."

Henry did so, and as he did, he immediately felt another knife at his throat on the right. Before he could think, her knee pressed down on his hand, pinning it to the chair arm, and he hissed in pain. If he let go of her left hand, she was free to stab him with either the left or right hand and would do so before he could make another move. It was an absolutely brilliant move, and he looked up at her with a smile.

"How did you think of such a thing?"

"I cannot say, really; I just did. It worked."

"More than, I would say," Henry replied as she stepped back away from him and put the knives down on the table. "Come here to me, Captain," he said.

"I am not the captain; you are."

"Not this time. You commanded this voyage, so that is you."

"I give it up to you then."

"That is fine, but before you do, I think you should give me some orders."

She raised an eyebrow. "Oh?"

"Yes. I have broken rules and thus should be punished."

Catherine looked at him and then started laughing hysterically, drawing the same from him. Reaching out, he grabbed her and pulled her into his lap, wrapping his arms around her as they laughed together. All was right in his world once more, and he was grateful.

Chapter 19

The thick fog seemed to swallow everything around it, from sound to light, to the very people themselves. Figures appeared and disappeared like phantoms in between the pools of light created by lamps, torches, and fires. As Catherine set foot on the bustling docks, she looked around her, face hidden beneath the hood of her cloak, just as it had been the night she'd left this same place over a year ago. It felt like another lifetime, another life, another person. The Catherine who was returning was nothing like the one who had left, and as far as she was concerned, that was a very good thing.

Henry joined her, taking her hand and kissing it. They'd docked earlier in the evening but had decided to wait aboard until nightfall. Barnes and Rogers had been set to the task of procuring rooms at an inn for the crew, where they were to remain with strict instructions from Henry to be on their best behavior and bring no notice or suspicion upon themselves. Anyone doing so would be disavowed and left behind. Catherine and Henry, along with Barnes, Rogers, and Evelyn, navigated through the mass of cargo, ships, and humanity to hire a carriage that would take them into London proper. The ride was silent, with Catherine lost in her own thoughts and Henry wary of danger.

When the carriage came to a stop, Barnes was out first,

followed by Henry and Catherine, while Rogers and Evelyn remained inside. Catherine nodded to Barnes, who knocked on the door as Catherine stood with Henry out of sight of whoever might answer. The sound of the bolt sliding back made Catherine's heart clench, but the sound of the familiar voice answering it almost made her weep.

"May I help you?" Burke asked, and Catherine didn't need to see her face to know what the expression on it was as she sized up Barnes.

"Yes, is Lord Merrick at home?" Barnes asked.

"He is at court with the king; you can seek him there."

"Will he be coming back here tonight?"

"No, so waiting will do you no good. Lord Merrick always remains in his rooms at court unless his family is in town, and they are not here."

"I was hoping you would say that."

"Whatever does that mean?"

Catherine stepped into view, pushing her hood back. "It means I can come home."

Burke gasped. "Sweet Jesus! Lady Catherine, is that … but how? Your father said —"

"He was wrong. May I come in? I will tell you all."

"Of course! This is still your home!" she declared, stepping back to let Catherine inside, but when Henry followed her, Burke's eyes went wide. "Captain?"

"The one and only. Hello again, Burke," Henry said.

"What in the world!"

When Burke shut the door, Catherine pushed propriety aside to hug the other woman, someone she'd known most of her life. Burke returned the affection before she began crying.

"Your father told us you were dead! Murdered by the Captain!" she exclaimed as she pulled back to look at Catherine.

"That is a scurrilous lie," Henry said. "As you can plainly see."

"Burke, my father is the one who tried to kill me, not Henry," Catherine said.

"What!"

"He clearly thinks I am dead, but as in many things, he was wrong. Though it was not through lack of effort on his part, beating me and then stabbing me."

"Catherine!" Burke cried out, dropping the formality and taking hold of her shoulders. "Your father can be terrible, but that is quite an accusation."

"It is the truth," Catherine said, looking her in the eyes. "I am here to set things right with the king, but I need my father to not know I am here."

"Which is why this man asked if your father was coming back."

"Exactly why. We need a place to stay, and I was sure I could trust you and the others to keep silent once you knew the truth of the matter."

"You know you can. We were always far more partial to you than to anyone else. Just the three of you?"

"No, two others are waiting outside."

"Bring them in, you daft child!"

Henry couldn't help his laugh. "Ah, that sounds like the Burke I remember."

"Oh, no. Do not try to be charming with me, Captain. You are the reason this all happened in the first place!"

"Burke," Catherine chided. "He is not. He may be the one who gave me the courage to leave, but he was not the cause. You know perfectly well what the truth about the duke was."

"Yes, that is true. I was terrified for you when we found out."

"Barnes, would you have the others come in?"

"Aye, Lady Catherine. I will have the trunks brought in as well."

"Thank you. Burke, I need to speak to you and the rest right away. Please gather them in the small parlor, would you?"

"Right away, my lady," Burke said, hurrying off.

"Home again, hm?" Henry said as Catherine let out a sigh of relief.

"Yes, but this time I am in control."

"Ooo, I do like the way you said that."

Catherine jabbed him with an elbow, the action combined with the wry smile on her lips making him laugh. "Hush. Come on."

Once Burke assembled the household and Catherine revealed herself, there were more tearful greetings before she explained what she needed from them. There was to be no hint that she was here, not a word spoken to anyone lest it put them all in grave danger. It was instantly agreed to, all of them happy to help her seek redress with the king after what her father had done.

"Hart, would you be so kind as to have water prepared for baths?"

"Of course, my lady."

"Mrs. James, would you be able to prepare a small meal for all of us?"

"Right away, my lady."

"Pogue, could you once again see to the Captain? And if it is not too much trouble for you, to Barnes and Rogers as well?"

Barnes and Rogers looked at each other, confused as to what was supposed to be seen to.

"Yes, my lady, I would be happy to."

"Good lad, Pogue," Henry said. "Good to see you again."

Pogue smiled. "If I am honest, it is good to see you, too, sir."

"Burke, I have a special task for you. Would you be so good as to train Evelyn how to perform your tasks? I will be needing her to do so when we return to New York."

Evelyn smiled, and Burke nodded. "Indeed, I can and would be happy to."

"Thank you. And could you see to it that the tailor and dressmaker come first thing?"

"Yes, my lady. Wait here while we prepare rooms for everyone."

"Of course," Catherine replied as Burke left the room and Barnes, Rogers, and Evelyn looked around them.

"This is where you lived?" Barnes asked.

"Sometimes," Catherine replied. "But often at court once I served the queen, or in the country."

"It is so beautiful," Evelyn breathed. "I have never seen anything like it."

"Catherine once told me there was a high price to pay for such opulence, and I thought I understood what she meant. But I am ashamed of how wrong I was," Henry said.

Catherine looked at him, her expression sad. "Do not be, for I was as wrong about you as you were about this. I gave all of this up because I refused to pay the price demanded of me, and I do not regret it."

Henry took her hand and kissed it. "We both walked away from our respective worlds, though it almost cost us our lives, and it has only made us stronger, I think."

Catherine smiled and released his hand, looking around her at the place she knew so well. A place that had once been her prison in so many ways and, for a time, was also Henry's. It was hard not to feel like a stranger here, and perhaps she was. At the same time, it was the perfect place to begin her plans right under her father's nose. She knew she could count on those here to keep her presence a secret, and that would allow her to line things up in safety.

When Burke returned, she led Barnes, Rogers, and Evelyn to the rooms they'd be occupying during their time here, and the trunks were taken up. Catherine made her way to her old room with Henry, and when the door shut behind them, she turned to look at him, unable to hide the swirl of emotions she felt over being here again.

"I know," Henry said as if he could read her thoughts. "I can only imagine how difficult this must be for you."

"And for you, too," she replied, sighing. "Back in a place that once served as your confinement."

"That is not how I see it. To me it is the place where I found myself again with the help of a beautiful young woman. It is the place where my life changed in ways I never expected, the place where I found you."

Catherine smiled and untied her cloak, pulling it from her shoulders and draping it over a chair. "That is a good way to think of it."

"You would have a hard time doing so, I would think. You have far more memories of this place and likely not all of them pleasant."

"Most of them are not," she said.

"That you could say such a thing with no trace of sadness bothers me more than I can say."

"I am sorry," she said as she turned to look at him with a frown. "I will not say it again."

"No, Sparrow, that is not what I meant. Do not ever tailor your words for me; you should always speak your true mind. What I meant is that it bothers me that such unhappiness was so much a part of your life that you think nothing of it."

"It was, but if I had not learned how to not let such things break me, I would not have been here for you to meet. I had to find a way to survive that, and I did."

"You did and have survived much more since."

"It is different, though. Physical survival versus the survival of mind, heart, and soul. So much damage can be done to those that never heal. Physical wounds fade, but those never do. You remember them always, and they always find a way to hurt you when you least expect it."

"That is a fair point," he said, removing his greatcoat and draping it over the same chair as Catherine's cloak before he wrapped his arms around her waist from behind. "But he cannot hurt you now, not with me here."

"I would like to see him try," Catherine said with a small chuckle.

"So would I."

"I never in my life would have believed I would have a man in this room with me."

"No? You would have married sometime."

"Yes, but I would likely never have returned here once I had."

"Hm. True. You may not have believed it, but did you imagine it?"

"Henry!"

"Come now, you can tell me," he said, turning her around in his arms. "Was it me? Someone else?"

"I ... well, I did not really understand what went on here, and I —"

"Ah, so you did!" Henry said, his smile teasing. "Tell me, my lovely, what did you imagine we would do here?"

"Talk, I suppose."

"Talk. Hmm," he said before he kissed her cheek. "I think you can do better than that."

"I really did not think of much."

"Oh, I do not know about that. After the tavern, did you ever imagine me here with you, kissing you in that way? Touching you?" he murmured against her neck between kisses.

Catherine closed her eyes, trying to focus on words because he was making it difficult to think. "Perhaps."

"Perhaps," he whispered in her ear, walking her slowly backward until the wall stopped them. "I know *I* thought about it, and well before that night."

A small gasp escaped her as she ran into the wall, the gentle weight of his body against hers making her heart race. "Did you?"

"I did indeed," he said, sliding his hands down her arms to her wrists, lifting them and pinning them to the wall. "I thought about how it might be to sneak in here the way you snuck in on me once. You would look at me in shock, but you would not ask me to leave. And when I pulled you close to me you did not pull away."

"What did I do?"

"You kissed me, and I did not hesitate to return the affection. I held you to the wall, similar to this, and it became a game. What could I do to you to make you cry out? I had a gentle hand over your mouth so you could muffle yourself, and I used everything I knew until your knees were so weak you could hardly stand. And then it ended in one of two ways."

Catherine's skin felt hot, and her stomach twisted at his words. She hadn't imagined such things then because she had no concept of them, but she certainly did now. "And what ways were those?"

"I am glad you asked," he said, the sound of his soft laugh as dark as his smile. "In one I lifted you so that you could wrap your legs around my hips, and I took you right there. In the other I took you to your bed and continued with my earlier game until I could take it no more, and by that time you were just as desirous of it as I was."

Catherine let out a small, involuntary moan as, at his last words, he pressed his hips against hers and placed a gentle bite at the intersection of her neck and her shoulder. "A good thing for you then."

"What is?"

"That we have time enough for both," she whispered before she kissed him and felt him melt against her.

"Christ Almighty, Catherine," he murmured against her lips when they parted. "How is it that you know precisely what to say to drive me mad and stop any thoughts I might have?"

"I learned from the best, did I not?"

Henry smiled, but there was nothing sweet about it. "You did. Mmm, think of the scandal this would surely be if they all knew. The prim and proper Catherine Merrick with a notorious pirate in her room with her, talking about all of the carnal things he wants to do to her and she to him. Think of what your father would say. Do you think his head would explode with rage? I hope so."

Catherine laughed before she gave him one of the long, slow kisses she knew set him on fire. "My father has no place here," she whispered, giving his lower lip a gentle nibble.

Henry's grip on her wrists tightened for a moment before he pulled her away from the wall, holding her against him as he quickly walked her to the bed and threw her onto it. Before she could recover, he was there, pinning her wrists to the bed with an almost hungry expression as his weight pressed her into the mattress. Catherine's breathing quickened as she looked up at him in surprise, and he switched his hands so that one held both of her wrists as the other covered her mouth.

"Then let us waste no more time, my lady, for the night is always shorter than we think, and it is time to banish the ghost of the scared girl who once occupied this space."

Chapter 20

The party was well underway at the palace, filled with the same faces, the same games, the same gossip, but that was all about to change. There was a storm coming that no one here would ever expect, least of all Lord Merrick himself, who sat on the dais with the king, the place he believed himself to be supremely entitled to. A place he would say he hadn't gotten to without hard work and sacrifice even if those sacrifices weren't always his. Catherine stood behind the curtain, watching him, in the same place she'd once stood after being parted from Henry. This time, however, everything was different. Though Henry stood behind her, just as he'd done then, he stood there as her husband, an outcome the girl who'd once stood here never could've imagined.

Just the sight of him made her both frightened and furious at once. This was the man who had tried to end her life, to take her from the only man in the world who understood her. The man whose actions led to the death of an unborn innocent. The child in her and the Catherine of that day still felt terror at the merest glimpse of him, but the rest of her roiled with barely contained rage. He'd tried to take Henry from her, and she'd refused to allow that to happen. Now, she refused to let him remain untainted by his numerous crimes, untouched so that he could go on hurting others.

Stepping away from the curtain, she took her place and nodded to the footman.

"Lady Catherine Merrick," the man called out.

The buzz of confusion in the room fell silent as Catherine walked out and stopped at the top of the stairs, curtsying to her king. Catherine Merrick was supposed to be dead, murdered by a criminal when her loving father had come to fetch her home. Yet here she stood, very clearly alive, resplendent in jewels she'd not left England with and a gown to match them, a gift from Henry that cost a mere pittance of his fortune. Her look had been carefully crafted for just this effect, proof that she was not only alive, but also thriving.

The king looked at her father in confusion before he stood. "Lady Catherine?"

"Your Majesty," she replied before she made her way down the stairs.

As she vacated the landing, Henry, Barnes, Evelyn, and Rogers appeared. All of them were dressed properly for court but remained where they were. The crowd parted for her, staring and whispering as she made her way toward the dais, and the fury in her father's face was gratifying.

"What are you doing here?" the king asked her. "You are supposed to be —"

"Dead, Your Majesty?" Catherine said with a smile. "Supposed to be, but as you can see, I am not, in spite of someone's best efforts, and that someone was *not* my husband."

Catherine didn't wait for the king to say anything before she looked at her father and threw something onto the table in front of him. The bag of coins hit the table with a thump and a rattle as she fixed him with a cold glare.

"There is the money for what plate you were not able to get back," Catherine said. "As that is all that is important to you, right?"

"Catherine, my darling," he replied, his tone laced with disdain and anger. "I am so glad to see you are safely recovered."

Catherine's laugh was bitter. "What a lie, and an unconvincing one at that. You are furious that I am not dead, are you not? You tried *so* hard; you thought I was when you left me, but I am stronger than that."

"How dare you try to —"

"Did I say you could speak!" Catherine said, raising her voice and bringing a shocked gasp from the crowd. "There is *nothing* you need to say, but there is plenty you need to hear, along with everyone else, for God only knows what other lies you have told."

"Lady Catherine, what is this about?" the king interjected.

"The truth, Your Majesty. My father is a liar and an attempted murderer, a greedy monster who will stop at nothing to get what he wants and keep what he thinks is his. Is that not right, Father? Oh, right, I seem to remember you telling me not to call you that right before you called me a whore."

There were scandalized whispers rustling through the courtiers now, but Catherine wasn't about to stop.

"You showed up at my home and demanded I give you back what was yours. I did so, but that was not good enough, was it? You wanted me dead. I had shamed you all because I refused to marry a man I knew would see me into an early grave. I very clearly remember you telling me that you did not care if I died, that what happened to me after my marriage was of no concern to you. Yet it was, was it not? I was married, but you very much cared now. Shall I tell them about how you beat me? Put a knife in my back?"

"That is a lie!"

"It is not, and I will strip down to nothing to show them all the scar it left if I need to! You tried to kill me, and you failed. You did succeed in murder, though, through the child I lost because of what you did to me," Catherine said, glaring at him.

A ripple of horror made its way around, but no one moved or spoke.

"But that was not enough, was it? Not for you. No, you

wanted revenge on my husband, and to cover your crime, you came here and lied to your sovereign. You got him to place a bounty on the head of the only man in the world who loved me, the one who had fought so hard to save me from the things you had done. A bounty that brought soldiers to our door to have him dragged back to Jamaica so Lieutenant Governor Morgan could collect it."

The king looked at Lord Merrick, realizing at that moment that he had, indeed, been lied to.

"I was not about to let you do that to him or to me, so I went after him. I went to Port Royal, and I got him back. I was almost too late, but I did it."

"You should be in the Tower, Catherine! You were foolish to come here! You should have stayed dead!"

"Do you think I fear you? That you can threaten me and I will cower before you like I used to do? You would be wrong. I held a man at knifepoint who has killed without mercy more times than you can imagine. I commanded a ship. I saved my husband by shooting the rope they were using to hang him. I have walked through hell, and you are *nothing*," she hissed. "May those coins bring you comfort in hell."

There was a large outburst at her last words, but she stared at her father in defiance before she turned and started back toward where Henry and the others waited.

"That is right, Catherine! Run. You are still the lying, thieving whore I told you that you were, and now you have shown them all just how right I was by showing up here with *him*. You are a disgrace!"

Catherine stopped and turned around, and almost immediately a knife buried itself in the table in front of her father, bringing a scream from those who had seen her throw it. Her father paled and took a step back, but Henry's smile was dark and proud.

"Coward," Catherine spat. "If you really believe yourself so righteous, then do what you should have done before: Challenge Henry. Do it. I dare you."

Henry stared at him, his gaze deadly serious. "Please do. I would *love* a chance to avenge my wife and my unborn child. I would love to kill you and then shove a pike up your arse before I paraded you like a stuck pig through the center of London."

"ENOUGH!" the king shouted. "Guard!"

Catherine's father offered her a smug smile.

"Arrest Lord Merrick and take him to the Tower on charges of murder and high treason."

"Your Majesty!" her father cried out in shock.

"You lied to me. You told me this child was dead, murdered, but you neglected to tell me it was really you who was the cause of it!"

"I had the right to seek redress for her theft!"

"Financially, Merrick! There is nothing in the law that allows for murder! You retrieved what was yours and she has paid for the rest, has she not? You tried to murder your own child, not because you were worried about some damned plate, but because of your own vanity! That you could be so cold to your own blood disgusts me. Your actions led to the death of an unborn innocent and very nearly led to the execution of an innocent man!"

"Innocent! You call him innocent? He is a murderer! Maybe not of her but of how many others?"

"He is what I say he is!" the king shouted in fury. "Take him!"

Lord Merrick was seized unceremoniously, dragged from the room protesting his innocence, and Catherine watched him go without an ounce of regret or sadness, though she managed to hold in the smile that threatened to show itself.

"Catherine! You come with me. NOW!"

Catherine curtsied and looked back at Henry, his face a mask of concern, before she followed the king in silence, shocked conversation following in her wake. They moved back into the palace and into the king's privy chamber.

"You have a great deal of nerve showing up here, Catherine."

"Perhaps, but you needed to know you had been lied to

and he needed to pay for his crimes. If you wish to punish me, so be it."

"Good Lord, girl, what makes you think I would want to punish you? You alerted me to a crime against you."

"I did steal, Your Majesty."

"You did, that is true, but I am willing to overlook it. I am sorry, Catherine. You should never have had to endure such a thing from anyone, much less your own father. I am glad you survived it, and I am deeply sorry your child did not."

"So am I, on both counts," Catherine said in a soft voice, her hard demeanor slipping for a moment.

"Have you had another?"

"No, and it is unsure if I ever will, but that is nothing any of us can control."

The king frowned. "No, but there *are* things within my power."

"Such as?"

"First of all, I will make sure your family is not tainted by your father's crimes. Your brother will take the title, and it will come to him unattainted. They will not suffer, and I will send for them immediately."

"Thank you, Your Majesty."

"Next, I am of a mind to make sure Captain Merrick will have no reason to be arrested again by giving him a full pardon."

Catherine gasped, her eyes going wide. "Your Majesty, I —"

"And I think, perhaps, for his service to the crown, a knighthood. Tell him nothing, for I wish to surprise him with it."

Catherine shook her head in disbelief.

"That, I believe, should be sufficient, do you not agree?"

"More than! You are most gracious, Your Majesty."

"You are living in the Colonies, are you?"

"Yes, Your Majesty, in New York. We have a beautiful farm there and were living quite happily until Henry was taken away to Jamaica. I even have a little spaniel, like the ones you have here," Catherine said, smiling. "Her name is Frances."

"Do you! That must be a small blessing. I know how much you loved the dogs here."

"She is the sweetest companion."

"I must admit, I was surprised when your flight came to light, but when word came back that you had married Henry Merrick, I was suddenly not at all surprised."

Catherine looked down for a moment, laughing. "I did not flee to marry him; it was just a bonus when I let him know where I was and he came to find me."

"The duke was humiliated."

"If I said I was sorry about it, I would be lying."

The king offered her a wry smile. "Truth be told, I think you picked the better option."

Catherine started laughing a bit harder, not bothering to hide it. "So do I."

"So, you shot the rope they were using to hang him, commandeered a ship, and can throw a knife with frightening accuracy. It sounds an intriguing tale, and you need to sit at the table with me and tell it. Let us reintroduce you to the court, shall we?"

Catherine followed the king out, and the crowd stopped, bowing and curtsying to him when he reappeared. He held out his hand to Catherine, who took it and let him lead her to his table.

"Captain Merrick!"

"Yes, Your Majesty," Henry replied, bowing again.

"I require your presence here at table, as well as your companions. I wish to hear all about this latest venture."

Henry raised an eyebrow, looking at Catherine, and she smiled to reassure him. "As you wish, Your Majesty."

With a gesture to the other three, he joined the king and Catherine at the table. Barnes, Rogers, and Evelyn looked overwhelmed and more than a little terrified.

"I know you have lives to get back to, but I am afraid I must needs ask you to remain at court for a short while. I must summon Lady Catherine's family to court in order to clean things up after today's scene. There will need to be time for the message to reach them and for them to make the journey here. I am sure they would like to see her and know she still lives."

"Of course, Your Majesty," Henry replied.

"Where are you lodging?"

"Merrick House, Your Majesty," Catherine said. "I knew it would be safe to stay there, as my father always remained here."

"Of course, and that is very clever of you. Look at you, Captain, you have come up in the world with a noble bride."

"I have in many ways, and her nobility is the least of those."

Chapter 21

"Catherine! It is a miracle!"

Standing up from the settee in the back parlor where she'd so often spent time with Henry during his imprisonment here, Catherine didn't know what to think when her mother hurried into the room, her arms out and tears streaming down her cheeks.

"Hello, lady mother," Catherine said, curtsying to her as Henry bowed respectfully.

Margaret stopped short and stared at her daughter. "Why do you greet me so?"

"Do you want the truth? Or do you want me to make up a more pleasant reason?"

Henry frowned but remained silent.

"Catherine … what … what do you mean, the truth?"

"I do not run into your arms because whenever I needed you, you were not there. You let him harm me, did nothing to stop it, and somehow I should fly into your embrace like some emotional, frightened child?"

"Catherine," Henry said, his voice soft as he checked her.

"No, she is right," Margaret said, and Catherine looked at her in surprise. "But it was not for the reasons she thinks, not because I did not want to."

"Oh?" Catherine asked.

"What he was doing to you, he was also doing to me. What

you did not see behind closed doors does not mean it never happened, Catherine. Do you remember days or weeks when I would not see you? It was because I was injured and had no wish to frighten any of you with the sight."

Catherine blinked, taken aback by her words. She did remember that, those moments of not seeing her mother for long stretches of time. They had always been told it was that she felt ill or some other reason.

"Hearing such a thing does not surprise me," Henry said. "Such practices rarely center on one person."

Catherine watched her mother take in the sight of Henry, looking him up and down with a curious expression. "So, you are he."

"Pardon?"

"The one who started all of this."

"I suppose I am, but if you wish for me to make apologies for it, Lady Merrick, none will be forthcoming."

"That does not surprise me," she replied, her tone cold. "Criminals are not often repentant. You have thrown our family into chaos, induced my daughter to flee, and now my husband is in the Tower!"

"Yes, he is," Henry replied, keeping his tone even, "but not for the reasons you seem to think. I have done nothing wrong here, so I have nothing to be repentant of. I did not induce your daughter to do anything, that was a choice she made quite on her own, and as you can see, she does not repent of it either."

"Mother, why do you think Father is where he is?" Catherine asked.

"I assume it has something to do with *him*," Margaret said, gesturing to Henry. "The one we thought had murdered you, that is what your father said! Lucky for you he was unsuccessful, but still you remain!"

"Henry did nothing of the sort," Catherine said, stepping in front of Henry as though she might somehow protect him. "It was *Father* who tried to murder me, Mother. Everything he told you Henry did to me? It is what *he* did, and *that* is why he is in the Tower. He lied to the king about my death so that Henry would be arrested and hanged to cover his own heinous acts."

"He ... what! No! He did not ..." Margaret floundered, looking between the two of them. "Why would he do such a thing?"

"I had shamed you all, he said, and he wanted to be rid of me."

Margaret swayed and braced herself against a chair, and Henry, despite her cold greeting, stepped forward to place a steadying hand on her back. "Catherine ... please ..." she said, beginning to cry again. "Why do you tell such lies!"

"Lies?" Catherine asked, incredulous. "After what you just told me, why is it so hard to believe he would do this?"

"To beat someone is one thing, but to murder your own child?"

"And yet that is exactly what he did, or at least what he tried to do. He admitted as much to the king, Mother."

"God have mercy upon us! What will happen to us now!" she wailed.

"Nothing. Charles will take the title, and life will go on. The king has assured me that it will not come to him attainted, and if he is not here with you, my assumption is he is getting the same news from the king now."

Margaret nodded through her tears, and Catherine crossed the small space between them and embraced her mother, feeling her mother grab hold of her as though she were drowning.

"You are free now," Catherine whispered in her ear. "Just as I am free. He can never harm any of us again."

"Yes," Margaret said, sniffling. "You are right, Catherine." Reaching up, she held her daughter's face in her hands. "You are stronger than I ever could be, and I do not know where you came by it. The point is that you survived and seem happy. I was inconsolable when I got the letter."

"Henry has never hurt me," Catherine said. "Never."

Margaret looked over at Henry. "I apologize to you, Captain, for my earlier behavior."

"Thank you," he replied. "I am guilty of a good many things, but harming my wife is not one of them, nor will it ever be."

"Come, Mother, let us get you situated, shall we?" Catherine said, gesturing toward the door.

"Thank you, Catherine."

***

An hour later, Catherine's brother arrived. Catherine and Henry were both there to meet him, paying him courtesy as the new Lord Merrick, along with the rest of the household. Henry surveyed the young man standing before them and surmised he couldn't be much older than he himself was. He looked sad, overwhelmed, and shaken. Henry couldn't really blame him, as the news he'd gotten was quite likely very distressing. Tall, he looked like his father, but with none of the cruelty or coldness. When he saw his sister, he stared at her for a long moment as though he'd seen a ghost.

"Kate," he whispered before he hurried forward and wrapped her in his arms, a genuine show of affection that Catherine didn't hesitate to return. "I am so sorry. For everything."

"So am I," she said, though the two of them remained holding each other for quite some time, and it was the first time Henry had ever seen Catherine seem truly close to anyone.

"We all thought … but thank God you are here and safe."

"Quite safe, Charles," she replied, smiling as she stepped away from him.

"Captain Merrick," Charles said, giving him a small nod. "I am able to meet you at last."

"Lord Merrick," Henry said, bowing.

"Shall we take some time together in the back parlor?" Catherine offered.

"Yes, I think it would be wise, for there is much to say. Burke?"

"Yes, Lord Merrick?" Burke replied.

"Would you be so kind as to send some refreshments?"

"Indeed, my lord."

Charles smiled at her. "Thank you. It is very good to see you again."

"It has certainly been a long time, Master Ch — I mean, Lord Merrick."

Charles chuckled and shook his head. "Fear not, for that is how you have known me for far longer, is it not? We will all get used to it."

Burke smiled and curtsied before she departed to fulfill his request, and Charles gestured toward the back hallway. The three of them walked in silence, and once the door shut behind them, he sighed heavily and rubbed his face.

"Are you all right, Charles?" Catherine asked, putting a hand on his arm.

"As all right as one can be when one finds out their father tried to murder their sister and is set for the block."

Catherine blinked. "The block …"

"What did you think would happen, Catherine? When the king told you I would take the title, did you assume he would just hand it to me?"

"I … I had not thought …" Catherine turned to look at Henry, her distress clear.

"Sparrow," Henry said, his voice gentle and calm, "you knew this would happen; it was why you came here, so he could pay for what he had done."

"Yes," she whispered, closing her eyes. "I just dislike being the cause of someone else's demise."

"As he meant to be the cause of yours, Kate?" Charles said. "He deserves it for what he did to you, for what he has done to all of us, and I am not sorry to see him finally get what is coming to him."

Henry looked at the young man with great curiosity, and Charles offered him a small smile.

"I know what you are wondering, Captain. I am not my father, nor have I ever been, despite his best efforts to make me so. I was furious when I heard he had tried to marry Kate off to the duke, and when I was then told she had fled after stealing the plate from her dowry, I was pleased to hear it."

"I will admit I am surprised by that."

"And I am not surprised you are. I assume Kate never spoke of us."

"No."

"Not because I did not want to!" Catherine interjected. "I just … it was …"

"It hurt less?"

"Yes. If I were to miss anyone, it would be you."

Charles reached out and ran a hand over her hair. "I missed you, too, but I would not trade your freedom for my selfish need to have you near."

Catherine reached out and took his hand, squeezing it.

"Kate, would you mind if the Captain and I spoke alone for a time?"

"No, of course. I will go check on Mother and let her know you have arrived."

"Thank you, sweeting. You are good to think of it, and I will send someone for you when we are ready for you to rejoin us."

Catherine nodded and walked to the door, stopping to glance over her shoulder at Henry before she departed. Burke came in as Catherine went out, setting the refreshments on the table and leaving as quietly as she had come. Charles went to the table, poured himself a cup of wine as well as one for Henry, and returned, holding it out.

"Thank you," Henry replied, taking it. "What was it you wished to speak about?"

"Many things, but first, I want you to know I bear you no ill will."

"That is good to hear. Your mother did not feel the same way, I am afraid."

Charles sighed and took a drink. "I am not surprised, but please be forgiving of her. She is so used to being under my father's thumb that her first reaction is always whatever she thinks his might be."

"For in that way she bears little risk of displeasing him and thus is spared the consequences of his wrath so that she may survive another day."

"Precisely."

"I am sorry for what has befallen everyone from the selfish actions of one man."

"I am sorry for what it took to get here, but I am not sorry for the end result. Please, sit."

Henry sat down in the chair, and Charles sat across from him. "Catherine did not speak of her family at all."

"As I said before, I am not surprised by it. There were four of us children."

"Were?"

"Yes. Two brothers between myself and Kate, and all of us close to each other. We took care of her, and perhaps that is why she became as she was. We taught her from our lessons, taught her to shoot, to use a rapier, things like that."

Henry raised an eyebrow. "A rapier?"

"Yes, she is rather good with it, to be honest."

"Did you teach her how to throw knives, too?"

Charles looked at him, intrigued. "We did. Why do you ask?"

Henry laughed. "When first I met her, I asked her if she could, and she told me no. Played as though she had no idea, then sunk two next to mine in the center when I dared her."

Charles laughed. "Sounds like Kate."

"She also buried one in the king's table in front of your father when he taunted her."

"I wish I could have seen it," Charles said, a sort of dark amusement in his expression. "Bet it scared him."

"She scared a great many people, I think."

"Good. Maybe they will think twice before any of them try to go after a Merrick again."

"Where are your other two brothers?"

"The youngest one died of fever several years ago. There was only a year and a half between him and Kate. She was ill, too, but she survived. When she found out he did not, it was weeks before she spoke a word to anyone."

"I am very sorry to hear it," Henry said, though the thought of Catherine in so much pain that she refused to speak was heartbreaking.

"George was the sweetest soul you could meet and unfailingly kind. I was sure he would go into the church one day, and I believe that was his wish."

"And the other?"

"William," Charles said, chuckling, "if you can believe it, is a captain in His Majesty's navy."

"What?" Henry said, his eyes wide.

"I do not know if he has ever been to Jamaica, but yes. Quite funny that she has married you."

"You mean a pirate?"

"Not a privateer?"

"I suppose if you want to get specific, yes."

"I remember Captain Sir Henry Morgan being quite offended at being called a pirate."

Henry rolled his eyes. "Yes, well, he can say whatever he wishes, but he knows damned well what he really is. We all do. I prefer not to lie to myself."

"That is refreshing."

"Catherine set him straight anyway."

"Wait ... what?" Charles asked, eyebrow raised.

"The king did not tell you?"

"No."

Henry grinned and recounted the tale of his being returned to Jamaica, Catherine's coming after him, her confrontation with Morgan, all of it, and by the end, Charles was laughing so hard he was wiping tears from his eyes.

"Christ, Catherine," he said, shaking his head. "She is something else."

"Spirited, some would say."

"I am glad you came and freed her. I think you were the only one who could."

"I think the king intended it to be otherwise, to use me to tame her by showing her I was not as she thought."

"Well, that was a mistake."

"It most certainly was."

"I will miss her a great deal, as I would have had she not come back or if she had truly died, but she is better off away from here with you, with someone who appreciates her."

"And I do."

"I know. I cannot say what I felt when the letter arrived," he said, his voice going quiet and his expression sad. "I prayed George was there to meet her, but I cried for days, I think. Drank a lot."

"I drank a lot, too, after I left her here."

Charles smiled and nodded. "As I said, I am glad for all of it. I have no intention of removing Catherine from our family tree, as I know Father intended to do. She will remain where she is, the first Merrick to settle in the new world."

"You will always be welcome," Henry said. "We have a large farm and a beautiful home that I have done my utmost to make something like this one. We can see all the way to sea from our ridge. I will be happy to return to it."

"It sounds like a piece of heaven. Perhaps someday I shall make the journey."

"KATIE!"

The commotion of someone calling out made both men stand up swiftly and make their way to the door of the parlor and out.

"KATIE!"

Catherine appeared at the top of the stairs and then let out a shriek of joy. "WILL!"

As Catherine hurried down the stairs, Henry looked to see a young man standing there in the officer's dress of the Royal Navy. Like Charles, he was tall, but he seemed to have taken the fair hair of his mother, unlike his siblings. Catherine jumped into his arms from the bottom of the stairs, and he wrapped her up in them, bursting into tears. The rush of genuine emotion shown by a brother realizing that his beloved youngest sibling was, indeed, alive and well was something Henry found exceedingly touching.

"Good Lord! Will! What are you doing here?" Charles asked.

"Charlie!" Will said as he loosed one arm from Catherine and shook his brother's hand. "We just came in, and the first thing waiting for me was an immediate summons from the king. He told me all, and I came straight here. I needed to see for myself that Katie was alive!"

"Perfect timing to come in from sea."

"Thank God for it," Will said before turning his attention back to Catherine and kissing her cheeks. "Christ above, Katie, whatever in the hell happened?"

"It is a long story," she sniffled.

"I have heard at least some of it. I am beyond thankful you are still with us. When I got the news …" he said, trailing off.

"Do not speak of it," Catherine said, silencing him with a gentle hand over his mouth. "It is not so."

"No, it is not," he said as she removed her hand, grinning at her.

"Will, I should like you to meet Captain Merrick," Charles said. "Kate's husband."

Will blinked and looked up. "Jesus."

Henry, unable to help himself, started laughing.

"Sorry," Will said, reaching out to shake his hand. "I was not expecting that."

"No offense taken," Henry said, smiling and shaking his hand. "I think you would normally consider me an enemy."

"No, not really," Will said, shrugging. "You sail under the English flag, so there would be no quarrel with you."

"I was just saying to the Captain that I did not think you had been to Jamaica, Will."

"I have not, no. I am usually around France and Spain or Ireland at times."

"Rough seas," Henry said.

"Especially around Ireland, but then I have heard the squalls in the Caribbean can sometimes put it to shame."

"That is most certainly true. I have sailed both."

"Have you!" Will said, intrigued.

"I wish Father had been so receptive of Henry," Catherine said with a wry smile.

Both Charles and William rolled their eyes. "Let us not worry about him, Kate," Charles said. "He is no longer a welcome presence here. Let us celebrate all being together again, shall we?"

"Yes! We must! Henry, we should go to the tavern in Southwark you took me to!" Catherine said in excitement.

Charles and William looked at him in shock.

"Sparrow, I do not think —"

"You took Katie to a tavern in Southwark?" Will asked.

"Ah. Yes."

Will grinned. "I like you already. Did she have anything?"

"Rum," Henry replied, laughing.

"Oh, excellent choice, Katie."

"I did not *have* a choice; it is what he gave me," Catherine replied, shooting a playful glare at Henry.

"Same thing," Will said, shrugging. "Likely better than whatever ale they had on hand. What do you say, Charlie?"

Charles seemed to consider it. "She *is* married now. Right, I am in. When we get there, she can tell us all about how she held a knife on Captain Morgan and shot the rope they were trying to hang her husband with."

Will's eyes went wide. "You did *what?*"

"It is an *excellent* story," Charles said, laughing. "Come on, let us go celebrate properly."

Chapter 22

The evening out with Catherine and her brothers had been more than entertaining, with Barnes, Rogers, and even Evelyn joining them. Henry felt as though he hadn't laughed that hard in years, and it was very easy to see where Catherine's personality had come from with her growing up with the two of them. Both men were jovial, easy, full of laughter and smiles, nothing like their father. He could also see why Catherine had chosen not to speak of them. Charles' assertion that "it would hurt less" made a great deal more sense. To have to think of them, speak of them, and know she'd never see them again, had to have been extraordinarily painful, and she'd solved it by trying to bury them instead.

William spoke of how he'd held a small funeral for her aboard his ship, the only thing he could do to wish her well, admitting that he'd hated Henry for what he'd done — or at least what they'd all *thought* he'd done. To learn the truth had been devastating but tempered by knowing she was really alive, and Henry made it known he held no ill will. He would've felt the same in the young man's place.

Catherine's stories of her latest exploits had her brothers crying with laughter, but they seemed neither scandalized nor surprised by them, with Will and Charles both buying her a drink for using what they'd taught her to set Henry free.

By the end of the evening, Henry was fairly certain that Will wouldn't be spending the night alone, thanks to Evelyn, who was quite clearly enamored of the young English captain. If Catherine noticed, she didn't seem to mind, but that didn't surprise him either.

Two days later, all were called back to court. Charles and William had to meet with the council and sort things out — with William given several weeks of leave under the current circumstances — and the queen wished to see Catherine. Afterward, Catherine talked him into a game while they waited, and it left Henry blindfolded and stumbling around a large room trying to find her.

"Catherine!" Henry called out, laughing, hands held out in front of him.

"Right here!" she said as she poked him, and then laughingly dodged his attempt to grab her.

Henry laughed and took a few steps forward. "Sparrow, where are you, little Sparrow? I *will* find you."

"Henry?"

Henry's laughter stopped at the sound of a familiar yet unfamiliar voice. It was one he hadn't heard in so long and yet he couldn't quite place it. His brow knitted together, and he pulled the blindfold off. When his eyes adjusted, he saw a small woman there, hands clasped over her heart, and he stared at her. He should know her, and when his mind caught up with his eyes, he realized he *did* know her.

"Mother," he whispered in disbelief.

"It is you! My Henry!" she cried out as she hurried forward to embrace him.

"How … how are you here?"

"Look at you! So handsome, a man! You were just a boy when you left us!" she said through tears. "The king sent for us. Can you imagine? The king!"

"Us?"

"Your father is here, your brothers and sisters."

Henry felt like he couldn't breathe. They were all here. The family he hadn't seen in so long he'd lost count. "But why?"

"I do not know," she said, "but I am grateful all the same! I thought you were dead, but here you are! Where have you been for so long?"

"Jamaica."

"Where the pirates are?"

"Mother, I *was* a pirate," Henry said with a small smile.

"You stop with your nonsense."

"Not nonsense. I was. I was good at it, too. But not anymore. Now I have a plantation in the colony of New York. I live there with my wife."

"You are married!"

"Yes, I am ..." but then he realized he'd not seen or heard Catherine. Where had she gone?

The rest of his family suddenly entered the room, and he was overwhelmed with joyous greetings and questions about where he'd been, so much so that Catherine's disappearance slipped his mind entirely. They were soon all directed to the rooms Lord Merrick occupied at the palace, and they marveled at the beauty of them, so far removed were they from what they knew. Refreshments were brought in, and Henry enjoyed getting reacquainted with his family. He told them about his journey from Wales to where he was now, all that he had seen and been through. In turn, there were stories from his father and mother, introductions to brothers and sisters who hadn't even been born when he'd left Wales, and news of the older ones.

Quite some time passed before the doors to the room opened and Catherine swept in. Her entrance caused them all to stand, bowing and curtseying, though he knew they had no idea who she was. For all they knew, she could be the queen. She certainly looked like one.

"Mother, Father, please meet my wife, Lady Catherine Merrick," Henry said.

His family looked at him, then at her. "*This* … is your wife, Son?" his father asked.

"It is," Henry said with a smile, taking her hand and kissing it. "Beloved, my family. The king sent for them; can you believe it? I have not seen them in … I do not remember how long."

"A great pleasure to meet all of you," Catherine said, her smile gentle, honest, and sweet. "And I knew they were coming. I asked the king for the favor of finding them and bringing them here to you."

"You did … oh, Catherine …" he said softly. There were no words for such a gift.

"Lady Catherine, the pleasure is ours," his father replied.

"A real lady!" one of his sisters replied.

"Better than that," Henry said. "An English Merrick."

"What! You married an English Merrick!" his father exclaimed.

"I did indeed," Henry said with a laugh. "But do not let her fool you. She is not as docile as she seems."

"Henry," Catherine said, nudging him, which only made him laugh harder. "The king requests your presence, Henry, and all of your family."

There were sharp gasps. "We are not anywhere near fit to be before the king," his mother said.

"Nonsense!" Catherine replied. "You are in your Sunday best, and that is all that is required. Come, we do not want to keep him waiting."

Henry looked at his family, as confused as they were, but followed Catherine all the same. He was led down the same long hallway he'd first come down as a prisoner, and the doors opened before them without them even needing to slow down, though it left no time for his family to stop and gawk at their surroundings. The doors to the throne room swept open, and Catherine dropped into a deep curtsy as Henry and his family all bowed or curtsied along with her.

"Your Majesty, I have brought Captain Merrick as you asked."

"Thank you, Lady Catherine. All of you, please rise," the

king said as he stepped down and surveyed all of them, and Henry noticed that both Charles and William were also here, as well as Barnes and Rogers. "I am glad to see all of you seem well and your journey was, I trust, tolerable?"

"Yes, Your Majesty," they all replied.

"It is an honor to be in your presence, Your Majesty," Henry's father said.

"I thank you. What is your name?"

"David, Your Majesty."

"And you are a farmer?"

"Yes, Your Majesty."

"Of what?"

"I raise sheep and cattle, Your Majesty."

"Excellent! And you, madame?"

"Mary, Your Majesty," his mother replied.

"Welcome to court, Mary."

"Thank you, Your Majesty."

The king took his time, going down the line and making introductions with Henry's siblings before he returned to stand before Henry. "Captain Merrick."

"Your Majesty."

"You are here for a reason, and it was Lady Catherine's wish that your family be in attendance."

"In attendance for what, Your Majesty?" Henry asked, cocking an eyebrow.

"For your knighting."

Henry stared at the king, even as his family gasped all around him. "Knighting?"

"Yes. Part of my reward to you. Do take a knee, Captain."

Henry did as he was instructed, too shocked to do otherwise.

The king snapped his fingers and held out his hand, and a sword was placed into it immediately. "Captain Merrick, before I confer upon you the knighthood in honor of your service to me, I also confer a full pardon upon you and upon those members of your crew who have decided to now retire and lead a quieter life in one of our colonies. This will mean no one is going to show up to drag you to prison … unless you do something else."

"I have no intention of doing so, Your Majesty," Henry said.

"Good to hear. Very well then, in the name of God, Saint Michael, and Saint George," the king said, tapping Henry first on the right shoulder, then the left, then the top of his head, "we do prefer and declare thee knight."

Henry heard his mother burst into tears behind him and tried to check his own emotion.

"Lord Merrick, if you will?" the king said.

Charles stepped forward. "It is my honor to confer upon you this medal," he said, slipping it around Henry's neck, "a token from our family in thanks for all you have done."

"Thank you, Lord Merrick," Henry said. "I am honored."

"Captain Merrick?" the king said, and Henry looked up. "Not you, the other one," he said as Catherine stifled a laugh in her hand.

William didn't bother trying, laughing as he stepped up to the still kneeling Henry. "And it is my honor to confer upon you, as a knight, your proper rank of captain in the Royal Navy, retired though you may be," he said as he held out the sash.

"I …" Henry shook his head as he took it and ran a thumb over the silk. "Thank you, Captain."

"With that done, rise you up, Sir Henry Merrick," the king said.

Henry stood, still in shock and not entirely sure what to say. Catherine stood beside her brothers, beaming. "Thank you all," he finally said. "It is an honor I never dreamed of."

"Well deserved after all you have been through," the king said. "A celebratory luncheon has been set for us; let us partake of it," the king said, smiling as he turned around and held out his arm to Catherine. "Lady Merrick?"

"Your Majesty," Catherine said in response to his use of her new style of address due to Henry's title, curtsying before she took his arm and the two of them walked toward the door at the back of the room, with Charles and William behind them.

Henry shook his head and grinned. A knight. When word of this reached Morgan, the man would surely choke on his tongue, and Henry felt it couldn't happen to a better person.

Chapter 23

Once they'd returned to Merrick House, Henry's sisters found great joy in trying on Catherine's jewelry and gowns at her invitation, staring at themselves in the looking glass, and Catherine loved helping them do it. Henry loved her for how sweet and welcoming she was to people who were so different than she was and with whom she had so little in common, though commonality was swiftly found. She never let them feel unworthy of being at Merrick House, or that they were lesser, because she didn't consider them to be. She called the tailor and dressmaker in so that each person might have a new set of court-worthy clothing and, with Charles' blessing, gave them the money meant for their father, which had been returned to the Merrick children. With it, they could afford a better home and better land and would never go hungry or cold.

There was much laughter as they tried to teach her Welsh words, and the English Merrick siblings taught them French, in turn. There was this strange sense of completeness for Henry in having everyone there together, and he knew it would be painful for both him and Catherine to leave everyone, for it would be unlikely they'd see any of them again. He very much enjoyed the company of both of Catherine's brothers, and it wasn't long before they felt like his brothers, too.

Not long after his knighting, the day came for the execution of Catherine's father. While Catherine and her mother remained behind along with Henry's family, Henry accompanied Charles and William to the event. When the man was marched onto the scaffold, he caught sight of his two sons standing off to the side with Henry, and his eyes narrowed as if they'd somehow betrayed him. The two young men, in their turn, stared back at him with nary a glimpse of sorrow in their eyes to see their father in such a state. From his conversations with them, he knew that neither one was sad to see this happen, not after all he'd done to them, to their mother, and to their sister.

The former Lord Merrick protested his sentence, declaring himself innocent of the charges leveled against him, insisting he'd been set up by Henry, who was the real assailant. It made Henry's blood boil to hear himself slandered, but Charles patted his shoulder to let him know they stood with him. In the end, it wouldn't really matter what was said; his words would die with him, carried off into the breeze to be forgotten, just as he would be. When the axe fell, none of the three men even flinched, turning away the moment it was done and departing, the cheers of the onlookers behind them.

That evening had been somber, and though Catherine shed no tears, he could tell she was conflicted about her feelings over the demise of her father. The Dowager Lady Merrick had wept, and he couldn't tell if it was relief or sadness, or perhaps a bit of both. She'd decided she'd depart to return to the country early the following morning, and she was sent off with hugs and kissed cheeks from all of her children, along with the promise from Charles that she had his blessing to remain living at the country house for as long as she desired and he'd visit her there or she could come to town and see him.

Henry, Catherine, and William sat in the back parlor that afternoon, engrossed in their varying activities while Henry's family enjoyed time in the Merrick House gardens. There was a comfortable silence broken only occasionally by William or

Henry calling the other's attention to something they read in one pamphlet or another, while Charles worked on getting himself caught up with Privy Council business after taking his father's place, and Catherine sat in the light of a window, working on blackwork for a shirt she was making for Henry.

"Lady Merrick," Hart said, stepping into the room. "There is a visitor for you."

"For me?" Catherine asked, looking up with a puzzled expression. "Who is it?"

"A Lord and Lady Wellesley, my lady."

Catherine gasped. "Frankie! Thank you, Hart, please do show them in!"

Hart nodded and departed, and Henry looked at Catherine, who was grinning. "Is it really, Sparrow?"

"Yes!"

"Who is this?" Charles asked.

"You remember Lady Frances, do you not?"

"Good heavens, yes! I had forgotten she had married!"

"I remember her, too!" William said. "She was a sweet girl."

The doors opened a moment later, and Frances practically bounced into the room. "Kitty!" she cried out in joy.

"Oh, Frankie!" Catherine said before she hurried to embrace her friend. "How I have missed you!"

"I have missed you, too!" Frances replied before she gasped. "Captain! You are here!"

"I am, indeed. Hello again, Lady Wellesley, it is wonderful to see you."

"And you! Oh my goodness! Charles and William, too!"

Both men bowed to her. "Lady Wellesley, you are looking very well," Charles said.

"Thank you, Ch — I mean, Lord Merrick. Sorry, I forgot."

"It is all right," Charles said, chuckling.

"I shall dispense with formality and say hello to you like the old friend you are, Frankie," Will said, kissing her hand.

"Ah, William, I am so glad you are home safe from sea, as

always! Oh, but let me introduce my husband, Lord Wellesley."

"Good afternoon to all of you," the young man said, bowing to them as they did so to him. "It is a pleasure to put faces to names after all my darling Frances has said about you."

"Are you sure you want your wife associated with such a scandalous family, Lord Wellesley?" William teased. "A father dead for the attempted murder of his own child and a daughter married to someone so notorious ... though she, herself, is now notorious for fleeing the country and marrying the man."

"William Merrick!" Frances said, indignant as she hugged Catherine close to her. "You take that back this very instant! Kitty is not notorious! She is full of adventure; that is all. And the other captain is a very nice man who taught us all how to play cards and win."

"Full of adventure?" Will asked. "Yes. Adventure and more than her fair share of mischief, I would argue."

Frances made a face at him, and Catherine laughed before Frances released her.

"What do you mean when you say he taught you to play cards and win, Frankie?" Charles asked.

"What she means is that I taught all of them how to play for keeps, how to watch for tells, and how not to get cheated," Henry said, smiling.

"You did a very good job of it, too, Captain," Lord Wellesley said. "Frances has quite cleaned up at many a gambling night, so I cannot and will not fault her for it."

"Good man," Henry laughed.

"But I am very glad to know you are all right, Kitty," Frances said, frowning. "You know I was worried when you left."

"Fear not, Lady Wellesley," Henry said. "Your letter did, indeed, make it to me safely."

"Oh, good! I am glad I chose the right man to take it. But then your father came back and said you had died and ..." she paused, her eyes welling with tears. "He said the Captain had done it, and I could not believe such a thing to be true, for the Captain we knew would never do any such thing!"

"And you would be quite right to think so," Henry replied. "I thank you for having faith in me, Lady Wellesley."

"You might as well call me Frankie as everyone else does."

"Very well."

"And you are welcome. I am surprised anyone who had seen you here believed it. We all knew you were in love with Kitty."

"What?" Henry asked, shocked.

"It was obvious," Frances said, laughing now. "At least to some of us. We made excuses for you many times when the men showed up to pull you off to something or other, telling them you could not be spared, for you were helping us with whatever we could come up with. That way, you would get to stay with us and with Kitty all day as you seemed to prefer."

"That is quite romantic of you, my dear one," Lord Wellesley said, "and entirely in character."

"Thank you, Frankie," Henry said. "You read that situation quite correctly."

"You chose to stay with the ladies all day?" William asked, incredulous. "Whatever for?"

"I found their company far more pleasant and entertaining and was rather tired of debasing myself. I have seen and participated in enough debauchery to last me a lifetime, so I was not missing out. Not to mention they often used me as a sort of bait to draw ladies and thus make them prey. Other times they would make bets on how long it might take me to convince one to join me."

Both Catherine and Frances looked troubled by the revelation, though the three other men in the room looked sheepish, and Henry knew full well they'd participated in such sport in their own turns.

"You should not need to perform like some trained animal," Catherine said.

"Of course not, which is why I preferred to stay with you."

"I cannot blame you for it in those circumstances," William admitted.

"Let us speak of something happier," Frances said.

"I have another friend named Frances," Catherine volunteered.

"You do?"

"Indeed. She is always so excited and has the sweetest disposition, just like you. Henry got her for me."

"He got you a friend? How?" Frances asked, puzzled.

"I got her a pup, just like the little spaniels the king has," Henry said, chuckling.

"You named a puppy after me!"

"It was the perfect name! She reminded me so much of you."

"Oh, I wish I could see her!"

"She is very sweet, and I am sure she would love you."

"I think I should like to play cards and see what Sir Henry has taught these ladies," Charles said. "The three of us against Sir Henry and the two ladies."

"I hope you are ready to lose some coin, Charles," Henry said, rubbing his hands together with a grin.

***

"Catherine," Henry said as he came into the bedroom later that evening. "There is something I need to discuss with you."

Catherine paused in running a comb through her hair and looked at his reflection in her looking glass. "Is something wrong?"

"No, not at all."

"All right, what is it?" she asked as she resumed her task.

"It is time we talk about returning home."

"Yes, I thought the same," she said, though she sighed. "I will hate to leave Will and Charles, but this is not our home."

"No, it is not, and William will be headed back out to sea soon enough. All the same, I know it will be difficult for you."

"It could not stay this way forever."

Henry crossed the room to the dressing table, leaning back against it and looking down at her. "I have been talking to my family, and I have convinced them to come with us."

Catherine blinked. "What?"

"There is plenty of land to be had, and their lives would be so much better away from Wales and its poverty. I want to help them, and this is the best way."

"It is impossible for me to argue with that."

"Does it bother you?"

"No, I like your family very much, and it will be nice to have some real family near to us."

Henry smiled and reached out to stroke her cheek. "You have enjoyed this time, a vignette of what it might have been like had your father been a kinder man."

"I have. I wish my brothers could come, too, but such a thing is impossible. Will is an officer, and Charles holds the family title and holdings now. He cannot leave, as it is up to him to carry our family line forward."

"I am sorry for it, Sparrow. I know how close the three of you are after having watched all of you together these weeks."

"Do not be, for I will take this borrowed time over having had nothing at all."

"How very like you to think of it in such a way. There is something else, however."

"Something else?"

"Sparrow, I … I want you to go home without me."

"What!"

"Do not fret, beloved. The reason I say so is that I want to accompany my family home to help them wrap up their lives, to sell their livestock, the land, all of it. While I do that, I want Barnes, Rogers, and the crew to take you and Evelyn home, then come back for me. By the time they return we will be waiting for them, and we will leave within a few days."

"But —"

"They will need my help, Catherine," Henry said gently. "I do not want to see them cheated or changing their minds because they feel overwhelmed at the thought. I may even bring a few animals back if I see some good ones to increase our stock. What I do not want is for you and the crew to remain idle here for weeks while we make the journey back, handle everything, and return. They need to get back to work."

"Yes, of course," Catherine said in a near whisper. "I just do not wish to be without you so long."

"I understand, and I feel the same, but this is the best way. I will miss you every moment we are apart."

"When did you want to do this?" Catherine asked, her tone one of resignation.

"Within the week. We need all the time we can get."

"So soon!"

"We need to keep ahead of the weather."

Catherine took a deep breath and sighed. "Then we shall be ready to depart."

By the end of the week, Henry stood on the deck of his ship, making last-minute checks to ensure all was ready for the journey that would take his beloved wife back to New York and away from him. It hurt, but he knew it was for the best and that Barnes and Rogers would keep her safe. William was also recalled, and with the king's permission, they would be meeting with his ship, who would escort them at least some of the way. Catherine's goodbyes to Charles were undertaken at Merrick House, tearful though they were, with promises to write as often as possible.

Once he was satisfied, he pulled Catherine into his arms one last time, holding her close to him and trying to drink in the feel of her, the scent of her, to hold him over until they were together again. Catherine's small frame shook with silent tears, and he said nothing, holding her until they eased. This would be difficult on them both, but it would be the last time this would ever need to happen.

"Fly safe, my Sparrow, and give everyone at home my love. We will be together again before you know it."

"Promise me."

"I promise as much as is within my control. You must go; you will lose the tide if you do not. See you soon, my love."

"See you soon," she whispered. Never goodbye. Goodbye was far too final.

Henry kissed her and then left her, shaking hands with Barnes and Rogers before returning to the dock. It was odd to be sending off his own ship, letting it leave him behind while it carried his most precious cargo. If anything went wrong, he would not be there to protect her, and though the thought troubled him, he pushed it out of his mind. He needed to believe that all would be well, or he would never let her leave. He heard the crew, under Barnes' command, start to call out the orders for departure, and when the wind caught the sails and lurched them forward onto the Thames, his heart lurched with it. Catherine ran to the stern, the farthest she could get, doing the same as he was, holding that last glimpse of the one she loved for as long as she could. Henry waved to her, and she waved back before they were obscured from view by another vessel.

"Safe journey, my love," he whispered.

Chapter 24

The sheer relief Henry felt as he once more set foot on the docks of the New York Colony was indescribable. He was home. Finally home. The place he'd thought he'd never see again that day in April when Morgan's men had dragged him away. It was nearing the end of September, and the air held a hint of the turn toward autumn. The leaves on the trees were beginning to turn color, and it was his favorite part of the year. He was glad his family's first sight of it would be at what he felt was its best. There was excitement amongst them as they disembarked behind him: a new place, a new country, a new start. He would settle them in an inn for now until they found a more permanent place.

The journey back had been smooth, though his heart had been in a constant state of anxiety during the days between when he and the family had returned to London and his ship and the crew returned. When he'd seen them, he'd wanted to weep in relief because he knew it meant his sweet Catherine was safely back on land and would be waiting for him. There had been as little delay as possible in reprovisioning, getting everyone on board and back out to sea.

Once he'd made sure his family was settled and comfortable, Henry helped the crew unload the cargo into wagons, though there wasn't much. The few things his family brought, some livestock, the rest of Catherine's clothing from Merrick House, as well as a few pieces Charles wished to send in the form of decoration as gifts. When the house came into view, he very nearly broke down to see it, feeling overwhelmed with the emotion of all that had happened since he'd left. He was down off the wagon before it even stopped, throwing the door open as he hurried inside.

"Sparrow!" he called out. "Sparrow, my love, where are you?"

It took less than a moment for Catherine to appear at the top of the stairs. "Henry!" she squealed in delight, hurrying down the stairs just behind Frances, who danced around him in squirming excitement.

Henry clutched her tightly to him once she was in his arms, and he silently thanked every deity he could think of for bringing him safely home to her once more. "Oh, my Sparrow, I have missed you more than I have words to convey."

"I have missed you, too! Thank God you are home at last!"

"I am, indeed, and have no intention of leaving again unless you are with me. I know this parting was my idea, and the best one, but I hated being apart from you all the same."

"Well, do not think I will allow you to do this again."

"As my lady commands," he said with a chuckle as he stepped back from her. It was only then that he noticed something different in the style of the clothing she wore and the difference in her figure, his eyes widening. "Catherine," he whispered.

"Seems our disagreement some months ago fixed more than one thing," she said, smiling.

Henry cupped her face gently, resting his forehead against hers and laughing through his tears. "You beautiful, brilliant girl. How long?"

"Almost five months gone."

Henry placed a hand on the slight swell of her stomach. "I can hardly believe it!"

"Hopefully being in such waters at the time of conception is not a bad influence."

"I am not sure the child would need that anyway. Pirate blood and all that."

"Can we at least *try* to keep it off of a ship when it is grown?"

"I promise nothing."

"I am shocked," Catherine said in that deadpan voice, the way she had once done in the parlor of Merrick House so long ago.

"I would be shocked if you were shocked."

"You are incorrigible."

"Guilty. But aside from seeing you again, this is the best thing I could have come home to. Come, let us go upstairs and catch up with each other. I could use a bath and the chance to lie beside my wife again for the first time in almost three months."

"I am looking forward to hearing everything," Catherine said, grinning as she took his arm and walked with him toward the stairs. "Though lying down seems like a trick."

"It might be."

"Then, by all means, lead the way, Captain."

"Gladly, my little Sparrow. Gladly."

ABOUT THE AUTHOR

A California native, Eilidh Miller, FSAScot, has a BA in English and studied history as an undeclared minor to better inform her literature studies. A Fellow with the Society of Antiquaries of Scotland, Eilidh is very active within Southern California's Scottish community, spending a great deal of time volunteering with the charitable organization St. Andrew's Society of Los Angeles.

A long-time historical reenactor, Eilidh loves research and educating the general public about historical events, as well as entertaining them with tidbits no one would believe if they weren't documented. She extends this same energy to her work, extensively researching the historical periods she includes in her writing to ensure that the information she presents is correct, even going so far as to travel internationally to access archives and scout locations.

She resides in Southern California with her husband, daughter, and her feisty Shiba Inu sidekick.

You can keep up with Eilidh on Twitter, Instagram, TikTok, or her website www.eilidhmiller.com. You can also join her reader group on Facebook, Eilidh Miller's Reading Lodge, to keep up to date on the next release, get exclusive content, teasers, and enter contests!

OTHER BOOKS BY THE AUTHOR

THE WATCHERS
THE WATCHERS SERIES: BOOK 1

ENEMIES OF THE MIND
THE WATCHERS SERIES: BOOK 2

ECHOES OF THE RISING
THE WATCHERS SERIES: BOOK 3

Made in the USA
Las Vegas, NV
29 June 2021

25698559R10152